THE GATHERING

THE GATHERING

ANNE ENRIGHT

THORNDIKE
WINDSOR
PARAGON

This Large Print edition is published by Thorndike Press, Waterville, Maine, USA and by BBC Audiobooks Ltd, Bath, England.

Thorndike Press is an imprint of The Gale Group.

Thorndike is a trademark and used herein under license.

Copyright © 2007 by Anne Enright.

The moral right of the author has been asserted.

LIBRARY OF CONGRESS CATALOGING-IN-PUBLICATION DATA

Enright, Anne, 1962–
    The gathering / by Anne Enright.
        p. cm. — (Thorndike Press large print reviewers' choice)
    ISBN-13: 978-1-4104-0315-5 (lg. print : alk. paper)
    ISBN-10: 1-4104-0315-7 (lg. print : alk. paper)
    1. Family secrets — Fiction. 2. Dublin (Ireland) — Fiction. 3. Domestic
fiction. 4. Large type books. I. Title.
PR6055.N73G38 2008
823'.914—dc22   2007037344

BRITISH LIBRARY CATALOGUING-IN-PUBLICATION DATA AVAILABLE

Published in 2008 in the U.S. by arrangement with Grove Atlantic, Inc.
Published in 2008 in the U.K. by arrangement with
The Random House Group Limited.

U.K. Hardcover: 978 1 405 68648 8 (Windsor Large Print)
U.K. Softcover: 978 1 405 68649 5 (Paragon Large Print)

Printed in the United States of America on permanent paper
10 9 8 7 6 5 4 3 2 1

THE GATHERING

1

I would like to write down what happened in my grandmother's house the summer I was eight or nine, but I am not sure if it really did happen. I need to bear witness to an uncertain event. I feel it roaring inside me — this thing that may not have taken place. I don't even know what name to put on it. I think you might call it a crime of the flesh, but the flesh is long fallen away and I am not sure what hurt may linger in the bones.

My brother Liam loved birds and, like all boys, he loved the bones of dead animals. I have no sons myself, so when I pass any small skull or skeleton I hesitate and think of him, how he admired their intricacies. A magpie's ancient arms coming through the mess of feathers; stubby and light and clean. That is the word we use about bones: *Clean.*

I tell my daughters to step back, obviously, from the mouse skull in the woodland or the dead finch that is weathering by the garden wall. I am not sure why. Though sometimes we find, on the beach, a cuttlefish bone so pure that I have to slip it in my pocket, and I comfort my hand with the secret white arc of it.

You can not libel the dead, I think, you can only console them.

So I offer Liam this picture: my two daughters running on the sandy rim of a stony beach, under a slow, turbulent sky, the shoulders of their coats shrugging behind them. Then I erase it. I close my eyes and roll with the sea's loud static. When I open them again, it is to call the girls back to the car.

Rebecca! Emily!

It does not matter. I do not know the truth, or I do not know how to tell the truth. All I have are stories, night thoughts, the sudden convictions that uncertainty spawns. All I have are ravings, more like. *She loved him!* I say. *She must have loved him!* I wait for the kind of sense that dawn makes, when you have not slept. I stay downstairs while the family breathes above me and I write it down, I lay them out in nice sentences, all my clean, white bones.

8

2

Some days I don't remember my mother. I look at her photograph and she escapes me. Or I see her on a Sunday, after lunch, and we spend a pleasant afternoon, and when I leave I find she has run through me like water.

'Goodbye,' she says, already fading. 'Goodbye my darling girl,' and she reaches her soft old face up, for a kiss. It still puts me in such a rage. The way, when I turn away, she seems to disappear, and when I look, I see only the edges. I think I would pass her in the street, if she ever bought a different coat. If my mother committed a crime there would be no witnesses — she is forgetfulness itself.

'Where's my purse?' she used to say when we were children — or it might be her keys, or her glasses. 'Did anyone see my purse?' becoming, for those few seconds, nearly there, as she went from hall, to sitting room, to kitchen and back again. Even then we did not look at her but everywhere else: she was an agitation behind us, a kind of collective guilt, as we cast about the room, knowing that our eyes would slip over the purse, which was brown and fat, even if it was quite clearly there.

Then Bea would find it. There is always one child who is able, not just to look, but also to see. The quiet one.

'Thank you. Darling.'

To be fair, my mother is such a vague person, it is possible she can't even see herself. It is possible that she trails her fingertip over a line of girls in an old photograph and can not tell herself apart. And, of all her children, I am the one who looks most like her own mother, my grandmother Ada. It must be confusing.

'Oh hello,' she said as she opened the hall door, the day I heard about Liam.

'Hello. Darling.' She might say the same to the cat.

'Come in. Come in,' as she stands in the doorway, and does not move to let me pass.

Of course she knows who I am, it is just my name that escapes her. Her eyes flick from side to side as she wipes one after another off her list.

'Hello, Mammy,' I say, just to give her a hint. And I make my way past her into the hall.

The house knows me. Always smaller than it should be; the walls run closer and more complicated than the ones you remember. The place is always too small.

Behind me, my mother opens the sitting room door.

'Will you have something? A cup of tea?'

But I do not want to go into the sitting room. I am not a visitor. This is my house too. I was inside it, as it grew; as the dining room was knocked into the kitchen, as the kitchen swallowed the back garden. It is the place where my dreams still happen.

Not that I would ever live here again. The place is all extension and no house. Even the cubby-hole beside the kitchen door has another door at the back of it, so you have to battle your way through coats and hoovers to get into the downstairs loo. You could not sell the place, I sometimes think, except as a site. Level it and start again.

The kitchen still smells the same — it hits me in the base of the skull, very dim and disgusting, under the fresh, primrose yellow paint. Cupboards full of old sheets; something cooked and dusty about the lagging around the immersion heater; the chair my father used to sit in, the arms shiny and cold with the human waste of many years. It makes me gag a little, and then I can not smell it any more. It just is. It is the smell of us.

I walk to the far counter and pick up the kettle, but when I go to fill it, the cuff of my coat catches on the running tap and the sleeve fills with water. I shake out my hand, and then my arm, and when the kettle is filled and plugged in I take off my coat, pulling the wet sleeve inside out and slapping it in the air.

My mother looks at this strange scene, as if it reminds her of something. Then she starts forward to where her tablets are pooled in a saucer, on the near counter. She takes them, one after the other, with a flaccid absent-mindedness of the tongue. She lifts her chin and swallows them dry while I rub my wet arm with my hand, and then run my damp hand through my hair.

A last, green capsule enters her mouth and she goes still, working her throat. She looks out the window for a moment. Then she turns to me, remiss.

'How are you. Darling?'

'Veronica!' I feel like shouting it at her. 'You called me Veronica!'

If only she would become visible, I think.

Then I could catch her and impress upon her the truth of the situation, the gravity of what she has done. But she remains hazy, unhittable, too much loved.

I have come to tell her that Liam has been found.

'Are you all right?'

'Oh, Mammy.'

The last time I cried in this kitchen I was seventeen years old, which is old for crying, though maybe not in our family, where everyone seemed to be every age, all at once. I sweep my wet forearm along the table of yellow pine, with its thick, plasticky sheen. I turn my face towards her and ready it to say the ritual thing (there is a kind of glee to it, too, I notice) but, 'Veronica!' she says, all of a sudden and she moves — almost rushes — to the kettle. She puts her hand on the bakelite handle as the bubbles thicken against the chrome, and she lifts it, still plugged in, splashing some water in to heat the pot.

He didn't even like her.

There is a nick in the wall, over by the door, where Liam threw a knife at our mother, and everyone laughed and shouted at him. It is there among the other anonymous dents and marks. Famous. The hole Liam made, after my mother ducked, and

13

before everyone started to roar.

What could she have said to him? What possible provocation could she have afforded him — this sweet woman? And Ernest then, or Mossie, one of the enforcers, wrestling him out through the back door and on to the grass for a kicking. We laughed at that too. And my lost brother, Liam, laughed: the knife thrower, the one who was being kicked, he laughed too, and he grabbed his older brother's ankle to topple him into the grass. Also me — I was also laughing, as I recall. My mother clucking a little, at the sight of it, and going about her business again. My sister Midge picking up the knife and waggling it out the window at the fighting boys, before slinging it into the sink full of washing-up. If nothing else, our family had fun.

My mother puts the lid on the teapot and looks at me.

I am a trembling mess from hip to knee. There is a terrible heat, a looseness in my innards that makes me want to dig my fists between my thighs. It is a confusing feeling — somewhere between diarrhoea and sex — this grief that is almost genital.

It must have been over some boyfriend, the last time I cried here. Ordinary, family tears meant nothing in this kitchen; they were just part of the general noise. The only thing that mattered was, *He rang* or, *He didn't ring.* Some catastrophe. The kind of thing that would have you scrabbling at the walls after five bottles of cider. *He left me.* Doubling over, clutching your midriff; howling and gagging. *He didn't even call to get his scarf back.* The boy with the turquoise eyes.

Because we are also — at a guess — great lovers, the Hegartys. All eye-to-eye and sudden fucking and never, ever, letting go. Apart from the ones who couldn't love at all. Which is most of us, too, in a way.

Which is most of us.

'It's about Liam,' I say.

'Liam?' she says. *'Liam?'*

My mother had twelve children and — as she told me one hard day — seven miscarriages. The holes in her head are not her fault. Even so, I have never forgiven her any of it. I just can't.

I have not forgiven her for my sister Margaret who we called Midge, until she died, aged forty-two, from pancreatic cancer. I do not forgive her my beautiful, drifting sister Bea. I do not forgive her my first brother Ernest, who was a priest in Peru, until he became a lapsed priest in Peru. I do not forgive her my brother Stevie, who is a little angel in heaven. I do not forgive her the whole tedious litany of Midge, Bea, Ernest, Stevie, Ita, Mossie, Liam, Veronica, Kitty, Alice and the twins, Ivor and Jem.

Such epic names she gave us — none of your Jimmy, Joe or Mick. The miscarriages might have got numbers, like '1962' or '1964', though perhaps she named them too, in her heart (Serena, Aifric, Mogue). I don't forgive her those dead children either. The way she didn't even keep a notebook, so you could tell who had what, when, and which jabs. Am I the only woman in Ireland still at risk from polio myelitis? No one knows. I don't forgive the endless hand-me-downs, and few toys, and Midge walloping us because my mother was too gentle, or busy, or absent, or pregnant to bother.

My sweetheart mother. My ageless girl.

No, when it comes down to it, I do not forgive her the sex. The stupidity of so much humping. Open and blind. Consequences, Mammy. *Consequences.*

'Liam,' I say, quite forcefully. And the riot in the kitchen quiets down as I do my duty, which is to tell one human being about another human being, the few and careful details of how they met their end.

'I am afraid he is dead, Mammy.'

'Oh,' she says. Which is just what I expected her to say. Which is exactly the sound I knew would come out of her mouth.

'Where?' she says.

'In England, Mammy. Where he was. They found him in Brighton.'

'What do you mean?' she says. 'What do you mean, "Brighton"?'

'Brighton in England, Mammy. It's a town in the south of England. It's near London.'

And then she hits me.

I don't think she has ever hit me before. I try to remember later, but I really think that she left the hitting to other people: Midge of course, who was always mopping something, and so would swipe the cloth at you, in passing, across your face, or neck, or the back of the legs, and the smell of the thing, I always thought, worse than the sting. Mossie, who was a psycho. Ernest, who was a thoughtful, flat-handed sort of man. As you went down the line, the hitting lost authority and petered out, though I had a bit of a phase, myself, with Alice and the twins, Ivor-and-Jem.

But my mother has one hand on the table, and she swings around with the other one to catch me on the side of the head. Not very hard. Not hard at all. Then she swings back, and grabs for the counter, and she suspends herself there, between the counter and the table; her head dipping below the spread of her arms. For a while she is silent, and then a terrible sound comes out of her. Quite soft. It seems to lift up off her back. She raises her head and turns to me, so that I can witness her face; the look on it, now, and the way it will never be the same again.

Don't tell Mammy. It was the mantra of our childhoods, or one of them. *Don't tell Mammy.* This from Midge, especially, but also from any one of the older ones. If something broke or was spilt, if Bea did not come home or Mossie went up to live in the attic, or Liam dropped acid, or Alice had sex, or Kitty bled buckets into her new school uniform, or any number of phone messages about delays, snarl-ups, problems with bus money and taxi money, and once, catastrophically, Liam's night in the cells. None of the messages relayed: the whispered conference in the hall, *Don't tell Mammy,* because 'Mammy' would — what? Expire? 'Mammy' would worry. Which seemed fine to me. It was, after all, of her own making, this family. It had all come — singly and painfully — out of her. And my father said it more than anyone; level, gallant, *There's no need to tell your mother now,* as if the reality of his bed was all the reality that this woman should be asked to bear.

After my mother reaches over and hits me, for the first time, at the age of seventy to my thirty nine, my mind surges, almost bursts, with the unfairness of it all. I think I will die of unfairness; I think it will be written on my death certificate. That this duty should devolve to me, for a start — because I am the careful one, of course. I have a car, an accommodating phone bill. I have daughters who are not obliged to fight over who is wearing the other one's knickers in the morning before they go to school. So I am the one who has to drive over to Mammy's and ring the doorbell and put myself in a convenient hitting position on the other side of her kitchen table. It is not as if I got these things by accident — husband, car, phone bill, daughters. So I am in a rage with every single one of my brothers and sisters, including Stevie, long dead, and Midge, recently dead, and I am boiling mad with Liam for being dead too, just now, when I need him most. Quite literally, I am beyond myself. I am so angry I have a second view of the kitchen, a high view, looking down: me with one wet sleeve rolled up, my bare forearm lying flat on the table, and on the other side of the table, my mother, cruciform, her head drooping from the little white triangle of her bare neck.

19

This is where Liam is. Up here. I feel him like a shout in the room. This is what he sees; my bare arm, our mother playing aeroplane between the counter and the table. Flying low.

'Mammy.'

The sound keeps coming out of her. I lift my arm.

'Mammy.'

She has no idea of how much has been done for her in the six days since the first phone call from Britain. She was spared all that: Kitty running around London and me around Dublin for dental records; his height, and the colour of his hair, and the tattoo on his right shoulder. None of this was read back to her as it was to me, this morning, by the very nice bean garda who called to the door, because I am the one who loved him most. I feel sorry for police-women — all they do is relatives, and prostitutes, and cups of tea.

There is saliva falling from my mother's bottom lip now, in gobs and strings. Her mouth keeps opening. She keeps trying to close it but her lips refuse to stay shut and, 'Gah. Gah,' she says.

I must go over and touch her. I must take her by the shoulders and lift her gently up and away. I will squeeze her arms back down by her sides as I push and guide her to a chair, and put sugar in her cup of tea, though she does not take sugar. I will do all this in deference to a grief that is biological, idiot, timeless.

She would cry the same for Ivor, less for Mossie, more for Ernest, and inconsolably, as we all would, for the lovely Jem. She would cry no matter what son he was. It occurs to me that we have got something wrong here, because I am the one who has lost something that can not be replaced. She has plenty more.

There were eleven months between me and Liam. We came out of her on each other's tails; one after the other, as fast as a gang-bang, as fast as an infidelity. Sometimes I think we overlapped in there, he just left early, to wait outside.

'Are you all right, Mammy? Will you have a cup of tea?'

She eyes me: very tiny, in the big chair. She gives me a narked look and her head twitches away. And it comes down on me like a curse. Who am I to touch, to handle and discard, the stuff of a mother's love?

I am Veronica Hegarty. Standing at the sink in my school uniform; fifteen maybe, sixteen years old; crying over a lost boy-friend and being comforted by a woman who can not, for the life of her, remember my name. I am Veronica Hegarty, thirty-nine, spooning sugar into a cup of tea for the loveliest woman in Dublin, who has just had some terrible news.

'I'm just going to ring Mrs Cluny.'

'Ring her?' she says. '*Ring* her?' Because Mrs Cluny only lives next door.

'Yes, Mammy,' and she suddenly remembers that her son is dead. She checks again to see if it could be true and I nod in a fake sort of way. No wonder she doesn't believe me. I hardly believe it myself.

3

The seeds of my brother's death were sown many years ago. The person who planted them is long dead — at least that's what I think. So if I want to tell Liam's story, then I have to start long before he was born. And, in fact, this is the tale that I would love to write: history is such a romantic place, with its jarveys and urchins and side-buttoned boots. If it would just stay still, I think, and settle down. If it would just stop sliding around in my head.

All right.

Lambert Nugent first saw my grandmother Ada Merriman in a hotel foyer in 1925. This is the moment I choose. It was seven o'clock in the evening. She was nineteen, he was twenty-three.

She walked into the foyer and did not look about her and sat in an oval-backed chair near the door. Lamb Nugent watched her through a rush of arrivals and instructions as she removed her left-hand glove and then picked off the right. She pulled a little bracelet out from under her sleeve, and the hand that held the gloves settled in her lap.

She was beautiful, of course.

It is hard to say what Lamb Nugent looked like, at twenty-three. He has been in the grave so long, it is hard to think of him innocent or sweating, when all of that is gone to dust.

What did she see in him?

He must be reassembled; click clack; his muscles hooked to bone and wrapped with fat, the whole skinned over and dressed in a suit of navy or brown — something about the cut of the lapels, maybe, that is a little too sharp, and the smell on his hands would be already a little finer than carbolic. He had it down, even then, the dour narcissism of the ordinary man, and all his acts of self-love were both subtle and exact. He did not preen. Lamb Nugent watched. Or he did not watch so much as let it enter into him — the world, in all its nuance of who owed what to whom.

Which is what he saw, presumably, when my grandmother walked in through the door. His baby eyes. His two black pupils, into which the double image of Ada Merriman walked, and sat. She was wearing blue, or so I imagine it. Her blue self settled in the grey folds of his brain, and it stayed there for the rest of his life.

It was five past seven. The talk in the foyer was of rain, and what to do with the jarvey and whether refreshments would be required; after which the knot of arrivals was pulled in a string through the front lounge door, and the two servants were left behind to wait; she in her neat chair, he with his elbow on the high reception desk, like a man standing at a bar.

In which position, they stayed for three and a half hours.

They belonged to the lower orders. Waiting was not a problem, for them.

Ada did not pretend to notice him, at first. This may have been the polite thing to do, but also I think he would have had it from the start, this trick of not existing much. And the rages he suffered in later life must have been, in 1925, the usual run of passions and young hopes. If Nugent suffered from anything, in those early days, it was decency. He was a decent man. He was not a man much used to hotels. He was not used to women who showed such twitching precision in the way they worked a glove. There was nothing in his history to prepare him for Ada Merriman. But, he was surprised to find, he was ready for her all the same.

Behind the high desk, the little concierge hung a key on his board, then clicked away to check a bell. He came back to the desk, wrote a note, and left again. A maid came out of the back kitchen carrying tea on a tray. She mounted the stairs and turned on to an upper corridor and never came back down. They were alone.

Such discretion. Because Dublin was full of proud women as well as decent men, and you could be loud about it or you might, like this pair, be easy and silent. And in the quietness of their attention they each realised the strength of the other and the fact that neither would be the first to walk away.

There are so few people given us to love. I want to tell my daughters this, that each time you fall in love it is important, even at nineteen. Especially at nineteen. And if you can, at nineteen, count the people you love on one hand, you will not, at forty, have run out of fingers on the other. There are so few people given us to love and they all stick.

So there is Nugent, stuck to Ada Merriman before the clock strikes the quarter-hour. And she to him, by implication — although she does not know it yet, or does not look as if she knows it. Meanwhile, the light fades and nothing happens. The maid who never came back downstairs comes through the foyer with another tray and she mounts the stairs again and disappears one more time into the dark of the top corridor. In the room behind the reception desk they hear someone open a door and enquire after a Miss Hackett. And Ada Merriman looks into the respectable middle distance, where Lamb Nugent does not believe a single word she says.

The air between them is too thin for love. The only thing that can be thrown across the air of Dublin town is a kind of jeering.

I know you.

But it is too late for all that. It has already happened. It happened when she walked in the door; when she looked about her, but only as far as the chair. It happened in the perfection with which she managed to be present but not seen. And all the rest was just agitation: first of all that she should notice him back (and she did — she noticed his stillness), and secondly that she should love him as he loved her; suddenly, completely, and beyond what had been allocated to them as their station.

Ada reads him with the side of her face; the down on her cheek bristles with all that she needs to know about the young man

27

who is standing on the other side of the room. It is the beginning of a blush, this knowledge, but Ada does not blush. She looks at her bracelet: a narrow chain in rose gold, with a T at the clasp, like the fob of a watch. She fingers this small anomaly — a male thing on her girl's wrist — and feels Nugent's disbelief weigh against her. Then she lifts her head very slightly to say, 'So?'

Quite brazen.

He might hate her now, though Nugent is too young, at twenty-three, to put a name on the emotion that sweeps through him and is gone, pulling in its wake a change of air. Something open. A zephyr. What is it?

Desire.

At thirteen minutes past seven desire breathes on the young lips of Lamb Nugent — hush! He feels its awful proximity. The need to move surges through him, but he does not move. He stands his ground while, across the room, Ada's stillness becomes triumphant. If he is very patient, she might look at him, now. If he is very humble, she might state her terms.

Or maybe she won't. Nothing has been said. No one has moved. It is possible that Nugent is imagining it all — or that I am. Maybe he is a pathetic thing at twenty-three; all hand-wrung tweed cap and

Adam's apple; maybe Ada doesn't even notice him there across the room.

But this is 1925. A man. A woman. She *must* know what lies ahead of them now. She knows because she is beautiful. She knows because of all the things that have happened since. She knows because she is my Granny, and when she put her hand on my cheek I felt the nearness of death and was comforted by it. There is nothing as tentative as an old woman's touch; as loving or as horrible.

Ada was a fantastic woman. I have no other word for her. For the set of her shoulders and the way she trotted off down the street, with her shopping bag flapping at her hip. Her hands were never empty, and you never saw what was in them; whatever was to be folded or washed or moved or wiped. You never noticed her eating either, because she was always listening to you, or talking; the food just disappeared; like it didn't actually go into a hole in her face. Her manners were perfect, in other words, and contagious. Even when I was eight years old, I knew she had charm.

But how did Nugent know it, before she ever opened her mouth to speak to him? I can only suppose that it did not matter, that there were phases and stages to his attachment (he hated her, after all, before a quarter past seven), each of which he must re-enact in longer cycles — years long, or decades — he must move from love to a kind of sneering, he must be smitten by hatred and touched by desire, he must find a final humility and so begin with love again. Each time around he would know more about her — more about himself perhaps — and nothing he learned would make any difference. By fourteen minutes past seven, they are back just where they began.

But what of love?

Nugent does move now, quite suddenly. He ducks his forehead down and rubs his hairline at the roots. Is it possible that she might love him too? That they return to the moment when she walked in the door, and rise above these petty concerns of exchange and loss?

Ah yes, says the side of Ada's sad face. And she thinks about love for a while.

Nugent feels it stir in the deep root of his penis; the future, or the beginning of the future. No one interrupts them, now. Someone has strangled the maid in an upstairs room; the puppet concierge is thrown on a chair. There are fourteen feet of carpet between them. Nugent thinks of the swell of his glans easing out from its sack of skin and Ada thinks about love, while the hotel clock slips, and softly grinds, and whirrs into the quarter-hour chimes.

Dee dee de dee dah!

Dah dah de dee dah!

Revived, summoned, the little concierge trots into the gloom of the foyer with a small footstool which he places under a lamp on the wall. He trots out again and comes back with a spill held aloft, its flame made dingy by the last light of day. He stands on the stool to remove the shade, turns on the jet, fumbles the spill and, before it is altogether too late, manages the flame to the gas. It hisses hollow and blue before settling into the yellow-green glow of the mantle, and the light dips and then bounces out into the room. The foyer is sick with the smell of gas, followed by the warm smell of burnt paper, as black flakes scatter from the man's quick fluttering fingers. He replaces the shade, moves the stool under the next lamp, and leaves.

In his absence, the room pulses darker. And darker again.

He returns. Nugent and Ada both look at him as he completes the ritual of the lamp and stool; his entrances and exits; his ghastly self-importance as he moves around the walls towards the fourth and final lamp, which is above the chair in which Ada sits. He sets the stool beside her feet, as though bowing, and eases himself away again. After a long moment he comes back with the flame he might, but did not, take from the fire burning in the grate. He didn't want to bend over in front of them, perhaps, though he has no compunction about making Ada stand. He pauses before her, dipping the spill one way and another, saving and coaxing the flame back along the paper. He looks to her face. And waits.

Ada's dress rustles loose from her lap as she rises to her feet. And it may as well have fallen altogether on the floor; the dress might have been made of water, it might have been a puddle of colour around her feet, so naked does she look now. Nugent stares quite frankly while she clasps her hands in front of her, and looks down. At first he pities her, and then he does not. He shifts at last, at the side of the desk, and takes comfort from the smell that escapes in a sigh from under his shirt. Thank God for that. It is not his fault.

He was at the Pro-Cathedral that morning, for early Mass. He walked in a line with other men for Holy Communion. The look on their faces was as hungry as poor men queuing for soup. And when he got up from his knees, he did so like a decent man: slow in the haunches, heavy with the weight of his life on this earth, sad for the people he loved. Brave.

It is Lent. Nugent has given up rashers, sausages and all kinds of offal for the duration, also strong drink. His body has been cleansed by the workings of his soul — so the smell that rises from under his shirt has something of the spring air in it, a whiff of early morning soap, the quiet ming of a day's toil. The cloth of his suit is decently worn and the collar of his shirt is decently clean, and his life stretches ahead of him decently waxing into a solid middle age.

With one small interruption — because there is nothing decent about the glint in his baby eye, looking at Ada Merriman in the foyer of the Belvedere Hotel.

She has looked back at him. Standing — as it were, naked — with her hands clasped in front of her, she has lifted her face and looked him in the eye.

This is the shock. The shock is the complete self of Ada Merriman. Her pupils widen to receive him; they rush open, and Nugent is glad of the support, beside him, of the desk's wooden wall.

Then they smile. Ada smiles. Like there is

some joke in the room, that she wants him to share.

Nugent looks at her. He wonders which part of her body she finds so amusing. Is it her breasts, or her throat? Either she does not realise she is naked (she is, after all, fully dressed), or else she does not care. She may be laughing at the little man who is lighting the lamps. Or she may be laughing at him — standing there like a gobdaw with a lump in his pants. And Nugent's eyes swell with the unfairness of it, and with the force of love denied.

Except — as the little lamplighter might tell him — she has not denied him anything yet. She has not denied him, at all.

The gas lights burble and faintly hiss as the stool is lifted and the man withdraws, angled slightly towards these lovers in cynical courtesy, as if he can see it all, the coupling (such squelchings), the money, the lies that they have already begun to tell. Oh, if it was a song you could sing it. If it was a song you could batter it out on the spoons. Especially in Dublin, in 1925.

This is all my romance, of course. Everyone had a beautiful grandmother — something to do with sepia and the orange blossom in their hair. Also the steady look in those old-fashioned eyes. We do not know how to be brave, any more, as a bride was brave in those days. Here is Ada's wedding picture: she wears the low veil of the 1920s and the silk of her dress shows its tender, hand-sewn stitches in a line of dents around the hem. She was pure and she burned. Ada Merriman, my modest, ardent grandmother, was the thing poets wrote about, in 1925.

She has my feet. Or I have hers: long, with scraggly toes. Also the large-boned ankles and endless, flat shins that made me feel so gawky at school, before I learned how to put them to use. I have an expensive body, I realised, sometime in 1979. It isn't a sex thing. Lawyers want to breed out of me and architects want me to sit on their new Eames chairs. Nothing too big at the front, just rangy and tall. So I dress up well, I suppose — though nothing would persuade me into a skirt that stopped mid-calf, to show my transvestite ankles and my poor knobbly toes.

So there is something pathetic about Ada's big feet in satin shoes. She is married. She is happy. Or so I fancy, as I put her photo back into the shoebox that holds all that remains of her story, now.

She did not marry Nugent, you will be relieved to hear. She married his friend

Charlie Spillane. And not just because he had a car.

But he never left her. My grandmother was Lamb Nugent's most imaginative act. I may not forgive him, but it is this — the way he stayed true to it — that defines the man most, for me.

4

I ring the bereavement people in Brighton and Hove from Mammy's phone in the hall, and they give me the number of an undertaker who, very nicely, takes my credit card details while I have it handy. There is the coffin to consider, of course, and for some reason I already know that I will go for the limed oak — a decision that is up to me, because I am the one who loved him most. And how much will all that cost? I think as I put down the phone.

Mrs Cluny comes in from next door, utterly silent. She swarms through the hall and into the kitchen and closes the door. After a little while, I hear my mother's voice start up, very low.

I don't have the patience for the old, circular dial, so I switch to my mobile and walk around the house as I go, ringing the lot of them, in Clontarf and Phibsboro, in Tucson, Arizona, to say, 'Bad news, about

Liam. Yes. Yes, I'm afraid so.' And, 'I'm in Mammy's. Shocked. Really shocked.' The news will be discussed along lines too slight and tender to trace. Jem will ring Ivor, and Ivor will ring Mossie's wife, and Ita will source Father Ernest, somewhere north of Arequipa. Then they will all ring back here later — or their wives will — for times and reasons and gory details and flights.

I walk through the dimness of our child-hood rooms and I touch nothing.

All the beds are dressed and ready. The girls slept upstairs and the boys on the ground floors (we had a system, you see). It is a warren. The twins' bunk-beds are in a little room on the left of the hall door — the one where baby Stevie died. On the other side of this room is a doorway to the garage extension, with its three single beds. Beyond that again is the garden passage, where Ernest slept on a mattress on the floor, then Mossie, when Ernest left, and Liam last of all.

The slanting roof of the passage is made of clear, corrugated perspex. The mattress is still there, pushing up against the yellow garden door, with its window of pebbled glass. Liam's Marc Bolan poster is gone, but you can still see the soiled tabs of Sello-tape dangling from the breeze-block wall.

I had my first ever cigarette in here.

I sit on the mattress, which is covered with a rough blue blanket, and I ring my last, baby brother.

'Hi Jem. No, everything's fine. I have bad news, though, about Liam.' And Jem, the youngest of us, the easiest and best loved, says, 'Well, at least that's done.'

I try Kitty's again and listen to the phone ringing in her empty London flat. I lie down and look at the corrugated perspex roof, and I wonder how you might undo all these sheds and extensions, take the place back to the house it once was. If it would be possible to unbuild it all and start again.

When Bea arrives, I open the hall door and take her by both forearms, and we swing around like this as she passes me in the dark hall. I follow her into the kitchen's yellow light and see that my mother has aged five, maybe ten years in the time it took me to make the calls.

'Goodnight, Mammy. Do you want to take something? Do you want a doctor now, for something to help you sleep?'

'No, no. No thanks.'

'I'm going over there, to sort things out,' I say.

'England?' she says. 'Now?'

'I'll ring, OK?'

Her cheek, when I kiss it, is terribly soft. I glance over at Bea who gives me a dark look, full of blame.

Don't tell Mammy.

Like it is all my fault.

My father used to sit in the kitchen watching telly until eleven o'clock, with the newspaper adrift in his lap. After the news he would fold the paper, get out of the chair, switch the telly off (no matter who was watching it) and make his way to bed. The milk bottles were rinsed and put on the step. One of the twins might be lifted on to a potty and tucked back into sleep. Then he would go into the room where he slept with my mother. She would already be in bed, reading and sighing since half past nine. There would be some muted talk, the sound of his keys and coins as he left them down. The rattle of his belt buckle. One shoe hitting the floor.

Silence.

There were girls at school whose families grew to a robust five or six. There were girls with seven or eight — which was thought a little enthusiastic — and then there were the pathetic ones like me, who had parents that were just helpless to it, and bred as naturally as they might shit.

Instead of turning left outside Mammy's, I turn right for the airport road. I don't think about where I am going, I think about the rain, the indicator, the drag of the rubber wiper against the glass. I think about nothing — there is nothing to think about. And then I think about a drink. Nothing messy. A fierce little naggin of whiskey, maybe, or gin. I float towards it in my nice Saab 9.3 — towards the idea of it, flowering in my mouth.

I am always thirsty when I leave that house — something to do with the unfairness of the place. But I won't drink. Not yet. Kitty was so slammed when she rang earlier that all I could hear down the line was a stupid yowling.

'Owjz. Hizz,' she said. 'Hizz. Hizj im. Ohsfs. Hi.' By which I was supposed to gather that a policewoman had just called to her door too. And, yes it was a bad wait; though not such a long one. The trick *being,* I wanted to say to her down the line, the trick being to get drunk after the news and not before. It is a thin line, Kitty, but we think it is important. Out here, in the real world, we think it makes a difference.

41

Fact / Conjecture. Dead / Alive. Drunk / Sober. Out in the world that is not the world of the Hegarty family, we think these things are Not The Same Thing.

I didn't say any of this, of course. I said, 'Huh huh ho God.'

And she said, 'Ay ghai Ay Hizj.'

And I said, 'Ho ho ho oh ho God.'

And this went on until a man took the receiver and said, 'Is that Kitty's sister?' in a nice South London accent. And I had to be polite to him, and apologise a little that my brother had died all over his Thursday afternoon.

I realise that I am driving the wrong way for home, so I stop and ring my husband Tom at the traffic lights and say I won't be back tonight. I don't want the girls to see me, or worry about me, until I have got this thing done.

He says everything will be fine, just fine. Everything will be fine. His voice is trembling a little and I realise that if I do not end the call he will tell me that he loves me, that this is the next thing he is going to say.

'It's all right,' I say. 'Bye bye. Bye bye.' And I pull back into the traffic and the airport road.

There is something wonderful about a death, how everything shuts down, and all the ways you thought you were vital are not even vaguely important. Your husband can feed the kids, he can work the new oven, he can find the sausages in the fridge, after all. And his important meeting was not important, not in the slightest. And the girls will be picked up from school, and dropped off again in the morning. Your eldest daughter can remember her inhaler, and your youngest will take her gym kit with her, and it is just as you suspected — most of the stuff that you do is just stupid, really stupid, most of the stuff you do is just nagging and whining and picking up for people who are too lazy even to love you, even that, let alone find their own shoes under their own bed; people who turn and accuse you — scream at you sometimes — when they can only find one shoe.

And I am crying by now, heading down the airport road, I am bawling my eyes out behind the wheel of my Saab 9.3, because even the meeting your husband has, the vital meeting, was not important (how could you ever, even for a moment, think such things were important?) and he loves you completely for the half an hour, or half a week in which your brother is freshly dead.

I should probably pull over but I do not pull over: I cry-drive all the way. At Collins

Avenue, a man stuck in the oncoming traffic looks across at me, sobbing and gagging in my posh tin box. He is two feet away from me. He is just there. He gives me a look of complete sympathy, and then he eases past. It has happened to us all.

And what amazes me as I hit the motorway is not the fact that everyone loses someone, but that everyone loves someone. It seems like such a massive waste of energy — and we all do it, all the people beetling along between the white lines, merging, converging, overtaking. We each love someone, even though they will die. And we keep loving them, even when they are not there to love any more. And there is no logic or use to any of this, that I can see.

In the airport, I drive round and round the car park, floor after floor, until I am out under the evening sky. Liam used to laugh at me for this. Everyone used to laugh at me. The way I always park in the space that is nearest the planes: and that space is up on the roof, out in the rain.

I turn the engine off and watch the drops shunting down the windscreen.

The last time I brought him here, I could not wait to see him gone.

Seriously. The last time I brought him here, I sat for a moment, looking straight ahead, and the bulk of him in the front seat beside me was remarkable: the dark heap of him, when I turned and spoke to the brother that I knew — Christ! this grey thing in an unwashed shirt, this horrible old fucker, that I turned to and said, 'So. Plenty of time.'

I walked him all the way to the departure gates and watched him go through. I wondered was it possible for him to come back out again. It occurred to me that it could not be against the law. You can go right up to the gate and change your mind. You can even spring out of your seat on the plane and change your mind and walk back the way you came, back out into Ireland, where you can make everyone miserable, for another little while.

Usually, people's brothers become less important, over time. Liam decided not to do this. He decided to stay important, to the end.

A plane roars low overhead and, when it is gone, I am hanging on to the steering wheel, with my mouth wide open. We stay locked like this for a while, me and the car, then I sit back up and open the door.

While I am doing this — my mute screaming in my convertible Saab in the airport car park in the rain — I can feel Liam laughing at me. Or I feel his absence laughing at me. Because, somewhere, over there to the side — the place you can't quite see — he is completely there, and not there at all. He is not unhappy, I realise, now that he is dead. But it is not just his *mood* I feel as a warmth at the base of my spine. It is his disappeared, dead, essential self. It is the very heart of him, all gone, or going now.

Goodbye Vee

Goodbye

Goodbye

I open the door and climb out into the rain.

5

Here is my grandfather, Charlie Spillane, driving up O'Connell Street towards his future wife in the Belvedere Hotel.

It is half past ten on a Tuesday night. It is Lent. A few profane couples drift out of the Gresham or the Savoy Grill to take the tram or start the walk home, but otherwise the town is quiet. Charlie's car is a thick grey and when it slips under a streetlamp a pool of blue leather opens to the night. The hood is down, the brasses gleam and Charlie's head gleams. It is a beautiful thing, this car — which is not quite Charlie's car: though he has had it so long we can assume the man who left it with him is not coming back.

This is the car that lived in Ada's garage when I was a child, a Bullnose Morris, with a cracked old hood, like the hood of a giant pram. By the time I saw it, there wasn't much of it left, even the doors were missing. I used to sit in the front seat and listen to the mice running through the engine, in the stillness of the summer afternoons.

Or, 'Vroom vroom!' Liam would say, beside me. 'Vroom vroom.'

In 1925 the car is still a beautiful thing. Charlie revs it along with tremendous shifting of gears and pedals — Nugent thinks he shouldn't be driving it at all, so ruinous is this pumping, grinding technique to clutch-springs and valves. The front brakes are split open in a pool of their own fluid, on a table in his digs — Nugent is not the owner of the car either, but he does love it. Standing in the foyer of the Belvedere Hotel, he listens for the engine without knowing what he is listening for. Charlie, meantime, is running about Dublin on the back brakes only, seeing a man about a dog.

He is a swerver, Charlie. He does not like endings. He does not even like beginning things. When he does fall in love it is only because he finds that it is already slipping away from him. He grabs Ada, in other words, just at the moment that she turns to go.

But Ada does not know Charlie yet. Ada Merriman stands in the foyer of the Belvedere Hotel and looks at Lamb Nugent, while outside, Charlie Spillane cruises into Great Denmark Street, towards the wife he has not yet met. He is about to pull in at the door of the Belvedere Hotel, he is nearly there, when the spire of the Findlater's Church puts him in mind of something, and he roars off to The Hut in Phibsboro, to see a man about a dog.

Nugent cocks an ear after the escaping motor. There is a pause as the engine fades, and then the silence starts to spread. It seeps into the foyer of the Belvedere; the distant rustle of streets turning over from day into evening, as the night deepens and the drinking begins — elsewhere. As women shush their babies, and men ease their feet out of boots, and girls who have been working all evening wash themselves in distant rooms and check a scrap of mirror, before going out to work again.

On the other side of the room, Ada's breathing is so shallow and mild she might be an angel occupying, for the moment, the figure of a doll. Her throat is a pillar, as the poet might say, and her lips are sculpted shut in the light.

A spent coal slips in the grate with a whispering 'chink'.

Here come the dead.

They hunker around the walls and edge towards the last heat of the fire: Nugent's sister Lizzy; his mother, who does not like being dead at all. Nugent's ghosts twitter, soft and unassuaged, while Ada's make no sound at all.

Why is that?

She is an orphan. Of course.

A face appears at the front-door glass, and pushes open the door. A quick, pokey little face, with a beard. It looks around, and withdraws. The dead are scattered, but after a moment they start to return and, as though Ada can not bear it, she rises swiftly and walks over to the desk, where she rings the bell.

Ding ding!

They are standing beside each other — at last! — Ada and Nugent at the desk, and she is amused by it. The freedom and the ease of her is insult and provocation to Nugent — poor Nugent, who feels the eighteen inches between them more keenly than any other measure of air. Who would push any part of himself into any part of her and find relief in it. Who might put his hands into her belly, to feel the heat and slither of her insides.

Do not mock.

'This much,' he wants to say. 'I already love you this much.'

'Hello. Hello in there.'

The concierge swims out from the darkness of his back room.

'Do you have such a thing for the jarvey as a hot rum? For the man outside?' She turns to Nugent and says, 'I don't know why I do it for him, he's never there when you're looking. Only to stop him sneaking off I suppose.'

Then she walks back towards her chair by the door. She is only nineteen after all. And he is only twenty-three.

'I have a friend who owns a car,' he says, all of a sudden.

'Do you?' She stops; interested and pert.

'He should be here any minute, he should be here by now.'

'I'd love a go in a car,' says Ada. 'I'd be mad for a go in a car.'

And she swivels about to sit in her chair.

Oh for a rope to pull it from under her — Nugent skidding across the room to catch her in his arms. They could kiss in black and white, she turning away for the caption:

Stop!!

Because it is not only Lent, but spring. How else would you have it? Ada Merriman is beautiful and Lamb Nugent is no better than he should be, and this is all we need to know — that when she walked in through the door, and sat with such quiet grace on that little oval-backed chair, he saw a life in which no one owed anyone a thing. Not a jot.

A car pulls up outside. Nugent hears the engine's throbbing and the look he gives to Ada turns to one of pain and farewell — as if their situation were in some way impossible. But it is not impossible, and the alarm that flares between them now is just another kind of delight.

There is nothing that they do alone. Not any more.

Together they turn, as Charlie Spillane arrives through the door, raffish with drink, hearty with promises broken and appointments missed. His eye checks Nugent leaning up against the front desk — then he casts about him until he sees the figure in blue, sitting at the wall by the door. Oh.

'Ma'am,' he says, doffing his (imagined) bowler hat, 'I hope this fellow has been keeping you amused.'

And Ada laughs.

Just like that. With a sweep of his arm, Charlie has changed the maths of it — of his future and of my past.

Here are the two friends, leaving Ada Merriman.

Charlie indicates the hotel door to his pal and walks outside. He sits back into the Bullnose Morris and picks up his driving gloves. Then he rubs his face with them. He rubs his face as a man who has stopped crying, after crying for a long time. Nugent climbs in beside him. Charlie gives her some choke, struggles over the sharp hump of the forgotten chock, and drives on.

Conways is dark. They circle the Rotunda and stop back on Parnell Street where they find a lock-in in the back room of the Blue Lion — an unholy pub. There is an air of recent hurt; the smell of something burnt coming out of the jakes in the yard.

'A bottle and a lemonade,' says Charlie.

They taste their drink and look with circumspection at the murderous clientele of the Blue Lion. Charlie has a small opinion about the car while Nugent examines the grain of the wood and the shine of the low brass rail.

On the way home, Nugent tilts out of his seat to stand with his head a little higher than the car's front window, and he lets the night air lap his face. As they bowl along the Green, he glances at the girls who are waiting, even in Lent, for the nobs to come out of the Shelbourne: a series of white ovals, their faces twist around like turning leaves, at the sound of a car.

He plumps back into his seat as they slide to a stop, some distance beyond his door.

'Give it a look, will you?' says Charlie, meaning the brake drum, split open on the table in Nugent's digs.

'I will,' he says, and waves Charlie off at the front door.

Inside, Nugent looks around his little room; the narrow bed, the window, with two lace curtains like hair parted over a little square face and tied on either side. He looks at his small table — the broken brakes of the Bullnose Morris, beautiful as a picture of apples in the moonlight. He starts to unbutton his shirt, standing in the darkness. His shirt opens one button at a time. It parts in a V over the flesh of his chest. Further and further down. And Nugent is on his knees. He pulls off his shirt on his knees, and swings it around behind him, so the buttons hit his back, once, twice; and then he starts his night prayers.

Here she comes.

Lizzy.

His sister. Younger than him. She died. The room they grew up in was full of the wet rattle of her chest; the horrible gurgle of phlegm and the shocking bright blood. Nugent can not forget the nightly rosary,

54

said at a terrible, safe distance from her bed; her white knuckles fumbling on the coverlet for the dropped beads, or the dark light in her eyes as she looked at him, like she saw right through to his bones. His own puberty going unnoticed — almost to himself — as her little breasts swelled under the night-dress. She moved towards death and womanhood at the same pace, the nipples like a spreading bruise, the breasts growing, and failing to grow, over lungs hard with disease. And so, she died.

Is that enough for him to think about, while he is on his knees?

That when he holds his penis in the night-time, it feels like her thin skin; always damp, never sweating. Because, in those days, people used to be mixed up together in the most disgusting ways.

6

This is how I live my life since Liam died. I stay up all night. I write, or I don't write. I walk the house.

Nothing settles here. Not even the dust.

We bought eight years ago, in 1990; a new five-bedroom detached. It's all a bit Tudor-red-brick-with-Queen-Anne-overtones, though there is, thank God, no portico and inside I have done it in oatmeal, cream, sandstone, slate. It is a daytime house so late at night I leave all the lights on with the dimmers turned up high and I walk from room to room. They open into each other so nicely. And I am alone. The girls are just a residue; a movie protruding from the mouth of the machine, a glitter lipstick beside the phone. Tom, my high-maintenance man, is upstairs dreaming his high-maintenance dreams of hurt and redemption in the world of corporate finance, and it is all nothing to do with me.

Oatmeal, cream, sandstone, slate.

I started with all sorts of pelmets when we moved in, even swags. I wanted the biggest floral I could find for the bay window at the front — can you imagine it? By the time I had the stuff sourced, I had already moved on to plain Roman blinds and now the garden is properly grown in I want . . . nothing. I spend my time looking at things and wishing them gone, clearing objects away.

This is how I live my life.

I stay up all night. At half eleven, if he is home, Tom puts his head around the door of the small study and says, 'Don't stay up all night!' as if he didn't know that I will not sleep with him, not for a good while yet, and perhaps never again — which is how all this started, in a way, my refusal to climb in beside my husband a month or so after Liam died, my inability to sleep in any other bed than the one we used to share. Because I will not have the girls find me in the spare room.

What else can I do? We could not afford a divorce. Besides I do not want to leave him. I can not sleep with him, that is all. So my husband is waiting for me to sleep with him again, and I am waiting for something else. I am waiting for things to become clear.

So we do nothing. We divide our time. At

least I do. I take what Tom has left me of the day — there is plenty of it — and I live in his sleep. At seven a.m., when his alarm goes off, I get into bed and he turns to me and complains at the coldness of my rump. He says, 'Did you stay up all night again?'

'Sorry.'

As if this was the problem. As if we would have sex, if it weren't for the coldness of my ass and the eternal, infernal awkwardness of our *schedules.*

He gets the girls up and out, and so I sleep until three when I drag my face around to the school gates. After which, I ferry them to their ballet or Irish dancing or horse riding, or just home, where they might be allowed to watch telly before tea. I limit the telly — I say it is for their own good, but really it is for me. I like to talk to them. If I don't talk to them I think I will die of something — call it irrelevance — I think I will just fade away.

So I get a daughter on the sofa and manhandle her into loving me a little: Rebecca who is so dippy and kind, or Emily, the cat, the Daddy's girl; a bit hopeless, a bit cold, and her Hegarty-blue eyes the place where my heart founders most. We cuddle up, and there is messing and chat, then there is shouting about homework, or uneaten food, or bedtimes, and at half past nine, when the shouting and the messing is over and they are asleep, I start to prowl.

They don't really want me, I think. They are just putting up with me for a while.

Sitting room to living room to dining room to kitchen, a single flow of space around the stairs; the ground floor is open plan with a small study tucked on the other side of the hall door. If Tom comes home I will go in there. Some nights I go online. But mostly, I write about Ada and Nugent in the Belvedere, endlessly, over and again.

At half past eleven, Tom puts his head around the door and says, 'Don't stay up all night!' and when his footsteps are gone, the world is mine.

And what a crazy world it is!

There are long stretches of time when I don't know what I am doing, or what I have done — nothing mostly, but sometimes it would be nice to know what kind of nothing that was. I might have a bout of cleaning around four. I do it like a thief, holding my breath as I scrub, stealing the dirt off the walls. I try not to drink before half past five, but I always do drink — from the top of the wine bottle to the last, little drop. It is the only way I know to make the day end.

Late at night, I hear voices in bursts and

snatches — like a radio switched on and switched off again, in another room. Incoherent, but quite cheerful. Stories bouncing off the walls. Scraps of lives, leaking through. Whisperings in the turn of a door handle. Birds on the roof. The occasional bleeping of a child's toy. And once, my brother's voice saying, 'Now. Now.'

I listened for him again, but he was gone.

As I open the fridge, my mind is subject to jolts and lapses; the stair you miss as you fall asleep. Portents. I feel the future falling through the roof of my mind and when I look nothing is there. A rope. Something dangling in a bag, that I can not touch.

I have all my regrets between pouring the wine and reaching for the glass.

Sometimes, I go up to look at my bed, without me in it. Tom sleeps on his back. He does not snore. Sometimes, when he is sad in his sleep, he turns on his side and his hands gather under his chin. My husband, twitching as he dreams.

Tom moves money around, electronically. Every time he does this, a tiny bit sticks to him. Day by day. Hour by hour. Minute by minute. Quite a lot of it, in the long run.

Liam, my brother, spent most of his working life as a hospital porter in the Hampstead Royal Free. He pushed beds down corridors and put cancerous lumps into bags and carried severed limbs down to the incinerator, and he enjoyed it, he said. He liked the company.

I used to be a journalist. I used to write about shopping (well someone has to). Now I look after the kids — what's that called?

Tom had sex with me the night of the wake — as if Liam's death had blown all the cobwebs away: the fuss and the kids and the big, busy job and the late nights spent strenuously not sleeping with other women. He was getting back to basics: telling me that he loved me, telling me that my brother might be dead but that he was very much alive. Exercising his right. I love my husband, but I lay there with one leg on either side of his dancing, country-boy hips and I did not feel alive. I felt like a chicken when it is quartered.

7

But let that wait. Let the poor chicken wait awhile.

Here I am on the Brighton line, on my way to collect my brother's body, or view it, or say hello to it, or goodbye, or whatever you do to a body you once loved. *Pay your respects.* It is a mellow autumn day. I look out the window and am surprised that the Downs exist. There has always been something childish about England for me.

Haywards Heath
Wivelsfield
Burgess Hill
Hassocks

Names so silly and twee they must be made up. The constant surprise of this land, that it is actually green and actually pleasant. That it is actually there. It moves past me, but at different speeds. In the middle distance a swathe of countryside moves serencly on, while the far hills run backwards slightly, in a narrow strip. I try to find the line along which the landscape holds still and changes its mind, thinking that travel is a contrary kind of thing, because moving towards a dead man is not moving at all.

Then my sister Bea rings.

'Hello?'

'Are you on roaming?'

'I don't know.'

'Well, if you're in England you're on roaming.'

'All right, I'm on roaming.'

'Well, I won't run up your bill,' she says. And she starts to talk.

Some ancient impulse of my mother's means that she wants the coffin brought back to the house before the removal, so Liam can lie in state in our ghastly front room. Though come to think of it I can't think of a better carpet for a corpse, as I say to Bea; all those oblongs of orange and brown.

'It's a *carpet*,' says Bea.

And I say, 'Oh come on.'

'Just do it,' she says.

'Do it?' I say, meaning, *I'm fucking paying for it.*

'It's how Daddy would have wanted it,' she says, meaning, *I am the keeper of the flame,* and I am so furious with her that I can not hear what I say, or what she says for another little while as the countryside, in all its different speeds and directions, runs past the window and we fight our way back to safe ground.

She is right, of course. Daddy grew up in the West — he always knew the right thing to do. He had *beautiful manners.* Which, if you ask me, was mostly a question of saying nothing, to anyone, ever. 'Hello, are you well', 'Goodbye now, take care', the whole human business had to be ritualised. 'I'm sorry for your trouble', 'Put that money away now', 'That's a lovely bit of ham', 'It is your noble call'. It bored me to tears, actually: all that control. The dignity of the man somewhat undermined by his crazed rate of reproduction. Daddy died of a heart attack in 1986, and mourners laughed about it in the church porch, like he had worn himself out with too much shagging. 'He would have been so proud to see you all,' one of the neighbours said. 'So proud. Sitting in a row, like steps and stairs.' I did not say it, but I did not think so — not particularly. I did not think he would have been *particularly* proud.

He did have beautiful Irish. The language was a romantic place, for him, and it is the place where I love him, even now.

He wasn't the worst. Daddy was a lecturer in the local teacher training college, so, between the long holidays and the short hours, he was often around; marshalling, ordering, directing traffic; carrying in boxes of winter vegetables from the early morning market like he was running a summer camp and not a family. Though all this must have stopped sometime too — by the time I was in secondary school we lived on sending the twins down to the corner shop for rashers; Ernest or Mossie jingling the change in his pocket to see if there was enough there for a fry-up. None of the Hegartys was mean. Even I, the coolest of the Hegartys, am not stingy. This is more than a social thing, it's like a religious taboo; a mean person still makes my skin crawl, I have to turn and look the other way.

So what does that make me?

I'm fucking paying for it.

A disruption of the natural order, that is what I am.

Meanwhile, the train chunters through England, clicketty-clack, and Bea talks on, sitting on my dead father's knee with a ribbon in her hair, like the good little girl she has always been, and I look at the hills, trying to grow up, trying to let my father die, trying to let my sister enter her adolescence (never mind menopause). And none of these things is possible. None of them. There is a line on the landscape that refuses to move, it slides backwards instead, and that is where I fix my eye.

'Good luck in Brighton,' Bea is saying, and I am yanked by her voice into the bushes whipping past.

'Thanks,' I say. 'Look after Mammy,' and I close my phone, wondering have I said the words 'body' or 'coffin' or 'corpse' into the nice English silence of the carriage, thinking I would rather eat shit than — what? — *angels on horseback* with the neighbours, around my brother's dead body in the old front room.

That fucking carpet.

And not just the neighbours, but the remnants too of Midge-Bea-Ernest-Stevie-Ita-Mossie-Liam-Veronica-Kitty-Alice-and-the-twins-Ivor-and-Jem. The dead, the pious and the office managers (also housewives, ex-journalists, failed actresses, anaesthetists, landscape gardeners, something in IT, and something else in IT). We will look around and say, One less. One less. While the kids run around, stripping the house

66

down to the bare plaster with the sound of their screams; Rebecca playing with her cousin Anuna, who is actually my grand-niece — so don't ask me how many times that is whatever it is 'removed'.

Oh! he was desperate — that is what we will say. He was a terrible messer. He was always full of it. He just couldn't get it together. He had a good heart. He was all there. He was the best of company, we will say. Oh! but the wit. He had a tongue in his head, there's no doubt about that! But he was very sensitive. It was a sensitivity thing with Liam. You wanted to look after him. He was not able for this world. Not really.

'Yes,' I will say. 'He was a messer.'

I don't know if it is my earliest, but certainly one of my strongest memories of Liam is of him peeing through a wire fence into a smooth lake of water on the other side.

'Wheee!'

The pee spattering against the mesh, and then not, while I skated past. Skates! When I remember them now, I think that Ada must have spoiled us, too.

8

When I was just eight and Liam was nearly nine, we were sent with our little sister, Kitty, to stay with Ada in Broadstone. This was just a few miles from where we lived — I know that now, of course, but when we were children it might as well have been Timbuctoo. It was a world unto itself; a little enclave of artisan cottages close to the centre of Dublin, that fitted together like Lego.

I think we might also have been sent there when Kitty was just a baby. There is a gap in my mother's reproducing around then, and I think of these as the dead children years, the ones that marked her and turned her into the creature I later knew.

I don't know what they called these episodes. Single women had 'breakdowns', but in those days married women just had more babies, or no more babies. Mammy got going again, anyway, with Alice in 1967 (what would we have done without Alice!) and right after that came Ivor and Jem. I suppose the unfairness of twins might have provoked her final bout of 'nerves'. Certainly there were always tranquillisers in there among the Brufen and warfarin on her saucer of pills, and she has been, as long as I have known her, subject to the shakes, and inexplicable difficulties, and sudden weeps.

I sometimes wonder what she was like before we had to go away, or if I knew what was lost when we returned each time — if some 'Mama' who danced with the sweeping brush and kissed the baby's tummy was replaced by this piece of benign human meat, sitting in a room.

Ada's house was very quiet. It was hard to forget the sound of your breath — going in, faltering out — until you were smothered, slightly, by your own hesitation. It was the quiet of a house that had no children and the rooms were full of things. There were things on mantelpieces and little things on tables, that you might not touch. There were drawers full of things that had not been used for years, or were only used once a year. All of these were separate from each other, and special, in a way that things were never separate at home.

Ada herself existed in a distinct way that my mother could not. She fought with Charlie or flirted with him in the kitchen. My parents never flirted, they did not seem capable of it.

'Turn the telly up now, so Daddy can hear the news.'

They spoke to each other through their children, like every other couple I knew. And if there were no sweet nothings there were no fights either — though sometimes a grinding tone came into their conversation that might have been a sign of private coldness or disgust. I don't know.

Maybe I am wrong. Maybe they talked to each other all the time, but there was something so intimate about their speech I could not hear it, or retain it — the way it is hard to remember the particular laugh of someone you have loved.

But Ada flirting with Charlie — I do remember that: Ada swaying from cooker to table, and singing as she laid Charlie's dinner down. And I remember her things — the chest of drawers on the upstairs landing that was full of swatches and scraps of cloth; sample books with pages that you could turn like the soft pages of a book that had no story, only one pattern and then the next. There was a cut-glass vase full of feathers on the mantelpiece in Ada's bedroom; I remember the creak of her straw hats, and the smell of the felt ones that she kept on the bottom of her wardrobe. All this probably from my prissy little-girl phase, at eight or nine, when I loved to fold and smooth and secrete things. Except for the inside smell of the hats, which I remember from the time when I was three.

We were only occasionally in the house, most of the time we ran around the streets or played around The Basin, an artificial lake whose water had once been used in the making of Irish whiskey. It was this fact that obliged Liam to piss into it, and this is the picture I have of him in my head, a small boy swinging up his behind to sling the arc of his pee up in the air, the urine spattering against the wire or pouring, suddenly easy, through a diamond in the mesh.

There was also the fortress of the bus station at Broadstone to besiege, a dark wall, like a cliff cut out of the hill, with a statue of the Virgin Mary set in at the top. We hung around the gates, and finally, one day, snuck in where the double deckers were parked in rows, dodging and creeping along their long sides, until — it must have been Liam, hardly me — one of us reached up to the door handle, set like a dial in a semicircle beside the door.

Whissh.

You could smell them off the blue leatherette of the seats, the people who sat here and got up again, in order that different people could sit here and get up again, minute after minute, day after day, with their shopping and their ordinary lives. And though we did not slash the seats or graffiti the ceilings, the bus was so stalled and empty as we ran through it, that it made us realise, all three of us, how outside of things we were, farmed out to our granny — who meant nothing to us, of a sudden — and missing our parents, who meant less and less. For a moment, as Liam clacked open the driver's half door, I had a spiralling sense that he could actually drive the thing, careening down to Constitution Hill, up through Phibsboro, to the place where our rightful family was growing up without us, and further beyond.

And then we were caught. I was upstairs and heard nothing except, in hindsight, Liam and Kitty's slapping sandals as they ran away, Liam turning at the last to shout at me, which sound I did hear, my own name coming, for some reason, from outside the bus, while inside there was the sound of a man on the stairs, and the sight of his hand on the chrome rail as he hauled himself up, step by step, his torso finally rising out of the stairwell like an expanding balloon. Once he was fully up he stopped, and looked at me. He wore a peaked cap and a standard issue blue shirt, buttoned to bursting over an enormous stomach, the kind of stomach that needed a belt to support it, as a breast might require a bra. He walked this stomach down the aisle at me, as I backed away, until I was tripped into sitting by the back seat of the bus. Then he pushed it at me — and even though I doubt all this can be strictly true, I do remember the surprising tautness and bounce of it, as he jabbed at my face with its leading white button: me wriggling under it finally, past his little legs and the ming of his busman's gabardine. Then off down the stairs.

'Out!' he shouted after me. 'Out!'

Various busmen turned to look as I sprinted for the gates, and then beyond.

There was only one way to go and that was down Constitution Hill, until I was out of breath, at which place I would, no doubt, meet Kitty and Liam. But I did not find them until I came to the gates of a church: Liam, even then, with some idea of sanctuary — that even a bus conductor in his uniform couldn't get to you here.

73

We went in to pray — and I really believe this to have happened on the same day — we knelt up near the altar with the idea of pursuit at our backs, and after our hearts had settled we looked at each other, the need to laugh shifting even as we looked into a higher, more spiritual thing. So it was with a sense of pious elation that we gave thanks for our deliverance at the altar of St Felix by lighting a candle each and then, when we could find no slot for our pennies, lighting two or three more, until a priest marked Kitty's upper arm with a ring of bruises, giving us, as he held on to her, a lecture on wickedness that was dense with rage. And I can not remember a single word of it, or what Ada later said about the state of Kitty's arm, though I do recall the thick, vivid quality of the priest's mouthing face, like undiluted fruit squash. And though common sense says that these two events should not have happened on the same day, I say that they did, and when a man followed me through the back streets of Venice, many years later, with his erection in his hand, I ducked into a church as though inviting something worse — instead of which, I got nothing: empty seats, mould on the wall, a piece of paper stuck under a muddy oil painting, with *'di Tintoretto'* written in biro. There was a dark side chapel with heaven itself painted on the ceiling, at least when you put in a 100-lire coin for the lights to come on. Otherwise all was shabby, and calm. There was no worse thing waiting to happen to me. I knelt with my back to the flaring white rectangle of the open door, but the street Italian did not come up behind me, a child did not walk out of the confession box with his cupped hands holding a jigger of sperm, no saint moved. I bent my head and prayed like a woman in a fifties film, I prayed that it would leave me, the choking sense that this was the way I would die, my face jammed in filthy gabardine, of navy or black, a stranger's cock in the back of my throat and what, what, what?

Something turning in my stomach. A knife. No knife.

It isn't real.

But ker-klunk. The lights in the side chapel came on, with a great noise, followed by the slow mechanical grind of someone's money running out. I knelt and watched Germans and English come in and figure out the lire box and switch heaven on, while at my back the Italian with his erection lingered at the open door of the church, or not. (What was he going to do with it anyway?) At any rate he failed to cross the threshold, and when I finished my desperate, atheistical praying jag, I turned and found that he was gone. Which was fine. Except that now, when I walked the streets, he was everywhere.

We were good children, mostly. I imagine that we were good children, in those days in Broadstone; a bit quiet, a bit worried, perhaps; Liam especially prone to sudden switches and changes of tack, but these were as often hilarious as awful, and though Kitty was a pain in the neck it was in a childish sort of way, and there was no harm in any of us, that I can think of — why would there be?

9

The man beside me on the train to Brighton lifts his pelvis slightly, and settles it back down. He is dozing in the flickering, sexual sunlight, lulled and unsettled by the movement of the train. I can sense the blood pooling in his lap; the thick oblong of his penis moving down the leg of his suit.

Here comes another one.

And then again, there is nothing to fuss about — a young businessman having a hard-on beside you on a train — even if you are recently bereaved. Given the state I am in, I find the hydraulics of it more than usually peculiar. Such small things to have such large consequences. I wonder, briefly, if Liam would still be alive if he had been born a woman and not a man. And there he is, suddenly, leering behind the tea trolley, in a Dick Emery headscarf and industrial support bra.

'Cooeee! I'm alive!'

And, 'No thanks,' I say to the perfectly respectable woman who offers, 'Refreshments?' as the man beside me reaches for a newspaper to hide his lap.

Harmless. Harmless. Harmless.

And I close my eyes.

Liam walked into my hospital room the evening after Rebecca was born. He just showed up, with a bunch of pink flowers from the downstairs shop. Tom was gone home to get some sleep and the phone calls were done and people were leaving me time to recover, but I was high as a kite, showing the baby off to nurses and cleaners, wondering was it a football match or a terrorist attack, that had all her admirers stuck in some traffic jam?

And there was Liam in the doorway — I didn't even know he was home. And there was I, propped up on the pillows in a heap of extra sweat with a baby — untouchably fine — in the plastic cot by my side.

He moved across the room to take a look and there was a solidity to him as he bent over the next generation, checking, in a proprietorial way, eyes, fingers, toes, the tiny pores on her nose plugged with yellow stuff that made me panic already about blackheads when she was grown.

'How are you?' he might have said.

I don't think we kissed. The Hegartys didn't start kissing until the late eighties and even then we stuck to Christmas.

'I'm fine,' I would have said back.

And he sat in the visitor's chair and looked at this new scene: mother and child.

'Was it all right?' I remember he said that, and I remember I said, 'Well, it's all right *now.*'

The walls were painted yellow and there was something thick and ecstatic about the sunshine, now that the baby was born.

I remember thinking how good he looked; how handsome he might seem walking down a street of strangers, my slightly fat brother. He was happy to see the baby. He was reduced, by the sight of her, to someone I knew in my bones.

The birth had given me back my sense of smell, which had been oddly thwarted while I was expecting, and so I was in an aromatic rush with my nose stuck into a glass of champagne that I refused to drink but sniffed all afternoon. I could tell, from one hour to the next, how the drink was spoiling as it met the air. This was the place where I existed — in the smell that drifted from the top of a pool of champagne — beside which, even Liam's clothes felt loud.

I told him our mother had phoned, and

that she had cried.

'Cried?' he said.

'She thought we were all barren,' I said, though I felt my betrayal in a tinge. I had been pleased enough to hear from her at the time.

We talked about her for a while.

He was eyeing the glass on the bedside locker, and I told him it was only a little aeroplane sort of bottle. But he finished it off for me before he left, warm and flat and grubby as it was with whatever pungent stuff was spilling out of my pores as I deflated slowly into the room. I didn't mind. I told him I was glad to have the smell of it gone.

Sitting on the Brighton train I am trying to put a timetable on my brother's drinking. Drink was not his problem, but it did become his problem, eventually, which was a relief to everyone concerned. 'I'm a bit worried about his drinking,' — so, after a while, no one could hear a thing he said, any more.

Quite right too, it was all complete shite. Alcohol wrecked him, as it does. But I am trying to put a time on it — when I stopped worrying about him and started to worry about his drinking instead. Maybe then — with my new baby opening her eyes, over and over, as if to check that the world was still there. That was probably the moment. Just then.

A drinker does not exist. Whatever they say, it is just the drink talking. Or they only exist in flashes. Sitting against a yellow wall looking at your favourite sister, who has just unsheathed herself of a child. A look in your eye like old times. The rest is not to be trusted.

I could smell the settler he had had before he came in the hospital door, I could smell his lunch-time wine and last night's beer. But there was also some metabolic shift, a sweetness to his blood and breath that I did not recognise. He didn't eat much, those last years, his body already cycling on alcohol. And sitting on the train to Brighton I wonder if he had diabetes, if that was what was wrong. I suddenly think that if only he would get his bloods done, we could do something about this, because maybe his drinking isn't the problem, after all.

Then I realise that he is dead.

And, of course, his drinking was an existential statement, how could I forget? There was certainly nothing *metabolic* about it. There was no cause.

Was he pissed when he died? Probably. And now, what tide runs in his veins? Blood, sea water, whiskey. He was a maniac on whiskey. He probably thought he was swimming to fucking France.

I close my eyes against the warm sunlight and doze beside the dozing stranger on the Brighton train.

10

Here's Ada and Charlie in bed a year later. Charlie as sleek as a seal with his long, plump, stomach; his languid genitals blushing pink against his fat, white thigh. It is Saturday morning, and every stray breeze, every shift from Ada under the eiderdown can tease him aloft, until an angle is reached — say, fifty degrees — that seems to him both stern and kind. He muses on it for a while — forty might be considered awkward, any lower merely blundering and shy — and then it is something he has to share, this question of degree. He swims back under the bedcovers to Ada's skinny shanks and she laughs and lifts her knees. They have done this so often in the last few hours that it is hard to tell the difference between outside and inside. Also the difference between the covers and the air of the room, between their clothes and their hands: everything seems to stroke them. They are a bundle of nerves, frayed at the ends. They are wearing each other away; both of them amazed by the thinness of skin that happens just there; how close they can be, blood to blood, so that the ticking, afterwards, of one inside the other, might be a joke, or a pulse — the beating in your veins of someone else's heart.

Of course Charlie, at thirty-three, has more sense than to end up inside Ada more often than he can help it (though sometimes, it is true, he can not help it at all), and so he hoists himself out at the last to flop like a drowning man, spilling sea water on the quay. And Ada is raw not just from love but also from the vinegar she uses in her special French bag; a present from Charlie — so outrageous and sly — after they were engaged. They are lovers. Even though they are married they are lovers. There is no talk of children: nothing happens in the dark. Their courtship was a violent affair; the engagement, it seemed, just an excuse to protract the sweetness, so by the time they got between legitimate sheets they were worn out from it all and looked to their wedding night as to a final wreck. Ada undressed by the side of the bed like a woman getting into a bath, Charlie squinted under the lamp to wind his watch.

After which, with a sudden, awful inter-
course Ada's eyes locked wide and open
— they found they had everything to learn,
after all.

'Don't worry.' It seems as though Charlie
has said nothing else since the day they met.
'Don't worry, you will come to no harm.'

Ada did not know why she trusted him,
but she did. And she was right. And that
itself was a kind of triumph for her; skinny,
practical Ada, with her weather eye. She
trusted him at once, and she never stopped
trusting him, even as, in time, he brought
the bailiffs to the door. Now, on this Saturday morning, she picks up his hand and sets
it down on her overused pubis, so the
weight and warmth of it will settle her back
together, somehow. Everything hurts a little.
They are not very good at this yet. They
have great intimations of what is to come.

The bed is a mahogany affair, with two
swags of little flowers joining in a bow on
the headboard. It is a little soft — obliging
the lovers, at some grinding extremity, to
take to the floor. But it is luxury to lie in
and Ada has come into her estate: her own
bed, with her own bottles and potions on
the chest of drawers, and all her things,
books and breakfast, about her. She is married. She can live in this bed. She can eat in

it, and read in, and take to it on a regular basis.

And if the bed is a palace to her, then Charlie is her magnificent fat guest. Against the rose pink of the eiderdown, his sandy hair is all aglow. It streams downwards, and swirls around his body's dents. It stops in a line around each ankle before leaping, like an escaping fire, in little tufts from toe to toe. Golden hair courses down his belly. It hangs in little beardlets from under each pap and fizzes out from under his arms. Ada never tires of it, how it runs in currents, like he has just risen from a bath — and the joke at the top, where his head has been rinsed altogether clear. Because Charlie is very bald.

He is the kind of man who looks like he should be wearing a bowler hat, but Charlie is vain of his pate — he used to sit me on his knee, as a child, to stroke it — and he often goes bareheaded, to give it the benefit of a breeze. He does favour a scarf, though, and has a tendency to growl and clear his throat, also to tap his chest, rewrap the scarf, and to settle and resettle the lapels of his camel-hair coat. Charlie is seldom without his coat. He fills a room in a way that is always confusing because, though he gives the impression of being small — the baldness, or maybe a stubbiness about his thighs — he is actually quite large and his refusal to settle may come from a concern that he will not fit. Charlie is only ever passing through. He never takes a cup of tea. It seems that he has information to impart though, after he has gone, it is often hard to know what that information might have been. His voice is low, and urgent, and very pleasant. He makes people feel warm and uncertain, as though they might have been conned — but of what? They look down to check their hands but nothing has been taken, there is nothing there to take. So he is not liked for it — not exactly. Charlie's charm is completely pointless. And no one knows where he is from.

Spillane is a Kerry name, but his accent is English, with a bit of Clare in there, and all of it Dublinified. There is no doubt, with his mangled vowels, that Charlie wanted to blend in — unless he wanted to stand out, in some way. Still, no one believed a word he said. I remember disbelieving him personally, at the age of eight.

There was something about a horse (there was always a horse). There was the Lord Leinster story, and the endless Shelbourne Hotel stories, and the 1916 Rising story which was sometimes referred to, but never actually told. 'Ah yes, Mr Spillane,' says the man in the shop, winking at me over the counter, 'that would have been in the Glory Days.'

What did Charlie buy me? A sherbert fizz. Of course.

I remember him best with my skin. The creeping delight as he bent down to whisper; the bristle of his moustache and the grease of his tweed. He tickled you with the idea that there was something hidden in his hand or pocket — and there never was. Charlie played Find the Lady with no lady: he just loved the flourish, and after the flourish he loved to leave.

Poor Charlie. His was the first corpse I ever saw; massive and still under Ada's rose-pink eiderdown. Which is why it is a kind of blasphemy to write of their marriage night in the same bed — though blasphemy seems to be my business here.

I would love to remember how he died — whether with a noise in the night, or a lengthening silence in the middle of the afternoon. It must have happened while we were staying there. It might even have been the reason we went back home. But such details and dates were too terrible for a child to take in, it seems, because my mind has blanked them out — but completely. All I remember is the aftermath, trying not to laugh as we were brought up to the room.

It must have been the February of 1968. I was still eight, Liam was nine, and we were going up to 'say goodbye' to Charlie. I think I knew, even at eight, that you can say good-bye all you like, but when someone is dead they're not going to say anything back, so Liam had to stiff-arm me up past the neighbours reciting the rosary on the stairs. My memory has them all bundled in shawls; Ada's back ascending in front of us corseted in black taffeta. But this was 1968: there would have been patterned headscarves and big-buttoned coats that smelt of the rain. Ada would have worn her navy Crimplene with white piping, that came out for all occasions, with a matching navy bolero jacket and one of those hats that look like a bubble of felt, punched in on one side.

The neighbours' feet stuck out a surprising distance from the step where they each knelt: their shoes waggled mid-air, and there was something tripping and wrong about this other ladder, made of shin-bones in support tights, at cross purposes to the staircase we were trying to climb.

A very loud woman was praying on the return. She saw me giggling with Liam and rolled a sad eyeball, like there are some things beyond rebuke. I remember that, all right; the slow-motion feeling of being utterly wrong-minded and unable to change. I did not, I realised then, want to go into my grandparents' room. Not at all.

A few more kneelers cluttered the second flight, and then, through the open door, I saw the end of the bed and the still, uneven lump of Charlie's feet. I remember the straightness of his legs as revealed through the expanding door frame, the horrible little peaks of his knees, then the merciful swoop of the eiderdown up his fantastic belly's rise. His hands were on his chest, knotted, and complacent, and tied together with rosary beads.

The beads looked too tight, they looked like they were digging into his flesh. These little fierce formalities at the end; a sort of revenge on him, for being dead.

Ada looked to check us behind her, and then moved out of the way to give us a better view. It was a view that I did not want to take.

Charlie did love to leave.

'Goodbye! Goodbye!' You never knew where he was going. He left in a fug of explanations that explained nothing at all. So Ada was proved right, at last — he was a most annoying man. You could tell by the way she twitched towards him as though to swat the dandruff from his lapel. And in fact there was something there — a fly crawling on the side of his neck. I thought it had come out from under his collar and I was much bothered by the idea of maggots — from that day on, really. It stopped my awful smiling at any rate, like Ada was going to swipe at me, and not the fly.

She watched it rise and shift away from him, and hit the roller blind, once, twice. Then it came back to the bed. I was standing behind her; I could feel the still, raw rage as she saw it circle, and scoot away, and then come back to settle again on Charlie's dead neck. It landed and ran across the skin, not bothered by the deep creases in the soft flesh, or by the few high strands of hair. Ada moved, or went to move, and the fly lifted and repeated its escape to the roller blind, this time finding a way around the bright edge of it to hit the window pane, where it buzzed and thumped. We listened to it for a while; the sound of the rosary outside, and the sound of the fly battering the glass. Ada was mortified. She looked to the corpse. She could not move. Then, of a sudden, she seemed to realise that this was her own bedroom, with her own husband in it, dead or not, and she simply walked around the bed. When she reached the window, she raised one hand and pressed the blind flat. The buzzing stopped. Ada the housewife, with a terrible spot on her blind. We children now exposed to Charlie's bald head, naked in death.

You might think there is something light about the dead — our lives feel so heavy to us, sometimes — but the dent Charlie's head made in the pillow was living and deep.

I remember him lying down in the Phoenix Park, his head like a rock in the grass. And I remember my hand in his mouth — the whole of my hand — while he garbled around it and laughed. I must have been very young, my hand all disappeared into this huge face and — somewhere else, it seemed — the surging chaos of his wet tongue, the gentle flats and tips of his molar teeth.

The skull is the bone that is nearest the air. This is what I realised as I looked at the skin on the dome of Charlie's head; it was bloodlessly transparent, and the tan was all on the surface, in the thinnest glaze. Ada was back from the window, urging us forward to view, or witness, or maybe even touch, this briefly sacred thing, our dead grandfather. And I suppose it is amazing. The viewing moment. When they have left, but are not yet gone. When you are not quite sure what it is you see.

So I did look — at him, or it. And it was all fine and unsurprising, except for the moustache. Charlie, alive, had the most wonderful white bush of a moustache, lemon-scented and turned slightly at the tips. My grandfather was the only man I knew with a toy on his face. His moustache moved and distracted and dazzled. It was a sleight of mouth. And now it was still, and hiding nothing at all.

There was no trick.

That was the thing that made me cry — waiting for Charlie's moustache to move, and finding that it did not move. There was no trick, after all. Ada back beside us whispering, 'Say goodbye, now,' and Liam, who was older than me by nearly a year, taking a step forward and then stopping, because he did not know what to do.

'Shush,' Ada said to me. 'Stop crying.'

I wonder did they take the blood out? I mean, I wonder if he was embalmed before he was laid out, was that the custom in those days? The blood that was pooling in his shoulders and buttocks, the blood that had fallen to the back of his head, seeking gravity, already wanting to leach down through the mattress: the blood that bruised or hardened in him now, as the front of him (you see it is true) grew infinitesimally lighter, and we stood there, letting him go: that blood, so heavy and sticky and wrong — I wonder if it was still inside him, because it is the same, or a quarter the same, as my own blood. If I cut myself, right now, I would see it running free.

It's funny, but I have never thought of myself as related to Charlie, even though he was my grandfather. He was a different kind of person. He danced with Ada in the kitchen. He didn't have a job you could put a name on. He wasn't always home.

None of the Hegartys got his dog-brown eyes, or his fine, high nose — though it is true that his grandsons all went bald, in time. And this is something Liam could not have foreseen as he stood there waiting to do the proper thing, as soon as he knew what the proper thing was to do. He did not see that he would die bald as a coot, though I think we both knew, as he leaned forward to touch Charlie's poor dead hand, that Liam would die.

He was on his way.

If you ask me what my brother looked like after he was dead, I can tell you that he looked like Mantegna's fore-shortened Christ, in paisley pyjamas. And this may be a general truth about the dead, or it may just be what happens when someone is lying on a high, mortuary table, with their feet towards the door. That is how I knew that Liam was dead, when I finally saw him in Brighton, the fact that he was too high off the ground, and the thing he was lying on was too hard and flat, because the dead are never uncomfortable — even as we start forward to make them so. I don't think I looked at the top of his head, or thought about his baldness, or thought about anything. And I was glad I had some practice in this whole business — the viewing business — because although I loved Charlie, it was with the easy, anxious love of a child, that is always ready to love someone new.

But, dead or alive, you don't spend time examining your brother's body, its shape or parts, or the texture of its skin. So I can not recall Liam in any detail. All I know is that he looked completely different dead, while Charlie looked very like himself. And, as I wondered at the stupid, secondhand paisley pyjamas, I realised that this is why we were hauled up those stairs in Broadstone at the age of eight and just nine — because Ada had seen this day coming. She knew all along. She wanted us to be prepared.

Or maybe her grief was so large that she

had to drag everyone into it, even us children. Maybe she wanted the whole world to witness, and be horrified.

I wasn't horrified, I just felt lonely. Not because Charlie was gone — I didn't care about Charlie, I hated Charlie, I hoped he was heaving with maggots under that suit. But because I didn't want to be in that room, and nobody cared. My feelings were not relevant — not just to the occasion, but to the whole business of being alive.

The rosary churned on in the stairwell, as Liam stepped back and I stood there and refused to move. Liam's hand on my forearm, already livid with decay; Ada behind my shoulders, whispering me forward.

I did not go.

My grandmother had no patience. She moved on my behalf and put her hand on the corpse; once on the wrist, briefly, and then — impulsively, it seemed — along the line of his jaw. She laid her hand from his ear to his chin, cupping the length of bone.

It was a while before we realised that she was stuck. And another while before someone came up behind her and pulled her palm away from the cold cheek, looking over his shoulder, as he did so, to say, 'That's enough now.'

Like it was all our fault — this embarrassment of dead flesh, and the still-breathing love that was in Ada's body, a love that did not know where to go.

'That's enough.'

Mr Nugent. Of course.

And now I remember Nugent there at the end, I must remember him in the room all along, sitting by the side of the wardrobe, so the fly, when it lifted from Charlie's neck went right past him, before curling around to the light of the window and the blind. He was leaning forward, when we first came in, with his elbows on his knees and his rosary beads dangling towards the floor, and the mahogany behind him was nearly as dark as his black suit.

I have never trusted men who pray. Woman have no option, of course — but what do men think about, when they are on their knees? I do not think it is in their nature to pray: they are too proud.

But there he was, sighing through the Hail Marys as we trooped in the door: me, who was supposed to be in charge, my brother, gangly and raw in his grey school jumper, and Kitty coming up behind. And now of course I must add Kitty in from the start, my little sister, trailing up the stairs behind us, because she must have been there too. Kitty did the business like she did her Holy

Communion — with her head down and her face piously cocked. Did she lay a daisy on Charlie's chest, a childish buttercup on the pillowslip? No. As I recall, Kitty stepped forward, said, 'Bye bye,' and turned to leave the room. She was six. She loved her audience. I should know, I had to twist her hair into rags every night, to keep the ringlets tight.

Nugent was there all along: for Liam's bravery and Kitty's cutey-pie piety and for the huge bubble of selfishness rising and bursting in my chest. The big, miserable fucking roar of it, telling me that I was alive.

I remember that all right. I remember Kitty's hair rags, though I can not, for the life of me, turn the memory of my sister around to look at her six-year-old face. I can not, for the life of me, remember Liam's face, though I will never forget his nine-year-old hand touching Charlie's dead hand — Liam's mottled purple while Charlie's was clear, because his body had already forgotten that it was winter, in that cold house. There are photographs. There is the hint of my brother's smile in my own mirror, a tone of voice I sometimes hit. I do not think we remember our family in any real sense. We live in them, instead.

The only things I am sure of are the things

I never saw — my little blasphemies — Ada and Charlie in their marriage bed, her pubis like the breast of an underfed chicken under his large hand, or the sad weight of his tackle as she reaches under his long belly to pull him closer in. The sun in the flowered curtains.

Happiness.

11

I was opening the car door for the girls one day before Liam died and, as it swung past, I saw my reflection in the window. It disappeared, and I looked into the dark cave of the car as the kids came out, or went back in to pick some piece of pink plastic junk off the floor. Then the reflection swung back again, swiftly, as I shut the door. The sun was breaking through high-contrast clouds, the sky in the window pane was a wonderful, thick blue, and in my dark face moving past was the streak of a smile. And I remember thinking, 'So, I am happy. That's nice to know.'

I am happy.

Rebecca is eight now, she looks like me. Emily is six, she has black hair and the ice blue eyes you get on the Atlantic seaboard — Hegarty eyes, only more so — and I think that, if we fix Emily's teeth, and if Rebecca stops being dippy and learns how to be tall, then they both have a chance of being truly lovely, some day.

My children have never walked down a street on their own. They have never shared a bed. They are a different breed. They seem to grow like plants, to be made of twig and blossom and not of meat.

And yet, their parents wear them out. The last time we went on holiday, there was some bickering over directions, and in the middle of it I glanced in the car mirror and saw Rebecca staring straight ahead. Her mouth had sunk inwards and I saw, with terrible prescience, the particular thing that would go wrong with her face, either quickly or slowly, the thing that could grab her prettiness away before she was grown.

I thought, *I have to keep her happy.* I have to be in love with her father and keep her happy, or this thing will happen to her, she will turn into one of those people that you pass every day on the street.

'How did you meet Daddy?' says Emily, my rival. 'How did you meet him?'

'I met him at a dance.'

'What were you wearing?' says her sister, who is always on my side.

'I was wearing . . .' It was a long time ago, I can not remember what I was wearing. I say, 'I was wearing a blue dress.'

This is probably not true, but they like it. And it is true that Tom was wearing a really sharp suit when I smiled at him, one night in Suzey Street — and kept smiling, in a melancholy way, until he finally stopped talking and just leaned in.

'How did you know it was him?' says Emily.

'What?'

'How did you know it was Daddy?'

'I just did,' I say. 'I just did.'

Which is true — but not in the way they might expect. I can't exactly tell them that he was living with another woman at the time, and that the moment I saw them together I knew two things. The first was that he did not belong to her, and the second was that he belonged to me.

I could make him happy. That was all. I knew that, in some exact way, I could make this man happy.

'I knew it was your Daddy, because he was so tall.'

This will do. It is true enough. I also liked the curve to his top lip, and the way his suit hung open as he leaned over to talk to me, the dent in his chest as he stooped, the mixture of arrogance and inclination.

Tall men, they are so unwieldy. They cave in, like you have undone some secret hinge.

But this is not what you tell your daughters ten years later: that their parents only had sex by accident, and it was weeks before they managed to get all their clothes off first. That their father was so maddened by guilt he actually frightened me — until the moment when I wasn't frightened any more. That we were swept away. That afterwards we talked about *her.* And when we finished talking about *her,* when *she* was finally gone, some six months later, we had triumphant, tender sex, and after that.

After that.

It was time to buy a house, I suppose. But the early, frantic stuff was important. And the other woman was important too. A little ruthlessness. A pact. A spill of blood. Because we each knew we had met our match, in terms of ambition, or damage — call it what you like — we knew we would put it all right one day with this: two beautiful daughters in two beautiful bedrooms. Tall, no doubt, and clever. Who would attend their destined private school, and who would each be mapped, discussed, mulled over, well loved.

At least that was the plan.

'And what happened then?'

'Then we got married.'

'And then what happened?'

'Then we had you!'

'Yes!!!'

And your father took one look at you and ran out the door. (And that is certainly not true. Look! he is still here.)

Tom was taught by the Jesuits — which explains it all, he says. He is very clear-sighted about the world, and yet he questions himself, constantly. He pushes himself hard, and is rarely satisfied. He is completely selfish, in other words, but in the poshest possible way. I look at him, a big, sexy streak of misery, with his face stuck in a glass of obscure Scotch, as he traces the watermark of failure that runs through his life, that is there on every page.

And when he looks at his children, I do not know what he sees. He loves them, but they are *in his way.* And, whether he loves me or not, I too am *in his way.* But he is wrong. I am not in his way. I never have been.

If this is a fight, then these are the facts: when Tom was starting out in his own business, and I had a small baby, I left that baby with a minder and worked day and night to keep up with the mortgage repayments. But when he began earning again, it was clear that his money was much more important than any money I might earn, that his job was an important job, that he couldn't be expected to be doing pick-ups and Pampers and snot and drop-offs with so much importance around. And, eventually, I gave up work so that we would not be so much *in his way.*

But although these are the facts, they are not completely true. I don't miss work, for example. Not in the slightest. Even now, I can't believe I wasted so much of my life writing about heated towel rails. Endless words. About the difference between mulberry leather and tan. About oatmeal, cream, sandstone, slate.

This is how we used to live our lives.

I walk in the door after a terrible day at the office and kiss my husband, who is shattered after a day of work and baby-minding. Then I take Rebecca from him and change her nappy and put cream on the rash, and I fight with him about this, or about the empty fridge, or the washing-up, and somehow the baby gets put down and around half nine when she is finally asleep, I come downstairs and get a large glass of wine and bitch heartily about my boss, then I tidy up and drink a bit too much and stay up a bit too late. At half eleven Tom clears his work from the kitchen table and says, 'Don't stay up all night,' and, after a while, I hang the dishcloth over the kitchen tap and go up to bed. I know how unhappy he is. There is no doubt that my husband is unhappy, but also excited with his new business, and surely the mess can not last. Other people have children. Other fathers do not feel, as he does, *unmanned* by it — by the lack of money and the mayhem, and the fact that there is no place here for his considerable charm.

I should allow him space for his considerable charm. I place my face against his back and reach around to cup the soft handful of his prick, because I have had a little too much wine, and I think he actually hates me now, I am so much to blame for it all.

And he either turns, or he doesn't.

And in the gap I realise that he is having sex with someone else.

No. In the gap I remember how much he wanted to have sex with someone else, when that someone else was me.

A week after Liam's funeral I look at my husband's body. Asleep. Alive. I want to see all of it. It is a warm night. I take off the covers quickly, and he moves and is still again.

Tom is sad in his sleep. His hands are gathered under his chin, his legs are impossibly long and large, they do not look bent so much as broken at the knee. The hollow under his ribcage slopes to a little low, pot-belly and the cushion of his scrotum rests in the V of his thighs. He is very pale.

I remember making love to this body: a cloud of hair around the bridge of his penis, when I looked down from above; the little roof of his underarm, like a nave without a church, when I looked up from below. This was back in the early days, when we could not get enough of each other and he traced a candy-stripe of moles around my body, rolling me over as he went, until I was completely unwound, and tipped from the bed on to the floor.

I remember the size and straightness of his collar-bones under his shirt, one night in the rain, in the early-early days, when it wasn't like sex so much as like killing someone or being killed.

There he is now, in our bed, still alive. The air goes into him and the air comes out. His toenails grow. His hair turns silently grey.

The last time I touched him was the night of Liam's wake. And I don't know what is wrong with me since, but I do not believe in my husband's body any more.

107

12

Bad news for Bea and my mother and all the vultures who will flock to 4 Griffith Way for the wake — which is that there will be another ten days at least to wait before they can feast on Liam's poor corpse, because of the paperwork involved.

I hear this from an undertaker who looks about nineteen. He touched my arm in the corridor of the Brighton and Hove mortuary and took me away, somehow, in a car or a taxi — whether I sat in the back or the front of it, I can not recall. But I know that I will remember this, the hinterland of the funeral parlour, suburban and pastel: a desk with a chair on either side and, up on a swivel stand, a laminated catalogue of coffins, all kinds and varieties of them, except, when I enquire for the sake of distraction, the eco-warrior's cardboard.

'Did he like all that?' says the boy in black.
'Not really. A bit.'

I know what I want, I have known all along, but it doesn't look well to be too previous, so I turn the pages for the hideous silk linings, ruchings and slubbings, like being buried in a cinema curtain just as the projector snaps on and starts playing *Looney Tunes.* I say some of all this out loud while my undertaker listens a little, and lets me take my time.

His mouth is a solid purplish red against the white of his skin. He has a tiny, wet hole in his ear where his earring should be but is not, while he is talking to the bereaved.

'No hurry,' he says.

I love this undertaker. He has that thing that young people got, sometime after I grew up. He does not pretend. He does not judge. He talks about the caskets in a 'whatever' sort of way, like it is all just shopping — the real questions are elsewhere.

'That's the one,' he says as I poke my finger at a plain limed oak, and I think that maybe one of my daughters will marry someone like this, someone who is able to sit easy with a woman in a room.

'I can't take the flight with him,' I say. 'It's just too . . .'

' "Would passengers requiring assistance please come to the front of the queue." '

And I laugh. Whatever he means.

'Really, it will be fine in the hold,' he says.

He is not good-looking. His mouth is too squished and full; he is too soft and unformed. But there is nothing wrong with him. I look at his hands and they do not disgust me, and his eyelids, when he closes them, flickering, in order to make a point about buffed steel as opposed to chrome, have a faint pattern on them of medieval veins. His clothes do not mock his body. You could unpeel him, and he would still be true.

I must ask his name again. (Azrael.)

He touched my arm while I stood by Liam's body and he led me away. He is the person who comes after you have seen the worst thing. He is the rest of my life.

After I arrived at Brighton station, I walked around for a while, thinking that I should play this the way it happened — I should start at the place where Liam walked into the sea — because there is an order to these things that has to be obeyed. So at lunch-time, I am walking along the prom and Liam is still, residually, alive, and I am imagining this place in the darkness, and the lapping around my waist of black salt water. Liam is in the air. The figures that pass are scribbled with the graffiti of his gaze: everything they have spills over, or droops. An overweight child with breasts — a boy, it seems. An old man with a scab under his nose. A woman with a widening tattoo. A parade of lax flies and stained trousers and bra straps showing under other, shoestring straps. The living, with all their smells and holes. Liam was always a great man for people's *holes,* and who stuck what into which *hole.*

He is back in my head like an expanding smell — a space that clears to allow him to look out of my eyes and be disgusted by arse or tit, or 'cold tit', even, by flesh that is never the right temperature or the right humidity, being too *sweaty,* or flesh that is *saggy,* or *hairy,* and the women, especially, who inhabit this sad human sack too craven or too beautiful (except, of course, for their *holes*), and in the end, who do you sleep with, who do you kiss? People with no pores? I say this to him, in my head. I argue it out, but I can't shake him, I can't win, as I pass old men and old women, with their eczemous creases, or lean over the railing, pulling in the sea air to keep the rising vomit down, while thinking of my brother's own flesh and how it will look in two months', then three months' time.

I look over the railing as though to examine the density and variety of brown stones on the beach below. And there it is: the open tang, the calling, the smell of the sea. Such a miracle, at the end of the Brighton line, with the town stacked behind me, and behind that all the weight of England, in her smoke and light, jammed to a halt here, just here, by the wide smell of the sea.

The first time we took the ferry, myself and Liam, it was the end of his second year, and my first, in UCD. We were going to work in London for the summer. We sat in the space between carriages, from Holyhead to Euston, watching a man — who turned out, by some freak, to be our own postman — squeeze oranges into a bottle of duty-free vodka. He was giving the vodka to a drunken girl he had met on the crossing, and he waved the bottle at us too, and we may or may not have taken it, but what I liked was the way he winked to us before turning back to the girl — who was completely rat-arsed — as if we were all in this together, the seduction business, the business of, 'Crikey! Quids in.'

Liam never gave us a wedding.

The Hegartys loved a wedding, and a few of us actually had them, small or large, and some of them secular, and in the centre of it all, this decorous thing, an honest man, a lovely girl, fucking, in the nicest possible

way, to cheers and the chink of glasses —
and this was a thing that Liam never learned
how to do, how to switch in and out of sex,
how to talk around it, or share it, so although there were girlfriends we never saw
them, or if we saw them he did not like us,
the Hegartys, to speak to them: a line of
spindly, droopy human beings who held his
hand and peered at us over his shoulder.
Liam liked nice women. He liked women
who were kind or gentle. He liked those
translucent girls. And he was quite right not
to share them with us, the Hegarty hyenas,
myself and Kitty singing, 'And they called it
puppy lo — oo — oo-ove' as soon as they
left the room.

The funny thing, apart from the horny
postman, about that first journey through
the British night for us — fresh off the boat,
fifty paces across our first foreign soil and
then stepping up again on to the iron floor
of the train — was that we always thought
that we were nearly there. We looked out
the window and, after a period of darkness,
there were so many lights we assumed they
were the coming lights of London town.
Except that we never arrived. And it seemed
to us that England was a single city from
one side to the other, without pause. Then,
in the morning, when we had finally, defi-

nitely, absolutely arrived, we stood at the mouth of the underground in Euston, thinking that a train had just pulled in, and we would be able to make our way down when the crowd was gone. After a while we realised that the rush of people was not going to ease, that there was no one, particular train. London was all flow, it had no edges, it was everywhere.

Liam never liked the English, or so he claimed. In this he was helped, he said, by the fact that the English did not like themselves.

Clever Liam.

And I can not manage to love them, this herd on the hoof down the Brighton front, all of them enjoying the sea where Liam drowned. But I manage not to hate them, even though they are alive and my brother is dead. And I wonder how I escaped it — Liam's hatred of this or that arbitrary thing. Queers one year, Americans the next.

Who should I hate?

We swam at night somewhere. When we were young, we swam at night, and I can not remember where that might have been.

I look out at the wide, shifting sea, and, just for a moment, I think I have a smaller life, alive as I am in this sunlight, than my brother, walking out in the darkness; blood and whiskey into salt sea. Liam, pissed, just the skin that separated himself from his yearning self. Just for a moment, I think that it is more heroic not to be.

I look at my hands on the railings, and they are old, and my child-battered body, that I was proud of, in a way, for the new people that came out of it, just feeding the grave, *just feeding the grave!* I want to shout it at these strangers, as they pass. I want to call for an end to procreation with a sandwich board and a megaphone — not that there are many children, I now notice, on the playground that is Brighton beach, at least not this Tuesday afternoon. England, the land of the fully grown.

But I really don't mind these people, one way or another, and I love the undertaker. My catalogue companion, my English boy. This trendy ease he has is almost spiritual. I wonder who he goes home to — friends he likes, or parents he likes — and how do you have sex with a guy like that. Does he have moods?

When I am done, and have felt his harmless hand in my own (old) hand, I stand on the pavement outside his funeral parlour and I open my mobile to ring my difficult, middle-aged husband when what I want to do instead is lie down, just there, across the boy's doorway, until he steps across my prone body and lifts me up.

Azrael.

'How are things?' I ask Tom, and he tells me that the girls are going to friends' houses after school, and everything is fine. It takes me a moment to figure out where he is.

'Are you at work?'

'Of course I'm at work.'

'Rebecca has her Irish dancing,' I say.

'Well. Not today, she doesn't.'

'She has her showcase.' I wail it out into the street, and disbelieve it at the same time. Because what Tom is saying (quite rightly) is that my concerns are not important, they are invented, they are something to keep me occupied while he does the serious stuff of earning money and being more properly alive.

'Where are you?' I say.

'I told you, I'm at work.'

'Where at work? Where are you, *at work?*'

He can't put the phone down on me because I am in Brighton and recently bereaved. There is a long pause.

'Come home,' he says. 'When will you be home?'

'What's it to you?'

'Everything,' he says. 'What do you think?' And it is my turn now, to cut the connection, and fold up my phone.

My boy undertaker is behind me with the door open, saying, 'Do you need another coffee? Is there someone I can call?'

He has put his earring back in; a little sleeper of gold.

'It's all right,' I say. 'It's just the way it goes.'

I fell in love, I am beginning to realise, in my early twenties, when I met and slept with a guy from Brooklyn called Michael Weiss. He was in Dublin for an MA in Irish studies or Celtic studies, or what have you — we despised those courses, they were just something the college did to get rich Americans, and so I was surprised to find myself in love with Michael Weiss; surprised too because he was not a tall American with big prairie bones, but an average-sized guy who smoked roll-ups and talked with a Brooklyn pebble in his mouth, part slur and part contemplation.

Sleeping with him was very sweet, the way he would prop himself up to look at you and talk. He loved to chat while he was touching you, he loved even to smoke in this endless lazy foreplay that was all foreign to me then. I was twenty years old. I wasn't used to sex that was so aimless and unspecific. I wasn't used to sex that was sober, I suppose, and all this talking just made me uncomfortable: I thought he didn't fancy me. I watched his face move and wished he would just get on with it — the astonishing bit, the thing we were both here for.

I think, in his ironic, slow way Michael Weiss knew that he couldn't hold on to me, and all he was doing in those drowsy afternoons was trying to talk me down, like a cat in a tree, or an air hostess in charge of the plane. 'You see that leh-ver to your right? I want you to ease that leh-ver down to forty-five degrees.'

And though we got through a surprising amount of it — sex, that is — all I can remember is my madness at the time, watching the day outside his window shift to dusk in jolts and patches. It was, perhaps, an adolescent thing; standing naked on the nylon carpet of his student bedsit and feeling the change of light to be impossible; like my skin was being stripped off, as the day gave way, in tics and lunges, to dark.

Michael's father was an artist and his mother was something else. I wasn't used to that either — most of the parents I knew were just parents — but he had this semi-famous father and this mother who made appointments and met people and dressed

up to go out, and so he had all of that drag-
ging behind him. It was hard for him to
know what he was going to do when he
grew up, because he had been grown up, at
a guess, since he was ten years old. He wrote
some poems, and they were probably quite
good poems, but the idea of getting anywhere was a problem for him. There was
money — not a lot of money, but some —
and he had decided I think, even then, just
to exist, and see what came his way.

So now he is just existing, as I am, though
probably somewhere more interesting than
Booterstown, Dublin 4. He is in Manhat-
tan, say, or the canyons of LA, and he is
taking his son to saxophone lessons, he is
turning up to his daughter's dance showcase
on a Thursday afternoon, and finding all of
that an important and amusing thing to do.

I went out with Michael Weiss for two
years, on and off; driven crazy by his languor
— made inadequate by it, and impatient for
the world ahead of us, that was full of things
to do. I was not sure what these things were,
but they would be better than just hanging
around all afternoon, kissing and smoking,
talking about — what? — whether Dirk
Bogarde was actually good-looking, and
how, or how not to be, a Jew.

Now, of course, my afternoons are spent

not watching the television, so I was un-
doubtedly right to distrust and finally leave
Michael Weiss for a better, faster life, the
one I have now, cooking for a man who
doesn't show up before nine and for two
girls who will shortly stop showing up too.
Having tear-streaked sex, once in a blue
moon, with my middle-aged husband; not
knowing whether to hit him or kiss him.

Switch on the light, I want to say. *Switch on
the light.*

But it is not just the sex, or remembered
sex, that makes me think I love Michael
Weiss from Brooklyn, now, seventeen years
too late. It is the way he refused to own me,
no matter how much I tried to be owned. It
was the way he would not take me, he would
only meet me, and that only ever halfway.

I think I am ready for that now. I think I
am ready to be met.

I am sitting at a street café table, with
perhaps my fifth latte of the day, when some
American kids pass by, two girls and a guy.
One of the girls is saying, 'You know what
really sucks? What really sucks are those
button flies, when you miss a button?' and
the guy says, 'And you're like . . . this, you
know?' with his hands crossed at the wrist
in front of his crotch, like a picture of the

flagellated Christ.

This is what they were like, the Americans at college in Dublin — clear and loudish and interesting, at least to themselves. Maybe it is what we were all like, though no one wore long-sleeved T-shirts under short-sleeved T-shirts in our day. And I don't know if 'sucks' was a big word back then. I think about the boy's gesture, and I wonder why it is such a horrible thing to say. If someone sucks, then they are the worst possible type. A spoiler. Such a social word, I think, a gang word, for a very private muscular motion.

This is the way my mind runs, as I fail to gather myself together and get back on a train to the airport while my brother is decanted and transported and embalmed (the whiskey must help), somewhere in the town behind me. I go into a few shops and try normality for a while, and end up sitting still while the loud world passes by, with a long coffee spoon in my mouth, sucking.

13

When I was in college, I decided that Ada had been a prostitute — the way you do. It must have been around the time she died. I remember discussing my theory with Michael Weiss, who liked it a lot, though, as he pointed out, it was just as possible that she had been a nun, which was in his opinion pretty much the same thing, probably because he came from Brooklyn.

Well, yes.

Michael Weiss was the kind of person who took milk in his tea one day and decided against it the next, and he would, no doubt, have driven me crazy over time. But I think he said something true about Ada, or about the distance between me and Ada. Because I, too, might as well have been from Brooklyn, looking at the mysterious fact of her life and deciding on the one story that would explain us all.

I don't think I made it to the removal,

when she died — I probably spent the evening in Belfield bar — and the questions of who owned the house and where the money would go, once Ada's body was taken out of it, were a matter of complete indifference to me. Though not this question, suddenly, of who or what she had been; the orphan, Ada Merriman.

I made it to the funeral all right. There is the frizz of my mother's hair in the row in front of me, with our father on one side and, on the other, her sister, our Aunt Rose. There was a third child, a brother called Brendan, but he was probably dead by then, so these were the sad remnants of Ada's luck: our zonked-out mother, Maureen, and Rose the art teacher, who dressed in Interesting Tweeds of emerald green and cobalt blue. The Hegarty siblings were in the row behind them: in-laws and babies were sieved out into further pews, and it is possible that we sat, even then, in order of age; 'steps and stairs' as people used to croon, though the staircase was now bocketty, with gaps and broken planks and disproportion between one fat stoop and the next. Grown up, we all looked like cuckoos, every single one of us: we all looked wrong.

Later, I stood at the edge of the crowd and watched my grandmother's coffin being lowered, with melancholy indifference. The Ada of recent years was an old lady living out her allotted span. She was nice, of course — she was my Gran — but she wasn't the woman who woke me at four in the morning with the answer to it all: the Hegarty conundrum, the reason we were all so fucked up and so very much here.

Lamb Nugent looks at Ada Merriman across the carpet of the Belvedere Hotel, and she looks right back at him, and the rest, as they say, is history.

Fifty-six years later we had tea and sandwiches followed by self-congratulation in her surprisingly little house in Broadstone; the sprawling second generation, the beginnings of the third, my mother weakly enthroned in the good room, her sister complaining in the kitchen about whatever caught her eye. By then, the things that go wrong with people's faces had gone thoroughly wrong with theirs; Rose's mouth pulled into a jag of disapproval, my mother's gaze now watery and vague. Ada might have been good with other people's children, but she was manifestly terrible with her own. But, 'Oh she was lovely,' they said, the neighbours and few remaining friends: two men — I now realise they were gay — who were kind to her, the daughter of a dead actress who used to be on the telly. And didn't Jimmy O'Dea send a basket of fruit on her birthday? And Frank Duff who was the actual head of the Legion of Mary called to her house every Christmas. Indeed he did: I remember him, it must have been the year we stayed there, arriving like a little spinster Santa Claus with a box of chocolates in a string bag. He handed it to Ada and pressed her forearm, like they had lived too much, each of them, to have anything left to say.

That Christmas morning was as clean and crisp as it always is — my memory will not allow it to rain. But neither will it allow us home to Griffith Way, because this was the year that we were farmed out to Ada, me and Liam and Kitty, and we did not see our mother, not even for Christmas, though our father did arrive with a smug-looking Bea some time in the afternoon.

'Mammy's still not herself,' she said, looking extra pious in her new tank top, a mohair thing in stripes of raspberry and blue. And in the evening, Mr Nugent dropped by with a box of jellied fruit, or jelly impersonating fruit, in semi-circles of orange and yellow and green.

I was still too close to these things to care about them, the year that Ada died. The past was a bore to me, Ada's death completely tedious, as we passed the sandwiches and suffered the overused air of these little rooms. And, 'Oh she was terribly nice, your Granny,' which was true, of course. Which was only true. And they sipped or refused their light sherries, and cleared the kitchen in a riot of grease-proof paper, and were gone, leaving my mother in her chair in the good room, my *uxorious* father standing beside her, slightly stooped; Auntie Rose upstairs sneaking a last fag out the bathroom window, because she still did not officially smoke, even though her mother was far too dead to care, and besides, she always knew.

It might seem a little indecent, but it was at this point we were sent up to Ada's bedroom, under instruction from our father to 'take what you like'; the Hegarty girls enjoying the quietest screaming match we ever had, choked with fury and hating each other in whispers. I ended up with some strings of jet beads, the black ostrich feathers from Ada's mantelpiece, and a little porcelain hand with a gap in the palm where she kept her rings. Someone else got the rings, of course — I didn't have a chance. Kitty always needed things more than you did, Bea always deserved them more, while poor Midge — well, Midge always refused everything until she was persuaded to grab the lot. So I left the house with a howl of regret for all I had been denied, though there was nothing there I actually wanted. I had baggsed, on a whim, Ada's swatches and books of cloth and they seemed such useless objects by the light of day that I pushed them into a bin on the street. I did not know how to want what she had left behind. I wanted out of there, that was all. I wanted a larger life.

Liam missed all of this, because after the summer we went to work in London, he did not come home. Or rather he turned up now and then, and went to a few lectures: I would bump into him in the restaurant or bar, and he always had somewhere else to stay, and after a few wild months he was gone.

It was his final year at college. Most nights, I missed the bus and stayed with Michael Weiss in his Donnybrook bedsit: two high rooms with a partition around the toilet that didn't reach the ceiling and another around the kitchenette. The door into the bedroom was missing, and there was a massive old wardrobe beached against the wall. I fell asleep between these hunks of darkness — the black wardrobe, and the open block of the door frame, through which my senses swung — the sex still warm and hurting between my thighs, and no rest to be had anywhere.

There were things I told Michael Weiss, that year, that I haven't told anyone since. It was 1981. Nothing had happened yet, in Ireland — is that a funny thing to say? Nothing had happened yet in my life except the need to get out of it. I obliged Michael Weiss to have whiskey — the theatrics of it — I obliged him, once, to manhandle me around the room and up and down the street to walk off an, admittedly small, overdose of paracetamol. I gave Michael Weiss a wonderful, hard time and I rode him rotten, when all he wanted to do was prop himself up on one arm, and look at my face, and talk me down.

My image of these nights is of a woman (myself) lying on a bed, with her back arched, and her mouth open, and her hand scrabbling for the wall. No sound.

14

I think of her when I do the dishes. Of
course I have a dishwasher, so if I ever have
to cry, it is not into the sink, quietly like
Ada. The sink was her place for this. Facing
out of the back of the house, something
about the endless potatoes that needed peeling, or the paltriness of the yard, but, like
all women maybe, Ada occasionally had a
little sniffle and then plink, plink, a few tears
would hit the water in the sink. Like all
women Ada sometimes had to wipe her
nose with her forearm because her hands
were wet. There is nothing surprising about
this. Though I have to say, I have a stainless-
steel Miele dishwasher. And if I have any
crying to do, I do it respectably, in front of
the TV.

Life was hard for my grandmother, I know
that now. The surprising thing was that,
most of the time, she did not cry, but just
got on with it instead.

Ada believed in very little. She believed in a clean house. But she did not believe, or ever suggest, that if you ate the pips an apple tree would grow out of your belly button. I don't think she would believe in my picture of 'the orphan Ada Merriman'; though it is technically true that her parents died before she was grown. Ada just didn't do all that *stuff.* There was something about imagining things, or even remembering them, that she found slightly distasteful — like gossip, only worse. These days, of course, I do little else. And it is all her fault. Because if I look to where my imagining started, it was at Ada's sink, in Broadstone.

There was a red plastic mesh pad for the rough work, a dense green cloth for the close work and a sponge for finishing up. There was a white cotton cloth for wiping the oilcloth, that was never to be used for wiping the dishes. There was a cloth for the floor, that was never placed on the oilcloth. I had to know all this, because I was the oldest girl in the house. It was my job to take over sink duty, and do the washing-up.

I didn't mind it so much. I liked being close to her.

But I did imagine things. Standing at that Belfast sink, with the view of the yard and the green door to the garage beyond, I imagined Ada with her suitcase at nine years old, or ten, or whatever age she was when her mother died and she faced the wide world alone. I tried to imagine a father for her, but I could not. I imagined my own mother dying at home in Griffith Way — over and over again, actually — Mammy died, and my father wept and died, and afterwards, when she was planted, I imagined great adventures for myself and Liam, now that we were orphans too.

All this while Ada had me rinse the plates in water straight from the kettle, and Charlie winked at me, when her back was turned.

She called me into her room one morning. She was going out somewhere, getting dressed up. She was also wearing, I remember, a finger-stall in bandage pink, pulled tight by a loop of elastic around her wrist. For some reason I think she'd had an accident with the sewing machine, but this seems too vicious, really, to be true. I have no recollection of punctured nails, at any rate, or screams and commotion from the little boxroom. (And the fact that I can conjure this now — the runaway needle, the agonising extraction of the woman from the machine — makes me think that Ada was right; there is something immoral about the mind's eye.)

Anyway, the finger-stall was on her finger and I was called up to the top room and, 'Come here,' she said, looking over her shoulder and lifting her skirt a little, at the back. 'Do me up.' And she turned her leg to me for the side view.

Her thigh was surprisingly little. It had an inky map of broken veins in a cluster, above the sag of her stocking, which was folded at the top to a thick orange band. Little white tabs dangled on concertinaed ribbon, from a place I could not see, or did not want to see, and it took me ages to realise what she was asking me to do. I had to crouch by the Gothic panels of her corset, and tether it to the stockings that were waiting beneath. I remember the soft clench of the rubber snaps around nylon that would not stay still, and the cool of her leg, and the sour smell of her respectability. And I imagined that every man who called to the door knew about these secret gaps between her clothes; the amazing two-leggedness of her, and the tight vault of her corset, all open to the air below.

And perhaps they did.

So when Frank Duff arrived at the door, I thought he was after her too.

'Just a little something, Ada. No, I insist! Just a little something small.'

Frank Duff that is, who was the actual head of the actual Legion of Mary, a religious organisation dedicated, in 1967, to inanity and the making of tea.

'God bless now. Happy Christmas to all your brood.' And he ran a loving hand down my cheek, catching my chin lightly, letting it go.

Mr Nugent coming later with the box of jellied fruit. Ignoring Ada and talking to the children instead. It was Christmas: it was our day.

In fact, Frank Duff spent his early years rescuing prostitutes off the streets of Dublin. This is what he was doing in 1925 — this dotey, clever man — he was organising missions; he was talking girls out of the brothels, and buying off their madams, and taking them on retreats. This was the Legion of Mary's first, great work. In the Lent of 1925, when Ada met Charlie, Frank Duff was saying a lot more than his prayers.

This I discovered, as I chased him through the college library stacks, working on an essay for my final college assessment, which I called (with no sense of irony, I think), 'Paying for Sex in the Irish Free State'. Because I was suddenly certain of many things. Including the fact that people fucked, that was one of the things they did: men fucked women — it did not happen the other way around — and this surprising mechanism was to change, not just my future, which was narrowing even as I looked at it, but also the wide and finished world of my past.

So I imagined for a while that Ada was one of Duff's mended whores. She was not a blowsy whore, of course — she was an orphan. She was barely a whore at all. She was a poor girl, who turned her face to the wall as the coins clinked on to the bedside table, and the dark shape of a man left the room.

Let us stick with this. A satin slip, with the lace a little torn. A picture of the Virgin put in a drawer, until he goes. A romance of falling. And shivering in the doctor's waiting room, clutching your wool coat at the neck, where the button has gone. A dusty, middle-class fantasy, of crinkled stockings, and TB, and hunkering to wash over a basin on the floor.

So there are priests in the front lounge of the Belvedere Hotel that evening in Lent: and a madam, and our man with the Milk Tray, Frank Duff. They are buying the madam off. Quietly. They are closing her down.

Outside, Ada and Nugent listen, and then forget to listen to the thin line of talk that trickles out of the front lounge. For a moment at least, they merely sit across from each other — the man from the Legion and the little seamstress-whore. What odds? She is beautiful. And he is no better than he should be. The city is quiet and the hotel is quiet, and there is no one here to tell Lamb Nugent that he will sit in this woman's good, front room for the rest of his life, holding out his little china cup for *More tea, Lamb?*

No one, that is, until Charlie Spillane walks in the door.

'Ma'am,' he says, tipping his non-existent hat. 'I hope this fellow has been keeping you amused.'

Michael Weiss, as I say, loved it — but as soon as he loved it, I changed my mind. As soon as he said the word 'prostitution' it shrank away, my little snail of a story poking its way out into the world. He never met Ada. He didn't have a clue what I was talking about. I was talking about family. I was talking about what we were doing, three times a night. I was talking about the meaty flower of my cunt, under his hand.

Meanwhile Liam turned up and left again. He had a room going in a dive in Stoke Newington, and he was twitchy about the exams; our father going beetroot when he talked about the waste of his talent and of the good money thrown away on fees.

'Tell that brother of yours. If you see him. Tell that brother of yours to face me if he can. Tell him from me.'

'Oh, what Daddy? Tell him what?'

'What do you mean, *what?*'

'All right. I'll tell him.'

'What?'

'I'll tell him.'

Mammy saying, 'Who? Tell who?'

The American part of Michael Weiss thought the Hegarty family a blast. He met Liam in the Belfield bar now and then, and the two of them got on in that surprising way that men have — the man you are sleeping with and your brother, for example, who look at each other, and nod, and *get on.* It drove me slightly bats, actually, watching the two of them go off for a game of pool, while I sat there on my own with a glass of Satzenbrau.

But we had some good nights, the three of us, myself and Liam doing a thing we started that first summer in London, which was telling stories about our family like they were all made up. We had a double act about Ernest's ordination, the horrible yellow soles of his feet as he lay prostrate on the altar, the sight of our mother, when all the voodoo was done, tottering across to dress him in his robes, and then later, at a sort of wedding reception, the two of them cutting the cake together, my brother and my mother, and kissing when it was done.

'I don't believe it,' said Michael Weiss. 'Your mother! I don't believe it!' and he might start in on something about his own bar mitzvah, which we, of course, ignored.

Though some of the things we found funny about our family he didn't find funny at all. My older baby brother Stevie — the one who died when he was two — 'She did it,' said Liam. 'She put a pillow over his face,' and we'd laugh our heads off. 'Well, come on, she was pregnant all the time. All the time.'

'Wouldn't you?'

It wasn't long before Michael wanted to call to the house. I didn't know how to explain to him that no one cared if he called or not, but everyone would laugh at him for a year if he showed up at the door. In the event he rang the bell with a very American corsage the night of the rag ball, and walked right in like Cary Grant, through the hall and the living-room extension, and beyond that to the extension that was the kitchen, my father hopping up out of his chair to shake the boy's hand, and, 'Oh. Hello,' said my mother, as she would say, *will say perhaps,* to the alien who beams himself down on to her lino, or the junkie with the knife, as she will say on her deathbed to the nurse, or to the opening tunnel of light.

'Oh. Hello.'

'Michael Weiss, sir,' said Michael Weiss, reaching out a frank and manly hand; my father, to his credit, swallowing the need to ask if this is a Jewish class of a name, though he asks it of me later.

'Weiss, isn't that a Jew name?' insisting that he can't be an anti-Semite when he doesn't know any *blithering* Jews.

'Well, you know one, now.'

All of this before I started to stay out all night and the fights came. You might wonder where he got the energy. My father had a flaring temper, but he rarely lost it with his daughters. He lost it with his sons, but only when they confronted him. Of course his sons confronted him all the time, but as far as his daughters were concerned, he could ignore all sorts of late-night homecomings as long as you didn't ask him for the taxi money, he could let you walk in pissed, as long as you went by him and straight up the stairs, he would fail to hear you throwing up in the toilet as long as you cleaned up afterwards, but when he asks you for a cigarette and you pull out a box of Durex, like a catastrophic schoolgirl, then he is obliged to erupt, and keep erupting, like Old Faithful, until you have found yourself *alternative accommodation.*

Apart from anything else they were illegal. Everyone had them. Whether we needed them or not.

There was nothing Daddy would not say. He had no sense of distance. He might have been talking to himself, almost. I was *whoring all over Dublin.* I was *second-hand goods,* I was *turning myself into a toilet* — I kid you not — though I think what he really wanted to say was that I was *not doing what I was told.*

The shouting happened two or three months before my finals. And though it was a bit of a laugh in its way, it did affect my exams — and I was serious about exams. Maybe this was why I felt so unconnected: there I was sitting in the kitchen thinking about Robespierre, not to mention Frank Duff, my father cooking up a rage — he was a small man, Daddy — and I suppose I did my fair share of shouting too, but a part of me was just looking at him, all fizzed up, the redness in his neck, while his face was chalk white, then the redness boiling up around his blue eyes, until his face was suddenly, uniformly red, and ranting. There was also the red dome of his bald head to consider. I remember thinking that he himself didn't believe what he was saying, and that it was this lack of belief, combined with my own, that drove him to such extremes.

Back in Belfield, my best friend Deirdre Moloney had just been thrown out by her mother for nothing at all: a very low-key sort of girl, she'd only ever had sex twice. Children were being chucked out all over Dublin. All our parents were mad, in those days. There was something about just the smell of us growing up that drove them completely insane.

For a few weeks, Daddy could not look at me, and this hurt me in the Daddy-loves-his-little-girl place; the place where you trust and flirt. But though it hurt, I found that I was able to draw on more ancient hurts than that — and this is how I survived. This is how we all survive. We default to the oldest scar.

What hurts now is the fact that Daddy is dead. He died in 1986. So he never did walk into a shop where they sold condoms by the cash register. He never had to change his mind, not even slightly. I think of him, too, when I palm the cuttlefish bone that Rebecca finds on the beach, because it reminds me of a mango pip; the fact that when Daddy died no one in Ireland ate mango, though I think kiwi was all the rage by then. And I feel I must console him for mangoes. I must console him for the distance we have moved from the place where he stopped.

His ghost, incidentally, could not give a damn about who I slept with. His ghost is beyond sex. And sometimes I think that so am I.

Still, there was Michael, before the storm, shaking my father's hand and my father not saying, 'Weiss? What class of a name is that, at all?'

Me coming into the kitchen in a bronze-coloured Jenny Vander dress, looking, at a guess, pretty good. The two of us walking away from the house where I grew up, Michael Weiss beside himself with delight.

'I don't believe it,' he said. 'I can't believe it. Everything you said. It's all true.'

And I was — I still am, even as I write this — mortified.

15

Ada's hall door was flat against the street. There was no garden or path up to it so people passed by, very close, without ever coming in. This arrangement was as implacable as Ada herself, and as exciting. She was, in my mind, always at cross purposes to the world.

In the summer, the door had a cream canvas cover, with thick and thin rust stripes. There was a horizontal mouth cut out for the letterbox, a long slit for the knocker, and a little round hole for the bell. The door underneath, if you lifted the cloth, was painted bottle green.

The house was in a terrace of identical little houses, each symmetrical to the next, so the doors cosied up to each other in pairs. We slept in the back of the house. I remember standing at the bedroom window and looking out at the little garage at the end of Ada's little garden, and at the lane beyond. We had two beds between the three of us, a wide one for the girls and a narrow one for Liam. The wallpaper was a pattern of blue-green flowers, bulbous and slightly metallic; they made the whole place writhe a little under my steady child's eye.

Here's me, at the age of three, with my ear pressed against the beige tin cliff of her washing machine, or looking in over the lip, to see the swirl and jerk of the clothes: Ada pushing stuff through the mangle (*Don't touch the mangle!*), the last soap hissing out while some dress, catastrophically wrecked, slowly slides, then shoots out from between the rollers, to drop into the bucket like a Crimplene turd.

Here's me eating Ada's rubber bathing hat whose famous yellow flowers appeared in my nappy the next day. Though, of course, it must have been Kitty's nappy — hardly mine, at the age of three. Ada shouting for Charlie, who looked over her shoulder and said, 'Where did we get such a clever girl?'

Of course I was jealous of my little sister, but I had a peculiar, fierce love for her too. It is not surprising that I steal her memories for my own. Though no man, I now realise, ever puts his hand into a dirty nappy, as I can see Charlie doing in my mind's eye, to pull out a posy of shitty yellow flowers.

Here's me, definitely, pulling the bathing cap over my face. I lick the salty inside of it, until it seals me up — the smell of Ada's hair in the sea. Then I start to drown in the pink light, that explodes with soft flowers of bright red, and a curiously bright black.

Did this happen? The world hurting as the cap is pulled away; Ada, outside of me, shouting. Me being pushed into her meagre breast, that tasted of Lux flakes and wool.

More probably, it was Liam put the hat over my face and nearly killed me. Or it was Kitty who got smothered by the two of us. We played at fainting all the time, which would place the hat — the delicious, fantastic pink bathing hat, with the floppy yellow flowers — in the world of an eight-year-old as opposed to the world of one who is only three.

Sometimes, in second-hand clothes shops, I look for objects like these, thinking that if I could hold the hat in my hands, if I could stretch it and smell it, then I would know which was which and who was who out of Kitty, and Liam, and me.

The second time we stayed at Ada's our father drove us across town on a traffic-free afternoon — it might have been a Sunday — with suitcases in the boot. And the thing that astonished me then was how he knew the way.

This is where the silence happened — as I stood in the back room and looked out at the garage and the lane. It was an over-whelming silence, like the air was made of wood, and the bulbous flowers of the back-room wallpaper both writhed a little and were entirely still, under my eight-year-old eye.

And — I don't know why this should fit in, but here is my father in the kitchen of Griffith Way, maybe six years later, holding the thickness of the wooden table like it was a bible, and he's shouting at Liam in a care-ful voice the lines, 'I loved your mother from the day I first set eyes on her. I worshipped the ground she walked upon.'

This would be Liam saying something completely insulting, at the age of thirteen or so. My father's lips thin and purple, his chest working like a bellows, squeezing it out, phrase by windy phrase.

'I LOVEd your MOTHer from the DAY I first set EYES on her. I WOrshipped the GROUND she WALKED upon.'

While Mossie read the paper, and I got on with my homework, and Midge cried about something else altogether and made a cup of tea.

He certainly meant it. My father, trembling, in that moment before something was flung or broken. Liam calling him a fucking baboon then, probably.

'You're a fucking baboon!'

And flying out of the room, before he could be caught and given a thump.

My father was a small man. And his chest always whistled and sang. And I remember nothing like I remember that silence after he closed Ada's front door and lowered himself into the front seat of the car and drove away.

Ada's little garden was probably just a yard, but we thought it an exciting place, with crab apple and nettles: the door to the garage was sometimes open and sometimes bolted, and the fact that you never knew if Mr Nugent was in there only added to the interest. Liam used the tools on the workbench or played with the wrecked car in there. I used to sit on the stitched blue leather of the front seat, which was tight in places and ripped in others. I didn't try to drive; the dash was too strange. I just used to slide up and down the upholstery, or squirm across the nice rows of stitching, and talk in a grand voice to whoever was driving, whether or not he was actually there.

Two double doors led out to the back lane, where there was another car up on blocks, a pastel blue and chrome affair with great American fins. Even now I can not see a derelict car without a pang. Mr Nugent came and left by the doors to the lane, and fiddled about on the workbench, or stuck his head under the bonnet of the American monster if the weather was fine. On a Friday he came round to the front door to knock, and he always had sweets for the children. He wore a hat, which he doffed when Ada opened the door. It was many years before I wondered at the formality of this arrangement, or what was going on.

Ada called him Nolly, though we all knew that what you called him was Mr Nugent, if you called him anything at all, which we didn't. Sometimes she called him Nolly May, she'd say it after he was gone, 'Oh, Nolly May,' pushing the chair he'd sat in back up against the wall. He didn't do much except sit there getting insulted by the wallpaper, but there was always a slight sweat on him, and he cleared his throat a lot, and you could tell how much he wanted Gran.

She had gorgeous manners, Gran. She liked to put things on a tray. She had opinions about lump sugar and where was the right place to keep your biscuit between bites, all of which made you feel really uncomfortable and very well loved. She made dresses in the boxroom upstairs, and sometimes she worked in the theatre, which is why everything had to be so respectable. It made for a kind of twisting of the air between herself and the actors who sometimes came for a fitting. They seemed to wring something out between, until — oh, go on! — the room was ripe with implication. Though she would put the crockery away after the same guest was gone and tell me that the stage was an interesting life but it made you very bitter. Or she would say something strangely memorable like, 'Sex gets you nowhere in this world. Remember that, sex will get you precisely No Where.'

Though Charlie was often away, she had us for company, and sometimes one of the actresses slept in the boxroom, if she had a show in town; squeezed in behind the tailor's dummy and the electric sewing machine. At least I think she slept in there. The dummy worked strangely on my imagination; I can not even get the door open in my head, now, to look inside.

Peggy McEvoy, that's what she was called. And she was engaged to someone on the telly.

And there was Nolly in the good room, clearing his throat and swallowing, while we ate the VoVos he brought, and the Blackjacks. I knew him by the taste of sweets and by the glint in his glasses, or the heaviness of his pockets, or the peculiar small growth flowering inside his ear. His hands were placed square on each knee, and he always leaned forward slightly, not resting quite on the back of the chair. He sat like someone who wasn't getting much sex, now that I see him in my mind's eye — and his glance was too casual, in a way that I also now recognise. Though he had, in his grim way, four children and a wife we never saw, called Kathleen. When Ada was out of the room he would get up out of the chair and walk over to the television and turn it off with a clunk. Then he would sit back down and look at us. After a minute he would manage something out of his pocket.

'It's not a toy.'

Though it was always something interesting. One day it was a white mouse — or, it must have been a rat — with red eyes and a pink tail, and he lifted my jumper at the wrist, to let it run up my sleeve and on to my chest: Ada coming in then to scream.

She served up tea on one of those little tables that had two more tables tucked into it, each smaller than the other. 'Put a cloth on the table nest,' she'd say to me. And 'Charlie says' this and 'Charlie says' that, she would say to Nolly May, setting the tray down or handing him over a cup of tea. This was our Granda Charlie she was talking about, who, when Nugent wasn't sitting there, was, 'What time did he go? Did you see him take the money from the shelf?'

I don't think Charlie drank (even his vices were old-fashioned), he just did everything else. Or nothing else. It was hard to say what he did, except absent himself. And sometimes he came back in different clothes.

'Oh, he treated her like a queen,' as they would say over the funeral cooked meats. They had a story, Ada and Charlie, that is for sure, in which they each played the most important roles, and when she walked across the room to him, you could tell how fated they felt, as if their love was a great burden to them as well as a joy.

One time I came into the front room and they were sitting on either end of the sofa, and he had her old foot in his lap, and was massaging it through the sheer of her stockings.

I couldn't tell you what Nugent did, though it has stuck somewhere in my head that he was a bookie, or a bookie's clerk, that he put on a grey cashmere coat from time to time, and got into a black car, and was driven to the race-course. All I really know is that he used the garage out the back for his old jalopies and you never knew if he was in there or not. I thought — if I thought anything at the time — that Ada allowed him to use it because she had no car of her own, and by that time, Charlie did not drive.

16

So here they all are, going to the races, finally. It is Easter Monday and every car in Dublin is making for Fairyhouse in a convoy, there are charabancs in a line down O'Connell Street and trains going every twenty minutes from the station at Broadstone.

The drab days of Lent are over, the Legion's mission has been triumphant, the brothels have been raided by the police, sprinkled with holy water, bought off by Frank Duff, and closed down. A great religious procession has been held and a cross raised in Purdon Street by the man himself, who stood up on a kitchen table and drove in the nail with a surprisingly large hammer. Twenty girls have been decanted into the Sancta Maria hostel and dried out at either end. Everyone has been praying day and night, night and day, until they are fed up with it, the whole city has had it up to here, they have suffered the ashes and kissed the rood and felt truly, deeply, spiritually *cleaned out:* Easter dawns, thanks be to Jay, and when they have eaten and laughed and looked at the daffodils they go to bed and make love (it's a long time, forty days) and have a big sleep and, the next morning, they all go off to the races.

It is Easter Monday, a still-tender time. It is the day Christ says, *'Noli me tangere,'* to the woman in the garden. Do not touch me. It is too soon. It is too soon to be touched.

Oh Nolly May.

Though maybe Ada makes some kind of attempt. Maybe she forgets, for a moment, that Charlie is the one she will love for evermore and does her best with Nugent. He is the one who invited her, after all; lingering after Mass, to mention the possibility of the outing. Of course she'd be going anyway, so it's not so much a tryst he is suggesting, as a lift.

'You said you'd like a go in a car,' he says looking down at the path between them.

She fixes her eyes on the same spot and lifts her eyebrows to say, 'Can I bring a friend?'

So Nugent is the lover in all this, Charlie is the transport, Ada is the wraith and lilith the lovely girl the fallen woman the sad

whore the poor orphan the safe bet, whatever way you look at it, and with her is Ellen, who is company for Charlie and just a
maid.

Nugent and Ada sit in the back of the
Morris and the daylight suits her surprisingly well. There is fresh blood in her cheeks
and her hair is thick in the wind, and he
feels stupidly easy there beside her, he feels
like he could just talk — her understanding
is so direct. A man could speak to a woman
like this and feel like a better person, he
could forget altogether the night thoughts
and the struggles of his conscience, the gap-
ing wound of his soul that opens — in some
dream or waking dream — in his chest.

It is gone, this queer fragment, it is
whipped away by the festive drive in an
open-topped car, in cavalcade with every
other car in Dublin, now that Lent is over,
and the races are on. Nugent's hand is
steady and the girl beside him is as frank
and poetical as an animal, and so he is safe.
With Ada, he is safe.

And so they drive — up the Navan Road,
past the Guinness estates where Charlie lifts
his imaginary hat to give a cheer for the
lovely brew.

'Hoo hoo,' he says. 'Hoo hoo!'

And they are having a grand time now,

singing a song — what is it? — 'The Harp that Once', 'Silent O Moyle' — big, open-air songs. Charlie belting them out in his fine English baritone, looking at everything but the road, so the view that Ada has is of his shoulder blades, covered in fat and resting on the top of the seat in front of her, the flutter of his scarf reaching for her as she sits behind, the tips of his waxed moustache, signalling over his shoulder, now and then, cheerful thoughts of manliness and cleanliness and, if you considered them long enough, a tickling sensation on the inside of your thighs.

But Ada, we are sure, does not think like this. Ada has suffered enough from our imputations. She turns to Nugent as he talks of the races to come, and the possible odds, and the need for a clear hand from the minister of finance in all of this, because everyone likes a flutter, it is as much an Irishman's right as any other Christian man.

It is surprising to hear so much out of him at one time. Ada gets the feeling that Nugent speaks all at once or not at all. He is the kind of man that women were told to 'draw out', in those days — hard work, in other words, and fantastically easy prey.

But it might be compassion as much as anything else, that leads her to touch him, there in the open-topped car. Or thought-lessness. She is only trying to draw his attention, but to what? Lord and Lady Talbot de Malahide driving the whole way on the wrong side of the road, with the chauffeur's gloved hand stuck to the horn. Or something quieter, a straw horse in a farmer's field propping up a sign that says, 'Drinks Here'.

It could be a response to something he has said, 'They've made such a hames of it already,' meaning, of course, the Free State government; or a more intimate comment, like, 'Personally, I've never minded a spot of rain.'

The impulse is, at any rate, to touch him.

How will she manage it? She will lay her finger on his arm. She will lay her whole palm on his forearm. Or, later, she might take the crook of his elbow under the hinge of her wrist, and link him as they walk to the rails. And whichever one of these she does, she will feel Nugent flinch away.

Here is Charlie in front of her, bowing as he presents the open mouth of a bag of boiled sweets.

'Oh, comfort me with apples,' he says, before remembering himself and turning to offer first choice to Ellen, the friendly, double-chinned maid.

For the rest of the afternoon Lamb Nugent looks after Ada, while the corners of her jaw squirt painful juice for Charlie's apple drops. He puts on a penny a time with Myrellson of Dame Street, who knows him and forbears. Pride of Arras for the three o'clock, in which Ballystockhard makes all the running, Ada saying, 'Is that mine, is that mine?' and Nugent saying, 'No, it's not yours.' All afternoon he watches his luck dribble away, Street Singer, Con Amore, Daisy's Boss — who is picking these nags? Oh, but they have to back Ellen's Bean for the Fairyhouse Plate, they just have to, and when the horse comes in second Ada has more sense than to say, 'What does that mean, "on the nose"?' Coolcannon falls at the second last and with it all his hopes, and then Ada finally gets lucky on Knocknageena.

Yaroo!

The whole party is, by now, so worn out by the surge and loss of each race, and by the endless waiting in between, that when Ada jumps and lifts her fists, nothing is hidden from any of them. She might stay like that — Ada ascending — frozen in victory, from her clenched hands to the tip of her down-pointed shoes. By the time she hits the ground again it has been settled: one of these men wants her to win, and the other wants her to lose.

And she knows it.

Ada's horse came first. But it was only a horse — it's not exactly her fault. So maybe it is her sense of justice that makes her choose Charlie, who is pleased for her, as opposed to Nugent who is insulted by her good luck. But there is no doubt — the choice has been made.

On the trip home, Ellen sings in the front seat; the shreds of her lovely voice coming back to them on the wind, 'When Other Lips', 'I Dreamt I Dwelt'. They understand each other completely, each person in this car. They sit and think what it all means: Charlie has won Ada, Nugent has lost her. And this stirs in them thoughts of other things.

Charlie, for example, is thinking about all the girls he has pushed to the brink of ruin before letting each of them go. He is bidding it all farewell, the ravishing, tawdry, endless *tristesse* of one woman or another, one woman or another, until a man had to address his member as you might a dribbling dog, 'Enough, sir! Enough!'

Ellen is thinking that she will never get married.

Nugent is trying to catch last night's

dream, sure that it was telling him that he had lost, already, before he ever tried. It was a dream about his soul, a gap opening in his chest — because the soul is a she — there is a girl flowering inside him, breaking through, there is a hole weeping nectar just above his heart, it is opening to his hand, there — just there — a place where all good things are, as hope and loving-kindness, a place he can find a gorgeous kind of rest, and enter or be entered, over and over again, over and again, finding as he does so, the soul's own sweet ecstasy, until he wakes to the horror of his blasphemous thoughts and the after-shock of his seed just spent, and waits, in the dark, for the mess to go cold.

I don't know what Ada was thinking in the car on the way home. She was probably doing the sums in her head, wondering why she had to fall for the one who had a hole in his pocket. But even so she holds out her hand to Charlie and says, 'Thank you for a lovely drive.'

And to Nugent, 'Thank you for a lovely day.'

She looks Nugent in the eye. And she knows what he sees. And she doesn't care.

I do not know why Ada married Charlie when it was Nugent who had her measure.

And though you could say that she did not marry Nugent because she did not like him, that is not really enough. We do not always like the people we love — we do not always have that choice.

Maybe that was her mistake. She thought she could choose. She thought she could marry someone she liked and be happy with him, and have happy children. She did not realise that every choice is fatal. For a woman like Ada, every choice is an error, as soon as it is made.

17

One day, Ada packed a basket and took us to the seaside on the train. Or, I should say, she wrapped a few sandwiches in the waxed paper from the sliced pan, and she put them into her string shopping bag — she was turning into something off the BBC there, for a minute, walking down a country lane in a long skirt, with gnats and dust motes dancing in the sunlight around her hair. So no. Though this was the general mood, or the remembered mood, of the expedition, Ada did not wear a long skirt with mutton-chop sleeves, she wore a dress (what a rush, to remember this, now), a small-print floral dress in lilac — very like a housecoat print, if it were not for the exotic background of inky black. The collar and cuffs were bordered with the same floral print, except the flowers here were aqua blue, and this gave the dress some distinction, though it was also an ordinary flowery dress, with a nip in the waist and a full-enough skirt, and a slight glaze on the cotton, that hush-shushed as she moved.

We sat on the train beside her all the way to Donabate, which was beside the sea, and we played with the leather pull on the top window, or opened the door to look down the length of the corridor, and then slid it shut again. Past the Hill of Howth and on to Malahide; the train moved into the flat sandy reaches of North County Dublin, which all the Hegartys knew meant 'market gardening' as Navan meant 'carpets' and Newbridge 'cutlery and ropes'. We looked out the window, wondering what 'market gardening' might look like if we passed it by, and we played on the seats, and were, I suppose, entirely happy.

We were going to a place called St Ita's, and then we were going to the sea. This first was a peculiar destination. We had a sister Ita who was, even then, the most disliked among us, as perhaps each of the girls were, at the moment their breasts began to grow.

St Ita was an early Irish nun who, out of love for the baby Jesus, prayed for the gift of nursing — and 'the milk came'. So it was not to a place we were travelling, that day in the train, but towards some fuddled idea of 'nursing', whatever that meant to me at eight years old: a woman tenderly bandaging an infant's mouth, or a nurse smiling and waiting — something odd and lovely behind the hanging watch and white cotton on her breast. It was into whiteness that we were travelling, clicketty-clack. And it is a whiteness I remember, when we finally arrived, a seared white sky, that met, in a final burn of white, a far, grey sea.

Meanwhile, I sat in the carriage beside Ada's floral skirt, pulling a string of plastic beads from my pursed lips, perhaps, and mouthing them back in again. It would have taken forty minutes at the most, this fantastic, endless trip by train. Kitty and I in differently coloured gingham prints, pink for her and green for me, and Liam, as boys always are, in shades of navy and grey. We chug along, bouncing nicely on the sprung seats, all together, as actors on stage. Then, off at the station! The steam hisses, and Ada is back in her mutton-chop sleeves, as we climb the steps up to the little village and the hump-backed bridge from which you can look at the tracks slicing off northwards to Rush and Lusk. There is a shop for ice-pops and you can smell the sea, but Ada has further to go and we stand at a bus stop and wait until a stranger pulls up in a mint-green car and we all climb in the back.

'You're going to the hospital?' says the man behind the wheel and Ada says, 'St Ita's, yes,' on a long exhalation. The stranger lets it lie, this heavy word now beside us in the car. He is not going as far as the gates, he says; he will let us down near enough. It is his habit, evidently, to pick people up at this bus stop, and I know by the way he says 'hospital' that St Ita's is not a hospital. If we were going to a hospital, then Ada would have said.

There is a girl sitting in the front passenger seat, about five years old. She has fantastically round eyes, no shoes, and no T-shirt, and she is sitting, happy as Larry with her father in the front seat. We look at each other when the car stops, and she keeps looking as we get out, like she would like to get out with us too, despite all her luck. And a part of me goes with her when the car drives away.

Another part of me is still, these years later, walking along the road where the stranger set us down. It is a long straight road, a country road; though it has a proper concrete path along one side, and it is along this concrete path we walk, the three children and the woman with her string bag. There is a ditch beside the path and after that a large and shivering cornfield. On the other side of the road, there is a line of wonderful, wrecked trees and a low stretch of bog. Halfway along our side, a bungalow stands in the middle of the field, and we wait to see if there is a path up to it, or whether it had been altogether abandoned in the midst of the corn.

Far ahead of us — and this was the longest, straightest road, at the age of eight, that I had ever been on — there is a man with two sticks, and he bundles himself along, one shoulder hunching over the top of the stick, and then the other, his legs working curiously against, or after this rhythm, like he is only using the sticks for show. He is a short man and very sturdy. He twists his hand at the wrist, as the hunched shoulder comes down, and the stick might waver a little before he switches to the other side. Hunch twist waver step. Hunch twist wobble step. There is nothing wrong with his legs, as far as I can see, except that they are slow, and the road is very long. Hunch, twist, yaw, step. Shoulder, hand, and maybe, yes, leg. And we should be overtaking him, but the road is too long, and Ada is slowed by one or other of us children, until with the distance and the excitement of the day, I think that there is some other thing wrong with the man with two sticks, something we won't know until we pass, a deformation of his face, or an expression that we can not yet see. We are closer but we are still not there, as he walks gainfully along, covering more ground than you would think for a man with two bad legs, and we might actually pass him except Kitty has skipped out on the road, or Ada is halted by the shiftings and manipulations required by the string bag, which contains, not just egg sandwiches in waxed paper, but also something else. There are other little parcels in there, that are too good for our picnic, old-lady parcels, done up in wrapping paper and Sellotape, one of them looks like a box of After Eights, and one is very misshapen, and could be anything at all. And Ada has them in a separate plastic bag inside the string bag, with a name scored in biro on the front. She is going to visit someone in the hospital, and then we are going to the beach. And of course I have known this all along — we are going to visit my Uncle Brendan, though because I am eight I do not understand that my uncle is necessarily Ada's son, or I do not know what that means — 'son'. But certainly I have known it all along that we are going to visit Uncle Brendan in St Ita's which isn't quite a hospital, and after that we are going to paddle in the sea.

Liam, especially, is frisky and lonely, he wants to walk on the other side and look down into the low field that is turning into bog, but Ada will not let him, he must stick to the path, because that is what it is for, and what would our mother say if Ada brought him back to her all broken by a car? And at the mention of our mother everything gets a little bit worse, because what is Liam to me except a 'brother' and what is he to Mammy except her 'son', and when I look up old two-sticks is gone, and we have passed the long gap in the corn, if there was a long gap in the corn, and the bungalow sails on in the middle of the field behind us, up to its gunwales in golden brown.

I don't remember the hospital. At a guess, Ada did not take us inside. There was a handball alley in the grounds and she left us there, and we played between its concrete walls. On the rise behind the alley there was a round tower, like the Irish round tower on our copybook covers, and beside that was a huge vase of stone, perhaps a hundred feet high, and that was a water tower, and they stood watch from the hill, like a fat woman and a thin man, looking far out over the sea. There it was, at the bottom of the hill. A strong sea, under a hard white sky. And we might have run down there, but Ada had charged us to stay put, so we played a little in the handball alley, doing nothing, just liking the shape of it, and being in it; the back wall and the two slanting side walls, like cutting the end off a shoebox. On one side were the round tower and the water tower, and on the other was a wall of red brick. We did not look at this wall, or at the dirty casement windows with no bars, where the lunatics were, and we did not think of what lunatics did when they saw children — eat them, I thought, suck at their ears and jibber — so we played at being Nice Children for the watching loonies until Ada came back with her string bag half empty, pleased in a thorough sort of way, to see us playing there.

'Come on,' she would have said, and we did not tell her about the one loony we saw walking up the path from the sea, slow and stupid and dirty and terrible, who looked right at us as he shambled by.

After that, there must have been the sea. Ada bringing us for red lemonade into a pub, that had a black roof with huge letters of white written across it. We must have caught the bus back to the station at the hospital gates, and taken the train back home.

18

At around this time, Liam became frightened at night, and though Kitty was supposed to sleep in the double bed with me, he would come across in the darkness and worm his way between us, elbowing her out and hissing at her to move into the bed he had left. Kitty looked so Victorian in her nightgown, her heels and ankles white on the floorboards, her hair mussed over a face made plump by sleep; I would almost miss her, the healing stillness of her breath on the next pillow, occupied now by Liam's face, his eyes blinking and large, his hands rolling under the bedclothes as he rummaged a place for himself there. He was never still. He sank down off the pillow and looked up at me, or hooshed back towards the headboard, he fussed and squirmed, or he would freeze, appalled — there was a face at the window, or imagine if there was a volcano under Dublin, or if you fell down a hole and your mouth was full of maggots. All this was delivered with great gusto, so, though everything he said was terrible, I remember these as happy nights, talking until dawn. He must have been smaller than me by then, because he always ended up rolled into the line where my body met the mattress, and I would have to wake up to push him away.

What did we talk about? I wish I knew. In our teens, we wrote slick and 'hilarious' letters to each other, any time we were parted, the summer he went to the Gaeltacht, or the time I went off on a French exchange.

'Meanwhile,' he writes from Gweedore, the year he was fourteen, 'we get numb bums from sitting on the beach and not drinking vodka, or "bhodhca" as it is called here. Billy Tobin got sent back up for speaking English so Michael and me have developed a way of speaking English <u>as if it is actually Irish</u> which is great fun and not very comprehensible. Iubhsaid try it iurselbh some time.'

He was the one who talked most, but I didn't mind. I wish I could remember what exactly he said, but conversation doesn't stick to my memory of Liam. We never sat, one across from the other in proper chairs, in a house or restaurant, or bar. We talked as brother and sister might, looking elsewhere, or we sat on the floor, smoking, with our backs against the same wall, and we talked incidentally while looking at the passers-by, thinking about other things. We talked a lot in the dark, differently arranged: side by side in the double bed at Ada's, top to toe once or twice at home, or perpendicular in the dive in Stoke Newington, with two beds heading into the same corner of the wall. I used to see the yellow patch around his mouth as the cigarette crackled and glowed — then the red tip flew in an arc, as if thrown away. It made me feel slightly nauseous, endlessly lurching for the catch, and staying still at the same time. I am very frightened of fire. It was the summer, and sometimes we were still talking when the sun came up — but I have no idea what these conversations were. I put a phrase into the bedroom air, like 'Joan Armatrading', and I think, *We would never talk about her.* I suppose we talked about family, though there was a privacy to these things too. What else — quantum mechanics?

We talked about anything and everything, maybe, and when I bumped my suitcase down the stairs of the dive in Stoke Newington, I knew that I would never have those conversations about *anything and everything* again.

This was my second summer in London. Liam had just missed his final exams, and I was earning money for my last year, temping in Elephant and Castle. He had found this place to stay, a three-storey over-basement, that no one really owned. There was a hot little reek in the living room, a mixture of PVC and piss and sardines; finally traced to the sockets that sparked and blew everything you plugged into them. Black flares of smoke stained the white plastic, and while you peered and sniffed at them, the carpet left wet ovals on your knees. I can not actually recall the bedding, on which, room by room, each tenant had poor man's sex, the bodies left afterwards in painterly abandon on the waves and wrinkles of the greying sheets. We were young, so I suppose it is possible that we were beautiful, though the miserable girl with her fishnet gloves just got on everyone's nerves, and the Australian guy had to just lose the tan or shut up or get out, each of them, as I picture them now, impossibly lovely, the hard little bones of her white shoulders shrugging and dipping as she pulled on her Gitanes: him, stripped to the waist in the kitchen, the central furrow on his torso pausing at his navel, before rushing, in a mess of blond hair, down his cheerful Australian shorts. These were the dilettantes of course, the tourists like myself, they did not twitch or yowl or throw punches, they did not sling their shit in packets out the windows in the middle of the night, because they forgot for a moment where they were. There was a dealer in the basement, but few enough drugs in the house itself, or maybe it was just that no one offered them to me — something about my sandy hair and narrow face, even then, that showed I was out of that particular loop. No one tried to shag me much either, though one night myself and the Australian got together, just because we could.

I think about this encounter from time to time — when, for instance, I decide I should just go out there and 'do it' — I remember it as you might remember a scene from a film, bodies moving together in the afternoon light, limbs pulled into slow angles, tongues arcing out. This despite the fact that it took place, I am sure of it, in darkness, after bad wine and candlelight in the overgrown back garden. Something about the event, even at the time, meant that it was experienced almost entirely from the outside; my young body, his young body, all the postures and motions, and, above us, my hovering gaze, perhaps even his hovering gaze, or both conjoined. So wonderfully, cleanly pornographic we were, and quite friendly, it was just like dancing, and I felt nothing more than a dancer might, except for a little fist of feeling where I held on to the Australian, anxious that we should make this scene, with all its careful variations, last a while.

We parted with a smile that was as good as a handshake, and I went back to my own bed and lay down. It stayed with me for a day, maybe two; the freedom and chaos of fucking whoever caught your eye, the clarity of it, until suddenly I was prostrate and speechless with love for the Australian, endlessly lying there and listening to the house, the footsteps going through it, the voices and whispers; sorting through their rise and fall for the dull chirrup of his voice. I realised, too, that I was not in love with him, but condemned instead to a lifetime of such false intensities, that I would have to love each man I slept with in order not to hate myself, and the squalor in the house became suddenly insupportable to me, the damp and the mould, the fights over stolen cornflakes, the slow distance between Liam and the fishnet girl, garbled anguish from the room next door, and the dealer in the basement getting blow-jobs like a one-man brothel, with another girl always trembling outside on the stair.

And still I lay there, in the funk of anybody's sheets, waiting for the Australian to knock on the door, or the weather to change; waiting for some distant gear to catch and move my life along. I believe, now, that I could have been lost, just then — not that I am, these days, in any way *found,* but I think if my life had stalled there, I would have been lost in a more disastrous way.

The room was officially Liam's, so one of the things I looked at in those two or three days when I did not eat, and could not think, and moved only in the middle of the night, was his bed, at a right angle to mine; a yellowing wool blanket with a thick pink stripe along the top. Liam was always mysteriously elsewhere: this perhaps one of the effects of our stay at Ada's, that if he made a home, it was only ever to leave it. I don't know why I didn't mind: I was jealous of his freedom, certainly, but I think I realised, even then, that the place he went to was always less interesting than the one he had left behind, or more terrible. Liam was prone to boredom and decline; he was too vague and restless to make a tragic object of himself, even then.

I want to say that I was too middle class for Stoke Newington — in the infinite gradations of these things — but that isn't quite true. No. I clicked my eyelids shut on the room and, when I opened them, I expected it to be gone, that is all: the maroon-coloured wreaths swinging across the wallpaper, the little turquoise skirting boards, the bare floor with a raw cut piece of carpet for a rug. When I opened my eyes, I wanted the room to be gone, or stripped, the house empty, the tenants dead, the beautiful and boring Australian turned to dust (or 'Greg' as he was called). I wanted Liam to rise out of his heap of blankets to say, 'Jesus, Vee, let's go and get a cup of coffee. Let's go home.'

This, though I knew that Liam would never come home now, either to this bed, or the bed in Griffith Way, or any other bed he made for himself, with the pillows plumped up, and the top sheet turned down.

He fought with people too — and here in Stoke Newington, it annoyed me for the first time. There was a problem with the rent — he put the envelope under the door he said, it was a white envelope, a long one, with the guy's name written on it in *red biro*.

When Liam got into detail, I knew he was lying, also that he was starting to convince himself; he could see the biro and remember writing with it, once he recalled that it was red. These aimless wranglings just led to more mess and whining: Liam thrown outside this or another door at four in the morning or two in the afternoon with, 'Oh for fuck's sake. Come on!'

He never fought with me. I was his sister. I was on his side.

But he would have thought the Australian a cheap enough trick, and I knew this too as I lay rigid in the room we shared, for three days that I can not remember, until I got up and packed my stuff and bumped my suitcase down the stairs.

I say that I did not leave the room for three days, but surely I had to drink sometimes, or go to the toilet. There was a problem with doors in the house: people were always putting locks on them, and the locks were always getting bust open, so the door to our room, as I see it in my mind's eye, swings a little to, and it is that gap that tormented me as I lay on the bed, the fact that when I opened my eyes, it was all still there.

I left Liam to the opening gap of the door, and to whatever was behind it. Something boring and horrible; Death, that rapist, who comes in and walks around, and will not say what it is he wants, until he takes it. And I wish I could remember what made me sit up and throw my things in the case, and leave: I fancy a piece of distant bird-song; the sense of someone calling me home, but the only person who might call was Liam and he was nowhere to be seen.

The suitcase was air-force blue; stiff, with rounded corners. It belonged to my friend Deirdre Moloney from college, the one whose mother would throw her out three months before her final exams. At this stage she still lived a twee little life, where things like suitcases and, say, walking boots, were readily to hand. So it was an air hostess's suitcase I carried down the stairs filled, just like an air hostess's, with dirty clothes and squeezed-out tubes of spermicidal jelly; in the middle of it all, the tiny, smothered sloshing of a mostly empty bottle of gin.

Bump bump bumpetty bump.

Liam was in some other house, like this one or worse, and he wasn't having a lot of sex, or drugs, or deep and spacey conversations. He was just the guy who stuck around, the one who would not go. He was the guy who could not be relied upon, the messer. 'Mick,' they called him. 'Oy, Mick!'

or the Rastas' soft, 'Hullo, Irish!'

Meanwhile, I wanted a shower. I wanted to be a girl. I wanted to have sex that meant something. I wanted a 2:1 in my arts degree. There was a path, I thought — I really thought that there must be a path — and Liam had wandered off it, and I wasn't going out there to look for him, not this time.

19

This was not the first time I left my brother, and it would not be the last. In his later, drinking years, I left him every time he arrived. But even before he hit the bottle, there were times when I just had to roll my eyes and walk away.

The problem with Liam was never something big. The problem with Liam was always a hundred small things. He had cigarettes but no matches, did I have matches? Yes, but the match breaks, the match doesn't strike, he can't light these cheap Albanian trash matches. Do I have a lighter? Fuck, he has spilt the matches. Why don't I have a lighter? He goes to find a lighter, rattling all the drawers in the kitchen. He walks out, leaving the back door open. He comes in the front door twenty minutes later with a lighter he found on the street — lying just outside the house actually — except that it is wet. He lights the oven from the pilot and lights his cigarette from the oven and burns his hand and after he has put his hand under the tap for a while he fusses in the cupboard for a baking tin and he puts the lighter — a cheap, plastic lighter — he actually puts it in the oven, and when I scream at him he shouts right back at me and there is a tussle at the oven door. After which, there is an hour of sulking because I do not trust him to dry a lighter in the oven without burning the house down. And after the sulk comes The Discussion.

Liam is clever.

No. Liam is dead.

Liam *was* clever, I should say.

Anyway. For someone who was blunderingly stupid most all of the time, my brother was very astute. And what he was astute about were other people's lives, their weaknesses and hopes, the little lies they like to tell themselves about why and whether they should ever get out of bed. This was Liam's great talent — exposing the lie.

Drink made him vicious, but even sober he could smell what was going on in a room, I swear it. After Tom's father died he did nothing but talk about rot. I saw Tom looking at him with a face that was completely blank, while Liam chuntered on about how long it took corpses to go off these days, because everyone was so full of E-numbers and preservatives. The thing is, I am not sure I even told him about my father-in-law dying, he just picked it up. Liam could be a completely shocking human being, but it was hard to say what exactly he had done to make you feel so off-key.

'What was all that about?' said Tom, when he left, pretending not to have understood a single word — because the place Liam worked best was under your skin. I don't think it was something he could control. It was like a contagion, he just had a contagious mind.

And then, he'd take a few drinks.

'Genital warts,' he said, with a sneer, into the clear air of our family sitting room, discoursing with much hilarity about how they traced a particular strain of them through a chain of infidelities in the Hampstead Royal Free. 'We called them the free warts,' he said, this followed by sluice-room japes, and shocked consultants' wives. Also patients in comas getting fucked, of course, or just waking up with sperm in their hair, and hey! Liam! you get everyone so excited, it's great to have you around.

Sober, he would miss buses and fail to

make connections and lose things or steal things. Though Liam didn't steal exactly — it was an intellectual problem for him, he just couldn't figure out why you had something and he didn't, and the only solution was to walk away with it, whatever stupid thing it was. Money sometimes, certainly from me, and probably from Kitty, though it is not something either of us would ever discuss, but also peculiar stuff. He took a phone off the wall of my kitchen in 1989, even though — or possibly because — I was renting at the time. Even though, and this is the stupidest thing, Irish phones did not plug into British Telecom. Liam, of course, would 'know someone' who could convert a phone, so the damn thing would be lying around his bedsit with the wires hanging out for God knows how long. All I know is that when I rang for the next six months, no one picked up an Irish, British, or any other phone. I also know that he took it because he sensed that he was going to disappear for a while, and he wanted to have something of mine with him, when it was time to leave. He wanted to keep the connection.

So I left him and he left me. What else are siblings supposed to do? The very first time was when we went to St Dympna's in

Broadstone. He went in one doorway, and I went in another, and though we were still sleeping in the same bed at night, during the day he was a boy and I was a girl, and he could not be seen to talk to me in the school yard. So whose fault was that?

This was 1967, the year that I grew taller than Liam, and I have remained so ever since. Other than the great bus-station adventure, nothing much happened in Broadstone. We mooched around the streets; two small raven-haired children with ice-blue eyes, and the lanky, sandy-haired one, which was me — this was the year I became dissatisfied with my hair, being stringy and underwashed. There were other intimations of adolescence. I stuck my face in the upstairs sink to see what killing yourself might be like, or I sewed the tips of my fingers together with one of Ada's needles, while Liam played with her cigarettes. Though I think all that happened later, in the surprising springtime, when we were still not gone home.

It was only supposed to be a summer holiday. One day the road was full of children and the next day they were gone, and we realised, myself and Liam and Kitty, that school had started without us. We had been left behind. We walked the streets past houses made intimate by silence. It seemed we could go anywhere. But we preferred to go back to our Gran's and sit a while.

There was sporadic talk of what to do with us. Ada would mention it to a neighbour on the doorstep — 'Do you have someone in St Dympna's?' Myself and Kitty finally trailing down behind her to the nun who would make room for us; Sister Benedict, a black-eyed, passionate woman who kissed us mightily and laid one childish cheek after another on her bosom, stroking us and talking to Ada, while we listened to the buzz of her voice and the amazing drum of her heart.

Looking down, I was fixated by her rosary beads, hanging to the floor, and by the great frankness of her toes, splayed in their monkish sandals beneath her robes.

She pushed me back, and knelt down in front of me, and held my head in her two large hands. She actually put them over my ears, so it was again in the echo of her body that I heard her say I was a beautiful girl and the school was so very, very happy to have me. I would be in her own class, she told me, I would be one of God's little soldiers — and this is how I remember my time with Benedict, as a time for marching, with all our desks in a row: Jesus in our hearts, and Mary looking over one shoulder, our Guardian Angel on the other side; God looking straight down, while the Holy Spirit dive-bombed the parting in our hair, exploding there in a harmless lick of flame. And there was no room anywhere for the Devil, who was a dark shadow over your left shoulder, just beyond the roll of your eye.

The best thing about Benedict was her name. She had chosen it, she said, after the monk who was fed by a raven in the desert, because when she was little there was grey mould and beetles in the bread. The school was named for Dympna, an ancient Irish princess who refused to marry her father. When her mother the queen died, Dympna's father looked all over the kingdom but could not find a bride. Then his eyes lit on his own daughter. Dympna escaped with her father-confessor, all the way to Belgium, where her father-the-king caught up with her and chopped her head off. What a fantastic story. St Dympna is the patron saint of the insane, Sister Benedict said, because her father was insane to want to marry her. Of course.

My own name, Veronica — an ugly enough thing I had always thought, it sounded like either the ointment or the disease — was one of her great favourites. St Veronica wiped the face of Christ on the road to Calvary and He left His face on her tea towel. Or the picture of His face. It was the first-ever photograph, she said.

I became quite fond of her; a figure leaning out of the crowd, both supplicatory and tender. I still think of her wherever wet towels are offered in Chinese restaurants and on old-fashioned airlines. We have lost the art of public tenderness, these small gestures of wiping and washing; we have forgotten how abjectly the body welcomes a formal touch. I knew my fate must be linked to Veronica's, in some way. Perhaps I would be a photographer. Perhaps there would come a moment when I would step out of the crowd, and then return — nothing more. I thought I might become a wiper of things when I grew up: blood, tears, all of that.

I confused Veronica with the bleeding woman of the gospels, the one of whom Christ said, 'Someone has touched me,' and confused her again with the woman to whom He said, *'Noli me tangere,'* which happened after the resurrection. 'Do not touch me.'

Why not?

Why should she not touch Him? Thomas touched Him, Thomas was invited to put

187

his hands inside His wounds. These things mattered to me very much, at the age of eight.

For a while, I practised with my own wounds and scabs, and was taken, each time, by the brightness of the red on the white toilet paper I used instead of Ada's tea towels. Children do not understand pain; they experiment with it, but you could almost say that they don't feel it, or do not know how to feel it, until they are grown. And even then, it seems we always feel pain for the wrong thing. Or so it has been with me.

I am not Veronica. Though I have done my fair share of *wiping,* in my day, and it is true that I am attracted to people who suffer, or men who suffer, my suffering husband, my suffering brother, the suffering figure of Mr Nugent. It is unfortunately true that happiness, in a man, does not do it, for me.

I remember a slow afternoon with Ada's sewing basket, trying acupuncture on my thigh, testing the depth of the needles as they went through fat and meat to the cartilage or the bone — maybe there was a tendon in there — I can't get interested in what goes where. I can't get interested in doctors, or bits, or gristle — give me the general anaesthetic, I say, give it to me now, *before* something goes wrong, and I also remember a night with Michael Weiss, hacking away at my inner leg, with a biro of all things, and then later, running through the ineffectual blue lines with his kitchen knife. And I remember the coolness of the cut.

And after a while.

After a while, the distant world came seeping back, beading at the edges, thick and red; rising up to join and flood the gap, then spilling slowly over the lip of flesh, with one engorged, delicious drop. The whole world came bleeding back, a world that consisted first of Michael Weiss, or at least his voice, going, *Would you just, would you please, would you ever just fucking stop!*

Such disgust. Such complete and utter disgust. *Are you pleased with yourself now?* Good, gentle, human Michael Weiss.

Oatmeal, cream, sandstone, slate.

There is no blood here. There is no blood in this house. But I am residually interested, you might say. I am residually interested, in the bleeding face of Christ, and the woman who may have existed, but who was certainly not called Veronica, who wiped the blood away and with it some of the hurt.

I don't go to Mass now, and have passed little of it on to my children, though Rebecca, at eight, is going through a pious phase, probably to thwart me. They are surprisingly tall — eight-year-olds. They are surprisingly like real people. Of course your own babies are always real to you, they are all there from the word go, but even strangers' children look like proper people by the age of eight, and, as if she has realised this, my eight-year-old has turned her new, fully human face to God.

Liam liked St Catherine of Siena, the sorelicker. He also liked three Roman saints with funny names who were turned upside down and had milk and mustard put up their noses, which killed them, apparently. It didn't seem to bother Kitty, as I recall.

20

As I write, I look out of the window and check with the corpse I have sitting in the Saab at the front gate. He is always there (it is always a he), a slumped figure in the front seat who turns out, on examination, to be the tilting headrest. But even though I know this, I am drawn to his stuffed, blank face, and wonder why he should be so patient. He lets his gaze rest endlessly on the dash, like a man who is listening to the radio and will not come into the house. A sign of the loneliness of men, and of their obduracy. He will not come into the house, my car corpse, the crash dummy in the front seat. He is waiting for the last of the football results.

I don't actually want him in the house, but that does not mean I am happy to always see him in my car, this man who talks to me, quite bluntly, of patience and ability to endure. And the possibility that people don't care about each other — or not really — that what they want most in life is *sport*.

I can stay up with him or I can go upstairs and sleep with my husband.

All night is a very long time.

I am in the horrors. It started sometime after the funeral, a week perhaps, after Tom tried to resurrect me by lying the length of my body and kissing and rubbing and all the rest. But I was over that — I had forgotten it. I was back to school runs and hoovering and ringing other-mothers for other-mother things, like play dates, and where to buy Rebecca's Irish dancing shoes. Everything was sad, but fine — good food, fresh air, a few too many glasses of wine, and off to bed. And then.

Here it comes — the four o'clock wake-up call. It creeps into me and I wake to the slow, slick, screaming heebiejeebies. What are they? *He is sleeping with someone else.* No, that isn't the four o'clock call. The four o'clock call is a much older, and more terrible, thing.

I can not feel the weight of my body on the bed. I can not feel the line of my skin along the sheet. I am swinging an inch or so off the mattress, and I do not believe in myself — in the way I breathe or turn —

and I do not believe in Tom beside me: that he is alive (sometimes I wake to find him dead, only to wake again). Or that he loves me. Or that any of our memories are mutual. So he lies there, separate, while I lose faith. He sleeps on his back. And one morning at — yes — four a.m., I wake to a livid tumescence on his prone body; a purple thing on the verge of decay. Tom is flung wide on his back, asleep like a dead saint, or a child. He is, anyway, beautifully asleep, with his palms turned skywards and loose by his sides, and a straining smile at the edge of his eyes, like what he sees in the centre of his blind forehead is so convincing, and fleeting, and lovely. I watch him for a while — so silly, such a silly idea to wake up to — but I can not check to see if it is true, the thing that I have dreamt on to the body of my sleeping husband; a cock so purple and dense it was a burden to him. He lies there, pressing his back into the mattress just to support it, this unbearable thing, that is stuck to him and moving away from him, while he sleeps on under it. Helpless. And full of pleasant thoughts.

And I turn around again and gather the covers about me, as the thing my husband is fucking in his sleep slowly recedes. A thing that might be me.

Or it might not be me. It might be Marilyn Monroe — dead or alive. It might be a slippery, plastic kind of girl, or a woman he knows from work, or it might be a child — his own daughter, why not? There are men who would do anything, asleep, and I am not sure what stops them when they wake. I do not know how they draw a line.

21

Here is another scene. It happens in Ada's house in Broadstone, much later. Years later. It is a scene where Ada wants to comfort Nugent because Nugent's life is not going well. Nugent's life is going very badly, and though nothing is said, Ada knows this because of the odour that hangs about him, and the way his shoulders stay straight while the rest of him sags down and away; she knows that growing old, with all its disappointments, does not suit Nugent.

She is not sure that it suits her either.

When she offers him tea, it is with a surprising wobble in the saucer, and he takes it quietly and sets it down. The biscuits are, in the circumstances, a little garish. With their fluffy white coconut sprinkled over pink marshmallow, the biscuits are a bit beside the point. Ada knows that he is sad, but she has yet to sympathise. Lamb Nugent has a wife, Kathleen, and four healthy children. He has no cause for complaint. What he asks is what Ada refuses most to give, he asks her to believe in his grief, the ordinary grief of a man with a wife he does not love overmuch and four children who he does not, for a moment, understand; the usual grief of men when they find that they have done nothing, and there is nothing left for them to do. He wants her to pity him his perfectly pleasant life, and the fact that it does not belong to him; the fact that he is a ghost in his own house, looking at his wife, who drives him up the wall, and his four children, who rob each breath as it comes out of his mouth. While he sits here with a woman too old to bed, the keeper of his treasures, the woman who will not love him, though she really knows she should.

And where is Charlie during all of this? He is off seeing a man about a dog.

So Ada eats the biscuits herself, one after the other, her eyes checking quickly around the room that her things are all as they should be, that the weather is improving, that the newspaper is still folded on the arm of the chair, waiting to be read. She is forty-seven, Nugent is fifty-one. They are, by the lights of the time, already very old.

Nugent sits in her front room and bleeds. There is nothing surprising about this: Ada presses the crumbs on her plate, sticking them to her forefinger before lifting them to her mouth. Why should it be worse for him than for any other man? But it is worse. He insists on it. He is tired of her now.

There is something she says that he fails to hear, or maybe he just decides not to reply. There is a lapse, at any rate, a flaw in the air between them, and Ada the housewife moves without thinking to make it right. She stands and busies herself a moment with the tray, turns again for an answer to whatever question it was: about the Spring Show, or the quality of the beach at Port Salon, and when Nugent tries to talk, but can not, she reaches out her hand and puts it on his shoulder.

That is all.

She reaches her hand to his shoulder and, in the manner of a person who knows her these many years, he looks up and lifts his hand to her hip. They stay like that for a moment, and then Ada dips to lift the tray, and turns to leave the room.

Or the tray has fallen and Ada's blouse is open under Nugent's fingers and they are half on the floor and half on the chair. What can it be like, to see her body after so many years? They are not used to nakedness; they have no selection of ordinary people's bodies in their heads, as we might garner just sitting on a summer beach. So the breast that he strains towards with his fifty-one-year-old mouth, might be beautiful or not, there is no way they have of telling, either of them: Ada's little pouch of a breast with its hard, upturned nipple, they do not, either of them, judge it for age or aesthetics, or for anything at all, the shock of it man-handled into the light enough to fill their minds as a car crash might fill yours or mine, so all that follows is slow and absolute and out of sequence, the drag of his private skin against her private skin, the butting of his penis against — is it her leg, or crotch, or belly? Has he wit enough to get her lying down? Is there a moment, as there might be these days, of decision, or request — because this is what the technicalities demand — or does it just happen? She is simply prone, neither pushed, nor helped, nor asked, and the thing already done, with Lamb Nugent spilled somewhere, outside or inside of Ada Merriman. They fix their clothing and nothing is said — is this possible? — that they have difficulty even remembering what has just happened between them, will always be hard put to say who wanted what or moved when, except for, now and again, a flash as they look one or other way to cross the street, or pause as the key goes in the door; a distant convulsion of hand and breast, the inside feel of mouth against mouth, and eyes that refuse to open in case daylight cry halt to what is happening again, briefly, as they step over the threshold or off the kerb?

It must have been bliss to lurch around like this, Nugent pulling her girdle up before coming in the silken hollow at the top of a leg that is, by the standards of the time, really very old. Still, I would like to allow them more. Ada has three children, Nugent four, and though it is possible to endure these bodily events as though they were happening to someone else (as my own mother might have done) I don't think it was in Ada's character, or in his, to be so innocent.

So. There is a turn in the conversation. Nugent stalls. Ada rises to fuss around the tray. She puts her hand out to console him, he lifts his hand to her hip, and their lives fork in front of them. They can let their hands stay, or they can let them drop. They are young again; back at that moment in life when someone else's body is a path that might be taken, with no chance of return.

They know too, that this moment is long past — they are not young, and there is nothing fateful about a coupling, when it is too late. What lies ahead is not so much a fork in the road as a small lay-by. They might do this, and it would not matter. Nothing would be changed by it; neither the future nor the past. Nugent would still have loved Ada, or wanted her, and Ada would still want Charlie, whether she loved him or not — whether, indeed, she ever loved anybody, or not. This is a difficult question for her to answer at forty-seven, and it is the one that is raised by Nugent's hand to her hip: the question of whether she ever loved anybody, her vagrant husband, or her children, or herself, or the parents she never had.

What of it? Ada does not love people so much as feed them and keep them clean, and this is a form of loving too, but he has sucked it out of her, this man with his four healthy children and his perfectly nice wife, he has taken her domestic love and found it wanting, and for a moment Ada does not recognise the lie — that all women are heartless because they are desired. For a moment, Ada stands there and thinks that it is true (and perhaps it is true), she has never loved a single soul. She is alone. There is nothing left for her to do.

By the time they move, it is all over. Ada's

love has been tried and found wanting, also Nugent's, also love in general — they are in agreement about this. So there is nothing consoling about the slide of her hand to the back of Nugent's melancholy head, or in the pull of his hand that brings her to her knees, as he shifts down from the low chair to join her on the floor, and there is something martyred in the lift of Ada's chin as she clears a place for his head on her shoulder and his face against her neck. And they move in this way, by shivering pauses and deliberate starts, through the body's chess until she is fully prepared, and on her own living-room floor, waiting.

I would like to think something else happened, when he entered her. But I do not know what. They were in love, suddenly. Or they were in pain. Or what?

They had a nice time.

They pulled the house down around their ears: God smashed in the grate, History, in tatters, festooned like Ada's tights on the fire-irons.

The bookie fucks the whore (I had forgotten she was a whore), and we are near to the truth of it here, we are getting to the *truth* of it — of man's essential bookieness and woman's essential whoreishness — we are pushing for it now as Nugent pushes into Ada, the fact of her baseness, the fact that *she wants it too.* Or is this enough? Would he not, to prove his point, need to do more?

I can twist them as far as you like, here on the page; make them endure all kinds of protraction, bliss, mindlessness, abjection, release. I can bend and reconfigure them in the rudest possible ways, but my heart fails me, there is something so banal about things that happen *behind closed doors,* these terrible transgressions that are just sex after all.

Just sex.

I would love to leave my body. Maybe this is what they are about, these questions of which or whose hole, the right fluids in the wrong places, these infantile confusions and small sadisms: they are a way of fighting our way out of all this meat (I would like to just swim out, you know? — shoot like a word out of my own mouth and disappear with a flick of my tail) because there is a limit to what you can fuck and with what, Nugent opening Ada's belly with his wicked, square fingers, delving into her cavities, taking with careful desire the beautiful lobes of her lungs and caressing — 'Oh,' gasps Ada, as the air rushes out of her — squeezing her pink lungs tight.

'Oh.'

I reach the end of what they might do, what they might have done, and it all shrivels back to this:

Ada reaches her hand to Nugent's shoulder and he, in the manner of a person who knows her these many years, looks up and lifts his hand to her hip. They stay like that for a moment, and then Ada dips to lift the tray, and turns to leave the room.

22

There are facts about the way that Liam died, that I wish I did not know. All the things I have forgotten in my life, and I can not forget these small details. I have forgotten my twenty-first birthday, also my eighteenth birthday, I have forgotten every New Year's Eve but two, I have forgotten what my dead brother looked like at the age of nine or ten or twelve, but I will never forget the three little facts the nice people in Brighton told me about the body that they pulled from the sea.

The first is that Liam was wearing a short fluorescent yellow jacket when he died, like the ones railway workers and cyclists wear.

The second is that he had stones in his pockets.

The third is that he had no underpants on under his jeans, and no socks in his leather shoes.

The tides in Brighton are fast and they

range far. He wore the jacket so he would be seen going into the water, and his body would be easily found. Liam, who could not organise a box of matches, was, on this occasion, fully organised.

The stones explain themselves.

It is the lack of underpants that makes me cry. Liam was never together, but he was always clean, and though he lived in various pits, they always had running water, he always knew where the nearest launderette might be found. He used an old-fashioned pink soap, with an industrial smell — I have no idea what it was called. I remember standing in the supermarket sniffing all the bars through the paper, ending up with some odourless stuff which he would not use. He put Coal Tar shampoo on his hair, and Listerine on his gums. He sprinkled anti-fungal powder everywhere and made demands for wet wipes beside the toilet. He flossed. His anti-perspirant would strip paint.

Liam took his underpants off because they were not clean. He took his socks off because they were not clean. He probably thought, as the cold water flooded his shoes, cleansing thoughts.

I know, as I write about these three things: the jacket, the stones, and my brother's nakedness underneath his clothes, that they require me to deal in facts. It is time to put an end to the shifting stories and the waking dreams. It is time to call an end to romance and just say what happened in Ada's house, the year that I was eight and Liam was barely nine.

Here is Ada's good front room in Broadstone. The door is painted a white gloss, going yellow. Inside, the room is papered a dusty pink. There is a clapped-out sofa and the two stiff wing-chairs, but Ada has put a fantastic array of cushions on the dark slip-covers, and instead of pictures on the walls she has signed theatre photographs in their frames. The room is slap up against this street, so there is a beige roller blind as well as lace curtains, and from ceiling to floor, there are drapes of theatrical red. The window is the first thing you see as you walk in, it makes everything else seem dim, except for the mirror over the mantelpiece which reflects a bright slice of room. The door opens inwards and is near the hall door, so you have to walk right in to see who is there: Charlie asleep on the sofa — sometimes in his pyjamas — or Ada reading in the wing-chair that is set against the window for good light, or Mr Nugent sitting in the other wing-chair, on a Friday, while Ada avoids him in the kitchen, putting biscuits on a plate.

Some weeks she was not there for him at all. You never really knew where she was. We didn't hang around Ada, who had a sharp enough way about her, and always had something to do. Ada liked her cup of tea, and when she sat for her cup of tea you could talk to her as much as you liked. The rest of the time we were, as all children were in those days, 'in the way'.

So I spent much of my time moving from room to room, looking for something or avoiding something, it was hard to say what.

'What are you doing there?' Ada would say. 'What are you doing *there?*'

There was a terrible boredom about the house, and I could never rid myself of it. Boredom lurked in the corners, and in the path to the garage, and in the little back yard. On this particular day I was variously bored on the stairs, or at the dining-room table, or in the hall, before I got bored again and decided to go into the good room.

What struck me was the strangeness of what I saw, when I opened the door. It was as if Mr Nugent's penis, which was sticking straight out of his flies, had grown strangely, and flowered at the tip to produce the large and unwieldy shape of a boy, that boy being my brother Liam, who, I finally saw, was not an extension of the man's member, set down mysteriously on the ground in front of him, but a shocked (of course he was shocked, I had opened the door) boy of nine, and the member not even that, but the boy's bare forearm, that made a bridge of flesh between himself and Mr Nugent. His hand was buried in the cloth, his fist clutched around something hidden there. They were not one thing, joined from open groin to shoulder, they were two people that I knew, Mr Nugent and Liam.

I am trying to remember what he looked like, but it is hard to recall the face of your brother as a child. And even though I know it is *true* that this happened, I do not know if I have the true picture in my mind's eye — the peculiar growth at the end of Mr Nugent's penis, the bridge of flesh between the man and boy. The image has too much yellow light in it, there are too many long shadows thrown. Mr Nugent is leaning back slightly, his hands are set square on either knee. I think it may be a false memory, because there is a terrible tangle of things that I have to fight through to get to it, in my head. And also because it is unbearable. Mr Nugent is leaning back in the chair, his chin is tucked in to his neck, his face pulled hard back with satisfaction, or pain. He looks like an old farmer getting his feet rubbed.

I don't know why his pleasure should be the most terrible thing in the room for me. The inwardness of it. The grimace it provokes like a man with a bad fart making its way through his guts, or a man who hears terrible news that is nonetheless funny. It is the struggle on Lamb Nugent's face that is unbearable, between the man who does not approve of this pleasure, and the one who is weak to it.

I have slept since with men who are like this — they give nothing away until the last, and then they whimper, as though something terrible had happened. The pleasure that overtakes them is like some kind of ambush. And you feel to blame, of course. You feel it is all your fault.

I say I have slept with 'men' but you know that is a sort of affectation, because what I mean is that when I sleep with Tom, that this is sometimes what he is like, yearning on the pull-back and hatred in the forward slam, and, 'What are you looking at?' he says, or a weird sarcasm at dinner with friends about coming, or me not coming, though you know I do come — at least I think I do — realising then, later, that what he wants, what my husband has always wanted, and the thing I will not give him, is my annihilation. This is the way his desire runs. It runs close to hatred. It is sometimes the same thing.

'What did I ever do to you?' I shout. 'Except love you? What did I ever do to you?' which question he finds too stupid for words.

I know all men aren't like this. Somewhere out there a hundred thousand Michael Weisses are walking their sons and daughters to saxophone lessons or piano lessons, living in some mellow American movie, where men are men and their hearts are easy. I know that these men exist, I have even met them, it is just that I could never love one, even if I tried. I love the ones who suffer, and they love me. They love to see me sitting on their nice Italian furniture, and they love to see me cry.

And I know how silly it is. You don't kill someone by having sex with them. You kill them with a knife, or a rope, or a hammer, or a gun. You strangle them with their tights. You do not kill them with a penis. So it is all — the I hate you, I love you, I hate — a dream of killing and dying, I understand that much; that when you roll away from each other to go to sleep, then the dream is over for another day.

There is also the pleasure of the boy to consider. There is also the question of who he hated, or who he loved. Though Liam, in this memory or image, had his habitual face on, which was an open face of plain white, with two looping black eyelashes over eyes so dilated that they looked navy blue.

He was terrified.

And before the scene became clear to me, I remember thinking, *So that's what the secret is.* The thing in a man's trousers — this is what it does when he is angry; it grows into the shape of a miserable child.

I remember it as being very cold. You remember the cold on some imaginary skin that does not quite coincide with your own and this is where I shiver, as I remember the dankness of the air that day in Ada's front room.

There is also a smell of Germolene, which will remain for me, for evermore, the smell of things going wrong.

I think, often, of Nugent looking at me when he realises that I am at the door. The boy's hand (surely it was moving) has stopped, and Nugent, leaning back from his difficult pleasure, takes a moment to notice this. For a moment, he wills the boy's hand on, imagines it moving, once, twice, until his mind trips over its obstinate stillness and he opens his eyes to see me standing there.

'Would you ever get out of that,' he says, and when Liam takes his poor hand out of the man's flies I feel that I have spoiled it for all concerned.

I pause as I write this, and place my own hand over my face, and lick the thick skin of my palm with a girl's tongue. I inhale. The odd comforts of the flesh. Of being me.

I have seen great bleakness in Liam's eyes, on that day and on many days since — but when Nugent saw me, a small girl in a school uniform holding the knob of the door, the look in his eye was one of very ordinary irritation.

'Would you ever get out of that.'

And I did. I closed the door and ran to the toilet upstairs, with an urge to pee and look at the pee coming out; to poke or scratch or rub when I was finished, and smell my fingers afterwards. At least, I assume that this is what I did if I was eight years old, but perhaps I just ran the taps and looked at the water, or trailed my fingertips over the bubbles of the bathroom glass, or walked the space in an absent-minded way, pulling back from the vertigo of the toilet bowl, and the white bath, so mysteriously full of air.

I look at my own children and I think you know everything at eight. But maybe I am wrong. You know everything at eight, but it is hidden from you, sealed up, in a way you have to cut yourself open to find.

23

I have taken to driving at night. It was my headrest ghost who first called me out of the house — I caught him in the corner of my eye and thought, for a moment, that he was gone. Then I saw that he was slumped forward against the dash, patient as a stricken pensioner, trying not to pee. I had folded the seat forward to get Emily's bicycle into the back, and did not set it straight when we came home. Now the seat had suffered a small but dreadful emergency out on the public roadway. I check the time: it is 3.30 a.m. At 3.45 the seat is still stuck. By 4.00 a.m. it has given up all pretence of a struggle, and is helplessly face down. I take my bottle of white out of the fridge a good half-hour before dawn and, on an impulse, pick up the car keys. Then, with glass, bottle and corkscrew I go out to my headrest ghost, in the rain.

When I open the passenger door and pull

the lever, the seat springs back, shocked and relieved. It stares for a moment, straight ahead. It is still game, my headrest ghost, like a thousand mechanical friends in a thousand cartoons. I sit in. The upholstery is cold. I pull the cork and pour myself a glass of wine, then I leave the bottle out on the tarmac and close the door. I relax into the seat and drink in its chilly embrace, quite happy; the whole encounter made private by the rain.

I do this a few times in the next week or so. I go out and drink in the car. Sometimes, it is not raining and it makes me feel quite breathless to walk out into the dark alone, there is something so bare about our little estate at night; the neighbours, each in their madness, asleep in a row. Nothing matters. The wheelchair child in number seven, and 'You Can't Park Here' in number ten, and my high-maintenance husband in number four, each dreaming their ordinary dreams.

I put the key in the ignition, just for the company of the air-conditioning, and I turn the radio on low. The urge to drive is very strong, but the wineglass, when I try it, will not balance in the cup holder. Still — and I am officially mad now, I am a mad house-wife — I ease the car away from the kerb and, drinking all the while, move around the estate in first gear. I want to fling the empty glass into somebody's front garden, but of course I do not do this. I pull over and set it down on the road, opposite the bottle, and through this little glass gateway I drive — past the carved granite boulder at the mouth of our enclave, and into the city beyond.

I am in a state of almost perfect fear as I work towards the centre of town; looking over my shoulder to check the emptiness in the car behind me, entering streets I have never entered before, always tending towards the sea. I hang on to the steering wheel, and brake too hard for the lights. I clip the kerb of a central island, and when the jolt clears my head I find that we are already, the car and me, on our way north, along the curve of Dublin Bay. I take satisfaction from the Hill of Howth, feeling, as I run the flat road along to it, that I am travelling over sand, that the tide still wants the ground under my wheels. In a car park at the top of the hill, I stop, and sit, and wait to be killed.

It is all getting a bit hectic now. I don't allow myself to leave the house for nights at a time, or I grab my stuff as soon as everything is still and I go. I do this maybe three or five times and wake out of a blank on the road behind the Sugarloaf, or running by a stud wall in Kildare. There is nothing illegal about driving, but it all feels forbidden to me, the housewife in her Saab, abandoning her children while they sleep, leaving them unprotected from their dreams.

Then, one night, I know the place I am avoiding and, with great and deliberate movements of the wheel, I overcome the car's natural reluctance and drive it all the way to Broadstone.

The streets are tiny. These are toy houses, children's houses. We could not have lived here. Where did we fit? Before I know it I am out on Constitution Hill facing a low wall with a grey Virgin Mary standing on the grey, round world, but it is not the fortress I remember, with the buses in rows at the top. The bus station is further down the hill, though it is on a height, and as I sink towards the river I see, on my left, the church where we were caught robbing candles. It is a Capuchin Friary, says the board outside, and I feel that the horrible priest could not have come from there, because these are friars, lovely people with bare feet in sandals in the middle of winter. But then, why not? It might have happened in a friary all the same.

I drive back up to Broadstone and find

myself, too quickly, at the small gate into the Basin where I park and get out of the car. There it is! This is the place where Liam peed — not, as I see now, through wire mesh, but through old-fashioned railings, though the rest of it is the same. It is all the same. The water is the same. And the path. This is where it happened.

I get back in the car and drive with no lights straight to Ada's house. I park in the first vacant spot, and I sit there for fifteen, twenty minutes, doing lots of urgent, awful remembering, before I realise that I am on the wrong street, though the number on the door is the same.

Tom meets me at the door. His nose flares at the fresh air on my coat and then he turns away.

I say, 'Where are the girls?'

He says, 'Where were you?'

I start to laugh. 'Ha ha,' I chuckle as I put my bag down on the counter, as I take off my coat, as I hang my coat under the stairs. He has dropped the girls to school and doubled back to confront me. From the bunched-up look of him I think he might give me a thump.

'Are you missing work, for this?' I say.

'Where were you?' he says, and I'd love to

say I was out, like he is out all the time. Doing, making, being — or even shagging. I'd love to say, 'I was just out shagging,' in a debonair sort of voice, but I don't want to think about how wan my body has become since I have taken to the darkness. I put my hand gently against his shirt front and the gesture is so graceful, even as I watch it, that it leads me, quite easily, to the buckle of the belt, which I tug with my other hand, and so, by softly pushing him away while pulling him forward, I contrive to blow my husband, in our own kitchen. On a school day.

This is real, I think. *This is real.*

Though I am not sure that it is, actually. When we are done, Tom plants a dry, thoughtful kiss in the middle of my forehead. He can not claim that he has been fobbed off — not after his official, all-time favourite thing — but he knows that he has been fobbed off, all the same. And it makes him angry.

'I just don't know where you're coming from,' he says. A corporate phrase from my corporate boy.

When he is gone, I go upstairs and lie down on Emily's bed. Then I get up and pull the duvet back and lie down again. I do not know what she smells like, she is like a perfume you have been wearing too long, she is still too close to the inside of me. So I can not smell her, quite, but I know that her smell is there as I lie down with the thought of her beside me. I want to run my hand down her exquisite back, and over her lovely little bum. I want to check that it is all still there, and nicely packed, and happy, that my daughter's muscles agree with her bones. I want to find the person that I built from my body's own stuff, and grew on ten thousand plates of organic sausages and sugar-free beans, and I want to squeeze every part of her tight, until she is moulded and compact. I want to finish the job of making her, because when she is fully made she will be strong.

24

I take the train back from Brighton, and I meet Kitty in a pub in the 'Gatwick Village', for the flight home. The place is unnerving, all the usual slop of pint glasses and ashtrays, but on miniature tables to allow room for the trolleys and backpacks and bags; men falling asleep over their beers, unshaven and sad. The pub itself just a pretence of a pub, a painted corner of the concourse, a differently coloured floor. There are no doors. I pick my way through the filth of baggage and delayed lives to find Kitty — a woman weirdly like my little sister, though much too old.

When I reach the table, I look down at the empty glasses in front of her and I ask, 'Are they all yours?'

'Oh for fuck's sake,' she says.

'Just asking.'

'Two of them are mine, the rest aren't mine. OK?'

'Do you want another one?'

'Yes thank you, I would love another one.'

I turn to wade back towards the bar, and hear her say, 'Bunny,' which is the name she had for me when she was a child. I turn back to embrace her, my back twisted, my torso held away, as she half-rises to receive the hug, her thighs trapped under the little table of wood. Her hair feels fake, like a wig, but I think it is just crisping up under the dye and Frizz-Ease. From a distance, it was just as curly and beautiful and black as it ever was, though when I check her face I see that it has collapsed, quite fundamentally, and all the distraction of blue eyes, and mischievous cheeks, and winning smile — the whole Celtic chipmunk — has melted as easy as wax, leaving the flesh hanging on to bones, bones, bones.

'How are you?' I say.

'*How* am I?'

'Yes. How are you?'

'Fine. I'm fine.'

'What is it, anyway?' I say.

'It's a G and T, thanks.'

'Yes, I thought it was.'

'Yes.'

It is many years, I think, since I have ordered a drink at a bar. The barman ignores me for the longest time. I feel like shouting at him that I am quite grown up and want to give him some money now. I want to say, 'My brother is dead! Serve me immediately!' but then, so what? Some people haven't seen their brothers in twenty years.

I get Kitty's gin and one for myself.

'English measures,' she says, holding the glass up and waggling it, like I am such a fool.

Kitty always goes on about being hit as a child, though the fact is that she was a complete brat: she always came back for more, and she often got it; not just from me and Liam, who actually liked her, but also from Mossie-the-psychotic, who taunted and enraged her into a total Shirley Temple. There was something transcendental about her rage at six or seven, her body rigid and her temper whizzing around the room, until she caught it, somehow, and stuffed it back into herself. After which, she exploded into a fire-breathing fluff-pot, a cartoon little sister; fists yammering against Mossie's chest. Which was just asking for trouble, because you shouldn't take things too far with Mossie. At least with myself and Liam, we only did it to tease.

And of course I feel guilty, when I think of it now, and I don't believe in hitting anybody, at all, ever, but I still find a twitch of something more than amusement when she is being a prissy little bitch like this. The toss of the head, some small superiority, it makes me wish she was six all over again.

I lift my glass to her, ever so slightly, and say, 'Cheers.'

She starts to cry as soon as we are on the plane; she weeps the whole way home. Pints of it. She moves from quiet leakage to sighs, heaves and judders, and then back again. It sounds to me like she is practising crying as much as actually doing it. I look out the window, while the air hostess kindly offers a brandy in her coffee and then charges five pounds sterling for it.

'Are you all right? Are you sure now?'

The man on the other side of her knows that someone has died. He wonders am I a social worker, or perhaps even a prison officer, and why am I not holding her hand. And I too wonder why I am not holding her hand, as I look down on the distant skin of the Irish sea. 'We slept in the same room for twenty years,' I want to tell him. 'Isn't that enough for you, isn't it already *above and beyond?*'

Liam, meanwhile, is sitting one row up

across the aisle. There is a slumbrous menace about his ghost that makes me realise how indifferent he was when he finally walked away from us all into the sea. I can feel his gaze on the skin of my cheek as he turns to look at me, uncanny and dead. I know what it is saying.

The truth. The dead want nothing else. It is the only thing that they require.

I look up too quickly, and he is gone.

There is a big white house on Lambay Island — Georgian, at a guess, and worth gazillions. I saw it first, it must have been, from the beach, the day we went with Ada to visit our mad Uncle Brendan. And it suddenly kicks into me, this fact of Ada's son lost to Largactyl and squalor. How many years of it? He probably died wondering who he actually was.

I search up the coastline for a beach, a bridge, an estuary, back again to a headland — and there it is: a pencil of a round tower, a fat vase of a water tower and, beside that again, a group of buildings surrounded by trees. I have just caught sight of it when I have lost it again, the plane banks and grabs a view of sky.

'What happened to Uncle Brendan?' I shout at Kitty, over the noise.

'What happened to Uncle Brendan?'

'Yes, Uncle Brendan.'

'What do you want to know about Uncle Brendan for?'

The plane opens its underbelly and we wait for the wheels to lock. Getting its little leggies straight, digging down its heels.

'He died,' says Kitty, relenting.

'Did he?'

'I quite liked him.'

'Did you?'

I was sure I had never met him, though now here he is, suddenly at the Christmas table in Griffith Way, a face made fantastic by falling jowls, his nostrils rimmed red and his eyes — his eyes when I think of them were tired and unpleasant, as though madness was a tedious business; nearly as tedious as Christmas. My memory puts him in an orange paper hat, with a glass of brandy in his shaking hand, but there was no alcohol in our house until Liam started smuggling it in, and there were no paper hats either.

Brendan is where we got our eyes from: Spillane eyes that met my father's Atlantic blue to give us our undiluted, alcoholic's eyes, of straight-no-chaser blue; beautiful and pathological and somehow absent, or absent-minded, until we 'turn them on', which is to say we notice someone and decide to give them the full blue.

(My own eyes are like Ada's, a sort of nothing grey they call *'liath'* in Irish when they write about stone walls or the sea. Alice got these rainy eyes too, as did Ivor and Midge. We were not true, electric Hegartys, but a sort of subspecies; the Firbolg of Griffith Way.)

Uncle Brendan is also where we got our mathematical streak — this, in fact, a fairly prosaic facility to do with remembering phone numbers and reprimanding girls at supermarket tills for overcharging on the mixed leaves. None of us have what Uncle Brendan had — this much we knew — because Uncle Brendan had Maths. We were always given to understand that our mother's brother was too good for this world.

And though Ernest reads up his String Theory by candlelight in the mountains of Peru, most of the clever Hegartys are just that — *clever,* which is to say unredeemed; earning more or less money than the next person and liable to smart remarks. I realise, as we land, that life in St Ita's was not a romantic one, but more likely a long, dirty business of watching the piss gather in your lap, and nearly knowing what you were thinking, from time to time.

'I know what I'm thinking!' says the mad man in my mind, banging the wooden arm of his armchair. 'I know what I'm thinking!' and the passing nurse says, 'Good for you!'

The airport terminal starts to slide past the window and it looks so much like a picture of a building, the whole ritual of landing feels so cinematic and fake, that I don't believe any of it for a while. Uncle Brendan is not dead now, or not properly dead, and there is something so skittish about the moving walkway, the escalators and the baggage carousels, something that will not adhere yet to Irish soil, that when I finally get the Saab out of the car park and hit the roundabout I turn north instead of south on the airport road.

It is only a few miles away, this place. The little bridge is still there, and the railway line, slicing north. After which, there is a sudden slack in my mental map and the road unravels in front of me. I am just beginning to lose hope when it snaps back into the road that I remember — just the same, long and straight. There is a concrete path along the left-hand side, a line of disastrous trees along the right, beyond them a ditch that gives way to a low-lying field, where a vivid, wet green inclines, here

228

and there, into a pool of water over grass.

Beyond the trees is the raw white light of the sky over water.

This is it. There is no shift between my mind's eye and my real eye. I try to slow down to the pace of my memory, but it is slipping by me too fast.

'Do you remember this road?' I say to Kitty.

'What road?'

'This road.'

'What about it?'

Already she has eaten up half the past. Half my life is gone before she decides to understand.

'Do I remember it?' says Kitty.

'Jesus,' I say.

'What?'

By now we are past the bungalow in its field of corn, though it is trimmed to stubble in the low autumn sun.

'The man with two sticks?'

And here, where she might well bring things to a pitch, Kitty just says, 'Oh.'

'Walking along here?'

'Here?' says Kitty. 'No, not here.'

At which moment I come to a halt, and make a right turn into the hospital drive.

It is as though we are driving through a sudden brief mist, on the other side of which is the past. I push along in second gear, leaning over the steering wheel as we pass a terrace of warden's cottages, the master's house perhaps, and then the hospital itself, which is built in Victorian red brick, and the size of a small town.

'Handicap Services,' says the sign and I think, with relief, that the lunatics have gone now. The lunatics have turned, quite naturally, to dust. People are not mad, any more. The lunatics are just a residue of skin in these rooms; scratched off, or hacked off, or maybe just shed: a million flakes of skin, a softness under the floorboards, a quality of light.

We pass a courtyard with a high chimney and a low boiler house, all in extravagant, industrial red brick. There are curious round windows on the boiler house, with the Star of David dividing the panes.

'Jesus,' says Kitty, thinking, as I am thinking for a second, that they are burning mental patients in there, just to keep the hospital radiators hot.

I pause at the handball alley, engine idling, and look at the round tower and the water tower beyond. But it is not possible to pull up the handbrake and get out into the naked air of the asylum, with the casement windows still watching in their rows. I inch towards a bungalow down by the sea, my fat tyres creeping over the gravel, then I do a three-point turn, and leave.

Once we are back out the gate, I scoot the few hundred yards to the sea itself, the public sea, the swimming sea. Salt water always makes me feel so sane; the height of the waves, and the flick of fish, and the huge press of it on the ocean floor all notwithstanding. There is a little housing estate coming down to the shore, a child on a bicycle, blank with curiosity, and, after I turn at the road's end, a grey wall enclosing a small field. And in that field — it is quite small — is a Celtic cross that says:

I get out of the car to look at it.

1922–1989
IN YOUR CHARITY,
PLEASE PRAY
FOR THE RESIDENTS OF
ST ITA'S HOSPITAL
BURIED IN THIS CEMETERY
MAY THEY REST IN PEACE

Just one cross — quite new — at the end of a little central path. A double row of saplings promise rowan trees to come. There are no markers, no separate graves. I wonder how many people were slung into the dirt of this field and realise, too late, that the place is boiling with corpses, the ground is knit out of their tangled bones.

I look back, helpless, at Kitty in the front seat of the car.

They have me by the thighs. I am gripped at the thighs by whatever feeling this is. A vague wind. It clutches at me, skitters between my clothes and my skin. It lifts every hair. It grazes my lip. And is gone.

25

I saw a man with tertiary syphilis at Mass, once. He was sitting in the seat in front of us, minding his own business until Mossie pointed him out, because Mossie was the kind of guy who knew about such things. The flaps of the man's ears had been eaten away; they had shrivelled back, like melted plastic. When he turned half-profile, you saw that the bridge of his nose had collapsed flat into his face, leaving a nub of flesh, low down where his nostrils were. His breathing was fussy and loud, but he did not look mad — Mossie said later they always went mad in the end. Still, there was no doubting the signs, on his face, of his history.

Kitty said it in the car on the way home from Mass. She must have been about eleven. She said, 'The man in front of us had tertiary syphilis.'

My father's head settled down into his neck as he drove, the whole back of him looked thicker. After a moment, my mother said, 'Oh.'

History is only biological — that's what I think. We pick and choose the facts about ourselves — where we came from and what it means. I sit and clean the skin from under my nails and think of the last manicure given to Liam by that gentle English undertaker boy, the black rubbings from off a bar; polish and sweat, spilt beer and other people's skin. What is written for the future is written in the body, the rest is only spoor.

I don't know when Liam's fate was written in his bones. And although Nugent was the first man to put his name there, for some reason, I don't think he was the last. Not because I saw anything else going on, but because this is the way these things work. Of course, no one knew how these things *worked* at the time. We looked at the likes of Liam and had a whole other story for it, a different set of words.

Pup, gurrier, monkey, thug, hopeless, useless, mad, messer.

Now he is dead, I have to say that Liam had his glamour days too.

My brother was unexpectedly beautiful at the age of fifteen — this, when I was still in the full grease and growth of adolescence.

'Where d'you get those rat's tails?' Ita would say about my hair, or, 'Why are your eyelids so red, do you think you've got *an infection?*'

Ita was going to be 'beautiful', she was going to 'get a man', so there was something indestructible about her looks from an early age. Meanwhile, my own face became less readable to me, from week to week. 'Where did you get that conk?' she said. Which was a good question, Ita, which was a very good question, thanks.

Liam had a funny hair thing going for a while and his lips flowered bizarrely and permanently one day when he was fourteen. But because he was small and, I suppose, 'pretty', his adolescence lasted about a week. At sixteen he was beautiful and bad, and the blue of his eyes was a dizzy thing. And though his restlessness made him finally unfit for the adult world, in his last years at school Liam was a princeling, a heartbreaker; he was beyond the rules.

As soon as Mossie left home Liam moved to the garden passage, where the walls were whitewashed, and there was rough-cut lino on the floor. This space had the advantage of an outside door, so you never knew if he was in there or not. He had a little cohort that hopped over the back wall and looked in the kitchen window from time to time;

boys mostly, and after a while, a few girls. He had a best friend, Willow, for hanging out and experiments — most of which seemed to involve stuffing things down their trousers pockets and looking idiotic any time I opened the door.

I didn't care. I was too old for them by then. I was busy doodling love-lorn fragments about Willow's older brother Tanner on the covers of my school folders. I wrote them in French, so no one would understand — except Mrs Gogarty, of course, who was the French teacher. *Mon amour est un petit oiseau brun/ Blessé par toi,/ Tanner.* She read it all upside down and looked at me fondly, and smiled. I hated her for this. I hated her finding me out and loving me a little (which she seemed to do). The thing is, there was great privacy in a big family. No one got into your stuff except to steal it or slag you off. No one ever pitied you, or *loved you a little,* except maybe Ernest whose pity was, even then, too deliberate to matter. And we thought this was an honourable way to live. I still do, in a way.

Meanwhile, I had two friends dropping in on the way home from school, of a sudden, and we had a fantastic good time — until Liam walked into the kitchen, when the good time got even better: Fidelma, who I didn't mind one way or the other and my best friend Jackie, who I did mind, actually. Apart from anything else, I thought, he was too short for her. We drank together outside midnight Mass one Easter, sitting in the field where they would build a school; passing a naggin of vodka, which we mixed in our mouths with a slug of fizzy orange. It was with some reluctance that I let it all happen — though it did have to happen, I knew that. Or not reluctance — what was the feeling? Loneliness. The sight of Liam turning into the quietness of my friend Jackie's face, in the dark. Meanwhile, Willow and I sat apart and swallowed loudly. Inside the church they passed the paschal flame from candle to candle until it looked like the whole place was on fire: then they switched on the fluorescent lights.

I haven't had vodka in years; even now there is something sweet and crotch-like about the smell of it, a big waft of earth and adolescence coming out of the glass and hitting you in the face. Jackie crying down the phone to me, and then Fidelma in her turn, until I shouted at Liam to leave my fucking friends alone. After which, he headed out for his Saturday-night solo and I hitched up with Joe Ninety — so-called because he was thirty years old — a man who, I now realise, wanted to break into me so badly he had to turn away from the kiss to push his forehead into the wall. I loved all that. Joe Ninety liked me to dress up and he got me into pubs, while Liam slid backwards from me, into his misspent youth.

One night Bea picked up the phone in the hall.

'Yes. Yes, it is,' she said and the whole house paused to listen. She got Daddy.

'Yes, it is,' he said. 'Right. Right. Right so.' Then he trudged upstairs and found his jacket and tie and went out into the autumn darkness, shutting the front door behind him.

He never went out at night.

An hour later, he walked back in the door as he had walked out of it, expressionless and sad. Behind him, Liam shrugged his shoulders and lifted his hands, to say there was no need for the welcoming committee. Later, he told us he had been bailed out of the local copshop, or prised out more like, by Daddy, and it was nothing — they just gave him a slap and sent him home.

We never found out why. Daddy wouldn't speak of it — not then or ever — and he treated Liam with a new, and complete, contempt. It was over for them: no more shouting, no more *leaning in* from Daddy, who used to stick out his forefinger and poke the boys in the hollow of the shoulder.

'What. Am I. After. *Saying* to you?'

Poke. Poke. *Poke.*

Sometimes I wonder why there wasn't murder in that kitchen.

'You're pushing it, Da. Don't push me now.'

But Daddy didn't even bother pushing Liam any more. The Gardai had rung the house and the shame of it was so total, there was nothing left to be said.

When I think of it now — such carry-on. Liam, in the kitchen, lifting his hair to show the dried patch of blood, and a streak of red from cheek to neck, where he had caught his face on the handle of the cell door. I remember it in vivid technicolour: his hair very black, and the streak very red, and eyes an undiluted blue. They just 'knocked him round a bit', he said, gave him 'a bit of a thump'.

And I said, 'Don't be so stupid.'

He looked at me.

I think, now, that what I meant was that if they hit him then it must have been his fault. I also meant that, if pushed, I would disbelieve him even though what he said was, strictly speaking, true.

If I am looking for the point when I

betrayed my brother, then it must be here, too. I looked at the raised flesh on his cheek and I decided not to believe him, if there was any 'believing' to be done. That was all.

I decided that he did not deserve to be believed.

'Don't be so stupid,' I said.

What else?

We used to laugh about things: foothering priests, and little boys' bollocks, and 'Come here and sit on my knee, little man,' and English choirboys and gay men's backsides, and anything really to do with innocence and bums, though nobody mentioned — now that I pause to list all this — nobody mentioned your *langer,* or your *wire,* or *getting your mickey licked.* Now why is that? Why did we think it was all hilarious, but only in certain, almost ritual, ways?

These conversations happened for a month or two one summer, and then they were gone. I liked them. I liked the silence after the laughter stopped. Liam's silence was like he had just peed himself but no one had noticed, so it was all magically OK. And my silence was the smallest possibility — taken up, and then set down again — of pointing out the wet patch.

For which pleasure, tiny but very keen, I would like to be forgiven. I would like to be forgiven, now, because I am very sorry for it.

If I believed in such a thing as confession I would go there and say that, not only did I laugh at my brother, but I let my brother laugh at himself, all his life. This laughing phase lasted through his cheerful drinking, and through his raucous drinking, and only petered out in the final stinking stage of his drinking. But he never gave it up completely — the idea that it was all a *complete joke.*

Liam never had any truck with self-pity, his own, or anyone else's. When someone was miserable — Kitty, for example — it was always for the wrong reasons as far as he was concerned. Don't get me wrong, Liam loved people who suffered — he loved the poor, the destitute, the lonely, the alcoholic, he pitied anyone with a problem, just so long as they didn't pity themselves. Which doesn't sound altogether fair to me. Which sounds like *pride,* to me.

I know I sound bitter, and Christ I wish I wasn't such a hard bitch sometimes, but my brother blamed me for twenty years or more. He blamed me for my nice house, with the nice white paint on the walls, and the nice daughters in their bedrooms of nice lilac and nicer pink. He blamed me for my golf-loving husband, though God knows it is many years since Tom had the free time for a round of golf. He treated me like I was selling out on something, though on what I do not know — because Liam did not allow *dreams* either, of course. My brother had strong ideas about justice, but he was unkind to every single person who tried to love him; mostly, and especially, to every woman he ever slept with, and still, after a lifetime of spreading the hurt around, he managed to blame me. And I managed to feel guilty. Now why is that?

This is what shame does. This is the anatomy and mechanism of a family — a whole fucking country — drowning in shame.

And, yes, sometimes I look at my nice walls and, like Liam, I say, 'Pull the whole thing down.' Especially after my nice bottle of nice Riesling. As if the world was built on a lie and that lie was very secret and very dirty. But I don't think empires or cities or even five-bedroom detached houses are built on the sordid fact that people have sex, I think they are built on the sordid fact that people have mortgages. Even so, my husband shags me the night of my brother's wake, and I wave my empty bottle at the Italian suedette seating system, and I too say, 'Let it all come down.'

One of the last times Liam was over, we were going open plan, actually — the back of the house was ripped out, and we were all camped in the front half, eating take-away. I think I blamed Liam, almost, and not the builders. He arrived in the middle of the rubble with a sad, too-tall woman, who seemed to have no opinions, not even about what she might want to eat. He drank constantly. After five days of it, they headed off to Mayo, and I hoped I would never see him again.

I have a picture from that visit, of Liam with Emily on his knee one night after her bath. He is a small grey heap of a man, settled back into an armchair that is covered in a dust sheet. Emily is two; naked, straight as a die, and more beautiful than I have words to say. Liam's hands are big, stuffed hands, wrapped around her middle, as he holds her on. Her bum is neat and sharp, sitting side-saddle on one of his thighs. Behind her, the cloth of his trousers wrinkles and sags around a crotch that is a mystery no one is interested in any more. His face is amused.

Liam understood Emily — they liked each other. Of Rebecca, who is more like me, he said, 'Pity about the teeth.'

I have to forgive that too, I suppose.

243

Pity about the teeth.

Soon after the Gardai took him in and our father got him out again, he threw the breadknife across the kitchen at my mother, who was probably just trying to say something nice, and the whole family piled into him, and kicked him around the back garden.

'Ya fucken eejit.'

'You missed, you thick.'

And there was great satisfaction to it, as I recall. Like a scab that needed to be picked. *He had it coming to him.*

(And perhaps, more secretly, so did she.)

But still I wondered, for a long time, what the cops had lifted him for. I thought about it a lot. It might have been for a broken window, or nicking drink in the offie, or just the look in his eye. Or it might have been for something I could not even guess at. There was a girl, Natalie, who was weepy and shouting at the corner of the road — maybe it was her. I thought there might have been some misunderstanding, that my father was obliged to straighten out with *further information* about the girl and her messy ways, and the length of her Saturday-night skirt.

In the end, I had to ask him. I said, 'Was

it Natalie? Was it that *wan?*' and he just looked at me.

What if he had raped her? Isn't that one of the things that men do? What if there was blood on her leg, tears on her face? Snot. What else?

I was sixteen and I knew nothing at all about sex. Isn't that strange? Whatever I knew of the mechanics of it was not available to me, somehow. I did not know how these things went. It seems that the years of my adolescence were years of increasing innocence, because by sixteen I was completely passionate and completely pure. We would all become poets, I thought, we would love mightily, and Liam, in his anger, would change the world.

Even so, there was something I couldn't quite get a handle on: something that was highly relevant, that I really needed to know. In the end I had to ask him.

'Was it Natalie — the cop thing?'

Liam looked at me. And the gap that opened between us was the gap that exists between a woman and a man — or so I thought, at sixteen — the difference between what a man might do, or want to do, sexually, what a woman might only guess at.

'Were you messing with her?' I said.

And he said, 'Don't be so thick.'

■ ■ ■ ■

There was a wood we walked through once. It was autumn, perhaps even that autumn. The trunks of the trees were grey and bright, and the leaves that clung to them were as theatrical an orange as leaves could get. It was an avenue of beech trees, I think now, with the roots lifting massively out of the earth in front of us.

That's all.

It was a romantic scene, walking along this avenue of orange leaves, so I would have been thinking of Tanner or Joe Ninety or whoever it was that week: I would have been thinking of the unknown man I was destined to love. Instead of which I was stuck, in all this beauty, with my brother.

There were mountains in the distance; massive with rock and heather. We walked under a high, pale sky and we felt, in this landscape, so small, and there was no one to judge. That's all. There was an immense feeling of Godlessness about it. Which made it sort of funny, in a way — all of it: the mountains and the pale sky and the overly orange leaves that refused to fall, in these, the closing days of our unholy alliance.

■ ■ ■ ■

What was the best time?

When Liam was fourteen or so, he had a bike and I had none and he used to give me a crossbar down to the shops or up to the local swimming pool. I don't know how he saw over my shoulder to do it. There was always a fight over the steering — me holding the handlebars rigid, him trying to pull them one way or the other, with his chin digging into my back, and my hair in his eyes. He cycled bandy, and my legs were stuck out to one side; so we were a thing of elbows and knees, the poke of handlebar ends and the vicious jab of stainless-steel pedals. You would think we did it for fun, but it was a fight from first to last.

After which, in the pool, we would ignore each other on the grounds of gender, and if there were no boys for him to hang out with, he swam alone, and if there were no girls I did the same. Sometimes we knew nobody, but we did not give up the chance of getting to know someone by ever speaking to each other. And if he did come over to me, with his skinny wet chest and his face all red in patches, I would be completely annoyed with him for blowing my cover.

247

Because who can be a mysterious object of the deep when their brother is hanging around, saying, 'You've got a snotter.'

'Shut up.'

'Big green one.'

'No, I haven't. Go away.'

'There it is.'

'Fuck off!! Go away!'

His skinny chest arching backwards. His messy, purple mouth going under. His foot churning water in my face, as he swims off to join the monstrous boys at the other end of the pool.

Natalie would have been there too, a fat little ten-year-old with a few pubic hairs like an old woman's chin — she lost the bottom of her bikini every time she dived off the edge of the pool. Four years later I ask Liam was he *messing with her,* and he gives me a look from a distance that I do not know how to cross.

I do now.

Now I know that the look in Liam's eye was the look of someone who knows they are alone. Because the world will never know what has happened to you, and what you carry around as a result of it. Even your sister — your saviour in a way, the girl who stands in the light of the hall — even she does not hold or remember the thing she saw. Because, by that stage, I think I had forgotten it entirely.

Over the next twenty years, the world around us changed and I remembered Mr Nugent. But I never would have made that shift on my own — if I hadn't been listening to the radio, and reading the paper, and hearing about what went on in schools and churches and in people's homes. It went on slap-bang in front of me and still I did not realise it. And for this, I am very sorry too.

26

Emily turns her cat's eyes to me.

'How did Uncle Liam die?' she says.

'He drowned,' I say.

'How did he drown?'

'He couldn't breathe in the water.'

'In the sea water?'

'Yes.'

It is important to be clear about these things — Emily needs to dismantle the world before she can put it together again. Rebecca's mind is a vaguer sort of machine, anxiety sets her adrift. Sometimes I wish she would focus up, but who is to say which is the better way to be?

'I can swim,' says Emily.

'Yes, you can swim, you're a great swimmer.'

'Couldn't he not swim?'

'Sweetie, he didn't want to.'

'Oh.'

'Do you want a hug?'

'No.'

'No *what?*'

'No thanks.'

'Well, I want a hug. Come here and give your poor mother a hug.'

And she comes over with outstretched arms and a big fake smile for the 'Poor Mummy' pantomime. I should think of her as selfish, but I don't — I think of her as utterly beautiful in her selfishness.

'I think it's OK to kill yourself,' she says into my chest. 'You know, when you're old.'

It is hard to remember that they don't mean to hurt — or don't know that they do. I push her back from me and I say, in a tear-thickened *shame-on-you* voice, 'Your Uncle Liam was not old, Emily. He was sick. Do you hear me? Your Uncle Liam was sick, in his head.'

She lingers at my knee and draws with her fingernail in the smooth nylon of my tights.

'Like seasick sick?'

'Oh forget it, all right? Just forget it.'

She jumps in to hug me, her victory won over all my *concerns.* And then she runs off to play.

For a week, I compose a great and poetic speech for my children about how there are little thoughts in your head that can grow until they eat your entire mind. Just tiny

251

little thoughts — they are like a cancer, there is no telling what triggers the spread, or who will be struck, and why some get it and others are spared.

I am all for sadness, I say, don't get me wrong. I am all for the ordinary life of the brain. But we fill up sometimes, like those little wooden birds that sit on a pole — we fill up with it, until *donk,* we tilt into the drink.

27

About a month after the funeral, Tom comes home as usual and he slings his coat into the sofa and sets his briefcase down, then he comes over to the dining area, working his tie loose, taking off his jacket, hanging it on the back of a hardback chair; he mooches over to the island to pick a piece of fruit from the bowl, and I think, *It never happened, Liam never died, it is all the same as it ever was.* Instead of which, I say, 'You'd fuck anything.'

'What?' he says.

I say, 'I don't know where it starts and where it ends, that's all. You'd fuck the nineteen-year-old waitress, or the fifteen-year-old who looks nineteen.'

'Sorry?'

'I don't know where the edges are, that's all. I don't know where you draw the line. Puberty, is that a line? It happens to girls at nine, now.'

'What are you talking about?' he says.

'Or not to your actual fucking. Of course. But just, you know, to your *desire.* To what you want. Is there a limit to what you want to fuck, out there?'

I have gone mad.

'Jesus Christ,' says Tom.

He plucks his jacket from the chair and heads for the front door, but I've got my bag and I'm there before him, scrabbling for the latch.

'You're not leaving,' I say.

'Get out of the way.'

'You're not leaving. I'm leaving. I am the one who is going to the fucking pub.'

I have the door open now, so there is a pathetic piece of push and shove in the porch — Hello, Booterstown! Tom, realising he is about to hit me otherwise, lifts his hands in the air. And there's my answer, I suppose, to the question of his impulses and his actions, and the gap between the two. If I wanted to see it. Which I do not.

'You can get the girls out in the morning,' I say.

Because this is where all our grand emotions end up, at who does the pick-ups and who does the porridge — at least it used to, until I gave in and tried to save my marriage by doing the lot. Christ, I could get bitter.

'What do you mean, "the morning"?'

I look at him, very hard. He lifts his hand to his lip, as though there might be something stuck there, which gives me the half a second I need to get over the threshold and back away from him down the drive.

'Where are you going?'

'I don't know,' I say.

And I go to the Shelbourne, on my credit card.

This is a mistake.

The place is full of people having a good time. They sit and drink and talk and laugh. They all seem bursting with it — whatever it is. With the whole business of being themselves. That guy Dickie Kennedy is drinking in a corner, and I remember the story about how he got his wife for 'deserting the family home'. And he also got the home.

I should be wearing my light green tweed skirt, tight across the thighs — that would show them. I should be sitting here in one of those posh wrap dresses. This is what I think about, on the brink of my marriage (or is it my sanity) in the Shelbourne bar — I think clothes would make a difference.

I sit and sip a gin and tonic from a heavy glass, and I realise that there are a limited number of ways for a woman like me to go.

Two years ago, I had a letter from Ernest. He was writing to tell me that he was leaving the priesthood, though he had decided to stay with his little school in the high mountains. And his bishop might have a few things to say about this, so he had decided not to tell his bishop — he was, in fact, telling no one except friends and family (but don't tell Mammy!) that it was no longer 'Father Ernest', but just plain old 'Ernest' again. Once a priest always a priest, of course — so he wasn't exactly telling lies by keeping his mouth shut. 'I have no place left to live but in my own heart,' he wrote, meaning he would conduct his life as before, but on privately different terms.

And I thought this was the stupidest stuff I had ever heard until, sitting on a stool in the Shelbourne bar, I wondered what might happen if I just carried on as usual, told no one, changed nothing, and decided not to be married after all.

And I wondered how many people around me are living with and sleeping with and laughing with their spouses on just this basis, and I wondered how sad they were. Not very, by the looks of it. Not sad at all.

The last time I saw Dickie Kennedy was out in his amazing house in Glenageary. It must have been after Rebecca was born. And God he was a savage. 'I see Brian's got his hands full,' he says, after some poor woman smoothes her skirt over a plump backside, because there seems to be no way she can reverse out of the room. We sit and listen to this stuff, and we eat mushroom risotto, followed by hake in a bright green sauce. The food is very good. Emer, the woman who made it all, has skin thickened to a hide by too much sun and too much cream. I am drawn to the V of her top as she shrugs, to see the whole business move and crease. She asks me some questions, and they are good questions, and I answer, and so the dinner proceeds to everyone's satisfaction. She is really quite witty. She gets a bit drunk. She tells a story about a woman we all know who took off her top in Dickie's office — the ugliness of her, you have no idea, the underwear — he came home *shaking.* And we all laugh. And then we go home.

Even Tom, in the car afterwards, gives himself a little shake, like he can not believe the contract that was being offered to us, just there.

'What was all that about?' When I get back

from dropping off the babysitter he is sitting in the living room, making his way through a bottle of whiskey, in the dark.

Or maybe this was another night. For a while, all those nights were the same.

'Do you want the light on?'

'No thanks.'

'Are you coming to bed?'

Here we go, again. Always after a few drinks, but sometimes even sober, we play the unhappiness game; endlessly round and round. Ding dong. Tighter and tighter. On and on.

'No, I'll just sit up a while.'

'It's up to you.'

'Yes.'

Push me pull you. Come here and I'll tell you how much I hate you. Hang on a minute while I leave you. All the while we know we are missing the point, whatever the point used to be. I know what it is now, though, because upstairs the baby shouts in her sleep. I move to go.

'Thanks,' he says.

'What?'

'Thanks for staying with me.'

'Oh, for God's sake.'

'No. Really.'

Or some version of the above — we rarely shout, myself and Tom, we just hate.

'I'll be back in a minute,' I say.

And one night — it might even have been this night, after the hake in green sauce, and Brian's plump wife, and the ugly woman in the bad underwear, and all the winning and the losing — Tom takes the cigarette out of his mouth. He holds it up, high under my chin, and he scrunches it in his fist. The smell, when he opens his hand, is small and terrible.

It clears my head.

The thing is, if I go up to Rebecca and kiss her, she will be happy. If I sit on the arm of the chair and kiss Tom, he will not be happy. So I stay with him for just a moment more, in the singed smell of his self-disgust. I hold his skull against my breast. I do this until Rebecca's wailing grows to the exact pitch that pulls me to my feet, every time. Then I go.

It was the children that did for us, at least for a while. I think he stopped hating me after I left work. Of course, Tom would say he never hated me, that he loved me all along. But I know hating when I see it. I know it, because there is a part of me that wants to be hated, too.

There must be.

Anyway.

It did get easier over the years, but it never really did get fixed.

I thought about this, as I sat in the Shelbourne bar — that I was living my life in inverted commas. I could pick up my keys and go 'home' where I could 'have sex' with my 'husband' just like lots of other people did. This is what I had been doing for years. And I didn't seem to mind the inverted commas, or even notice that I was living in them, until my brother died.

28

The British, I decide, only bury people when they are so dead, you need another word for it. The British wait so long for a funeral that people gather not so much to mourn, as to complain that the corpse is still hanging around. There is a queue, they say on the phone (the British love a queue). They do not gather until the emotion is gone.

What else am I to make of the ten days we have to wait for paperwork; the death certificates and removal orders, that have to find their separate ways into the one envelope that will accompany my brother on his journey home.

Meanwhile, as computers wait and printers jam, as coroner's assistants go to the gym, and registrars wrestle with the collapse of their central heating systems, Liam lies in some unspecified foreign fridge, and I — we all — get on with things. From time to time, as I move about the house, I am gripped by the thought that I have, shamefully, forgotten something: there is a tampon seeping into the water of the downstairs toilet; I have left half a biscuit on the arm of a chair, or forgotten to finish my tea. I can feel it going cold in my mouth, as I hunt around and finally find the empty cup.

Every day I go over to Griffith Way and sit in a formal sort of way with my mother, and Bea if she is there, or Kitty. We talk about ordinary things. Or we settle her in front of the television set and retreat to the kitchen, where Kitty — where we all — look diminished, overgrown. I am shocked by the amount of products we need, each of us slicked up and greased down, until there is no surface free of cosmetic matt or sheen. This is what it is to be middle-aged in the place where we once were children, and now, highlights notwithstanding, we are being treated like children again, not so much by our mother, as by death itself. Except we are very good children this time around.

I am a good daughter. I am a very good daughter. In some sort of middle-class fit, I go into Kilkenny Design and buy my mother a beautiful, spider-woven, cashmere shawl, in cream.

She takes it out of the bag, entranced for

a moment by the idea that she might look like an old lady off the telly.

So this is what they give you, when your children die.

She lets me put it across her, but her rounded old shoulders reject it, as does the set of her jaw. She pulls it down into her lap, saying, 'It would make a lovely christening shawl, wouldn't it? Ciara has one on the way.' Because, although she never quite knows us when she sees us in the flesh, my mother counts over her progeny and their progeny to the third generation; she shifts through their names with pleasure and ease.

'She's due in February, isn't she? Very cold.'

All the Hegarty babies are baptised, because to do otherwise would be to rob this woman of what she rightfully owns, her little treasure of souls — we all traipse dutifully up to the font and hand them over. I didn't mind, actually, but I thought Jem was pushing it. Who knows what the Hegartys believe? Mossie-the-psychotic goes to Mass every day during Lent, but we only know this because he tells us, being psychotic. The rest of us do our praying alone.

I take the shawl from her, folding it and putting it back in the paper bag, saying as I do so, 'Would you take something for yourself, Mammy, just once.' And she gives me a beaky look, as if to say, *What? You want me to be like you?*

I don't know what is wrong with being me. And I don't know if she would like me better, if she could remember my name. Mammy was always free to choose which ones she did and did not love. The boys first, of course, and after the boys, whichever of the girls were good.

I was not good. I am not sure why. It is not that I ever did anything out of the way. I just didn't buy it, and neither did Liam. We just didn't buy the whole Hegarty *poor Mammy* thing.

Poor Mammy sits and watches afternoon TV, as she does, and will do, before and after the death of any other human being. It is impossible to say what she is thinking about. When she speaks it is of things that happened long ago, before any of us came into the world: the adventure of the milkman's horse, the day she set fire to the living-room carpet in Broadstone, her mother Ada at the thin end of the month, making a stew that was only vegetables — jungle stew, she called it, the carrots were 'tiger meat' and the parsnips 'camel chews'.

Around us, the house is empty and tatty; a warren of partitions, scuttling with the ghosts of the children we once were. Three dead — we are nearly a normal family now. A couple more and we will be just the right size.

I had a guy in to clean the carpets once, and he told me he was the last of twenty-one. All big families are the same. I meet them sometimes at parties or in pubs, we announce ourselves and then we grieve Billy in Boston, and Jimmy-Joe in Jo'burg, doing well — the dead first, then the lost, and then the mad.

There is always a drunk. There is always someone who has been interfered with, as a child. There is always a colossal success, with several houses in various countries to which no one is ever invited. There is a mysterious sister. These are just trends, of course, and, like trends, they shift. Because our families contain everything and, late at night, everything makes sense. We pity our mothers, what they had to put up with in bed or in the kitchen, and we hate them or we worship them, but we always cry for them — at least I do. The imponderable pain of my mother, against which I have hardened my heart. Just one glass over the odds and I will thump the table, like the rest of them, and howl for her too.

This is what, over the years, my mother

has made:

1) Cups of tea.

My mother has wet, in her lifetime, many thousands of pots of tea — she never made anything else, really. And we always fought over it. Midge liked hers stewed; Ernest, weak. Mossie liked to wave the pot around, but it was Ita who splashed me once, swinging it round in an arc — I can still see the dirty ribbon of water looping towards me, the line of pain across my midriff, and how cold the cotton was, as I tried to peel it off.

Who's for tea?

Strange to say, she only made two alcoholics, of the actual would-you-ever-try-AA variety. But all the Hegartys are thirsty. All the Hegartys would *kill* for a decent cup of tea.

2) Descendants.

Most of the girls are genetic culs-de-sac and who would blame them, though Midge had six — she had them early and she had them often; her first coinciding with Mammy's last (it's not a competition, you know). Jem has two lovely babies. Mossie, the psychotic, has three careful children who have never left the family home in Clontarf.

3) Money.

No one has a proper job, except Bea who works as an office manager in a big estate

266

agent's in town, also Mossie who is an anaesthetist (we suspect that someday he will leave the gas on that tiny bit too long). But the rest of us just have euphemisms. Ita is a *homemaker,* Kitty is an *actress,* I am a *night owl,* Alice is a *gardener.* Both Ivor and Jem work in *multimedia,* which is the biggest euphemism of them all. Ernest is a *priest* (I rest my case).

4) Heterosexuals.

'Are you all straight?' my friend Frank once said to me, in tones of great disbelief.

'Hmmmmm . . .' I said.

Midge? Not really relevant, is it? Once you are dead. Or, alternatively, once you've married a pub manager and bought a house in Churchtown. Midge was a mother; she was a wiper, a walloper, a panicker, a hoarder of pains, especially her biggest and last. She might have been gay or straight or sheep-shagging, it is too sad to think about, really. What Midge *desired,* never mattered in the slightest. As for the rest of them: half of Bea's boyfriends are gay, but I don't think she is. Ernest is celibate. Kitty sleeps with lots of men, and she loves each of them and they are all married. Is that a sexual orientation? It should be — the little bitch. She only shags the impossible dream.

No one knows about Alice. But everyone

knows about the twins Ivor and Jem who have very pleasant, normal sex (hurray!) — not with each other, I hasten to add, but with their partners, one of whom is a girl from Surrey and one of whom is a nice German radio producer (male).

Meanwhile, Baby Stevie has little angel sex, up there in heaven, naked with the rest of the cherubs. He is queer as all get out. They make little noises when they kiss. It sounds just like their name. *Putti. Putti. Putti.*

None of us is straight. It is not that the Hegartys don't know what they want, it is that they don't know *how* to want. Something about their wanting went catastrophically astray.

This is what I sense as I look up the stairs to the room where we were all conceived: I sense the chaos of our fate — or not so much a chaos as a vagueness — the way that no one could find a groove. And I remember how proud we were. And how loyal. And the way we all stuck together. And wasn't that just *great?*

I always knew where everyone was. I used to sit on the window sill of our room, curled up against the fragile sheet of glass and track the entire house: Ita at the bathroom mirror, Midge at the sink. Mossie scratching his scalp into the seam of his biology book, Liam keeping company in the garden passage. Even at night I could tell who was where: each room cold and differently stale as the whole, soured day unloaded itself through my brothers' sleeping skin; the scent of my mother's tablets in the upstairs toilet, after she went in there to pee.

They are waking up. They are coming back home.

Bea, Ernest, Ita, Mossie, Kitty, maybe Alice and definitely the twins, Ivor and Jem.

They will thunder in overhead, in the huge bellies of planes. Ivor from Berlin and Jem from London, Ita from Tucson, the mysterious Alice from God knows where. Maybe even Father Ernest in a stripy ethnic hat, in from Lima via Amsterdam.

A hosting of the Hegartys. God help us all.

We will do the Hegarty thing. We will be brave and decent and hearty, we will cry and suffer through. There will be no *bollocks,* because the Hegartys don't do *bollocks;* the great thing about being dragged up is that there is no one to blame. We are entirely free range. We are human beings in the raw. Some survive better than others, that is all.

29

The body still has not arrived.

Tom leaves the property supplement out on the kitchen table, with rings and ticks around derelict bits of the inner city. He underlines the words 'In need of refurbishment'. I think he means me. I also think — thanks, Tom — that this is a great thing to do when your brother-in-law dies.

I go in to exchange Mammy's shawl and wander around town, and after a while I find myself crying on the escalator in Brown Thomas, which is only a shop. And the fact that makes me cry is that there is nothing here that I can not buy. I can buy bedlinen, or I can buy a bed. I can buy posh jeans for the girls or a Miu Miu jacket for myself, if it doesn't look too boxy. I can buy the plastic Brabantia storage jars that I am now staring at on the third floor, that I actually might need for pasta and rice and lentils and pumpkin seeds and all sorts of dry goods, expecially the ones that are never cooked or used that live on my top shelf. I try to count. Should I get one for the polenta, that has been sitting in its packet for the last five years, waiting for the day when we would need all the dry goods we could get? What about the chickpeas? The jars are half price. I need nine, I think. I start piling them into the crook of my left arm, crying a little more now, as I imagine the flood, plague and nuclear bomb that has us locked in the house eating five-year-old polenta. If anyone asks me, I can tell them that I am crying for the end of the world. And suddenly I want to throw the nine Brabantia storage jars into the air and shout, or go over to the till and empty my bag on to the counter, and say, *What about the starving people in Africa, with their bellies out and their eyes running with pus?* because I can buy anything at all in this shop. My brother has just died and I can buy anything at all.

'You need a challenge,' says Rebecca, primly, being eight.

And I say, 'Sure haven't I got you?'

Are they good children? Are they decent human beings? In the main. Though Emily is a bit of a cat, and cats, I always think, only jump into your lap to check if you are cold enough, yet, to eat.

Sometimes I wonder about Michael Weiss — whether he too has succumbed, with a high maintenance wife, and kids who live the middle-class dream, but with *avidity,* as my pair do. And I feel he would be able to manage that; he would be able to manage the world of pink, of liking Barbies but not too much, and buying them, or not bothering to buy them after all.

Liam never went into a shop.

So, in honour of Liam, I put the storage jars back and I drive home, pointing out all the changes to him, now that he is dead.

'Look at that row of street lamps!' I say.

He is not convinced.

I used to do this when he was still alive, actually: all the little changes and irritations, residential parking, gridlock, the seven million orange cones between here and Kinnegad, all of these things I pointed out to him, because he was living five hundred miles away. And though he came back in a sporadic way and took his holidays in the West, all of these changes went on without him. And though not one of them meant anything much, I was sad at the way he had been left behind. Liam existed in the seventies, somehow. He might, in reality, have been more cosmopolitan than we were — cooking curries over in London, having all sorts of amazing friends — but when he came home, he always seemed a bit of a throwback, a hick.

My emigrant brother makes an old-fashioned ghost, and when he died, I dressed him in worn-out wellington boots, as the Irish seventies dipped back into the fifties in my mind.

30

I am expecting the house to be crammed, but Bea shakes her head slightly by the door.

'Just us, really,' she says. 'A few neighbours.'

'What do you expect?' I want to say. 'Who's going to come and look at a dead body in your living room, when there isn't even a decent glass of wine in the house?' But I do not say this. Tom is behind me. He has taken my elbow, and is using it like a joystick to steer me around her, and I would be annoyed, but his grip is so old-fashioned. No one holds you like that any more, except Frank at work who was gay, and is now dead.

'It's all in the eyes,' he said once, as he eased me into some awful corporate bash. And, *Poor Frank,* I think. *Why did I not grieve for Frank?* And I realise, suddenly and with great conviction, that I must carpet the upstairs, Frank would have been all for it.

And get a cleaner again. I must get a cleaner to deal with the extra fluff. Then I remember Rebecca's asthma — as I always do at this point — and before I finish remembering this I am looking at Liam's dead body in the front room.

Haven't we met before?

I can see the exact colour of the new carpet I want. 'Driftwood', I think they call it.

Why do you keep following me around?

The room is almost empty. There is no one here that I can talk to about children's lungs or carpet colours, about weaves and nubbles and seagrass or percentages of wool. Dead or alive. Liam does not care about such things. I sit down. They have put him in a navy suit with a blue shirt — like a Garda. He would have liked that.

Who dressed him?

The young English undertaker, with the full mouth and the pierced ear; talking on his mobile to his girlfriend as he lifts the heavy head to slip the tie around.

The suit, I am sure, will be on the bill.

I expected the coffin to be set across the room, but there is not enough space for this. Liam's head points towards the closed curtains and there are candles behind him, set on high stands. I can not see his face properly from where I sit. The wood of the coffin angles down, slicing across the bulge of his cheek. I can see a dip in the bone where his eyes must go, but I do not get up to see if this dip is correctly filled, or if the lids are closed. This lift and fall of bone is all I want to see of him, for the moment, thank you very much.

The armchairs and the sofa have been pushed back, but Mrs Cluny, who has paused to pray, has chosen to sit on one of the hard chairs brought in from the kitchen. Kitty is on duty by the far wall in case a mourner should be left indecently alone with the corpse, in case the corpse should be left indecently alone. She looks at me as I perch on the arm of the sofa and she rolls her eyes. After a minute she comes over and says, quietly, 'Will you stay?'

'No,' I tell her. She does not understand. The whole business is finished for me now, it is beyond finished. I just want to get the damn thing buried and out of the way.

I say, 'I'll get Ita or someone. No. I can't. I have the kids.'

'Oh, the kids,' she says, slightly too loud.

'Yeah, you know. Kids.'

And in fact Rebecca is in the room of a sudden, backing towards me until she bumps into my knees.

'Where's your father?'

When I look over, I see Emily swinging out of the door handles with her eyes fixed on the coffin and her shoe kicking the paint.

'Would you stop that,' I say.

She doesn't.

'Will you *stop* leaving scuff marks on your Granny's door.'

Then I realise where we are.

'It's all right,' I tell her. 'He's dead.' Which is not, when I think about it, the most comforting thing I could say.

In a sudden flare of kilt and sandy-coloured hair Rebecca is back at the door, and they are both gone. I hear them laughing in the hall, then running up the stairs, although they should not be running upstairs. I have a surge of rage against Tom who insisted on bringing the children but can not be bothered to mind them, not even with a corpse in the house, after which someone pushes the mute button again, and it is some time before I notice that Kitty has gone and I am the only living Hegarty in the room. I don't know how long this lasts, but I feel like it is a long time, tracing the girls' whispered hysteria through the upstairs — tied to them, wherever they go, and tied too to this piece of garbage in the front room. The back of the house is dense with the sound of people I do not want to meet, and so I stay where I am, and decide not to complain.

So this is how Ernest finds me when he walks in the door, fresh off the plane. He is so incontrovertibly himself — it is some moments before I stop seeing him, my big brother, and pull back to see what he looks like, these days. He looks good, I find. His clothes are a bit sad, but at the top of the anorak and polyester slacks is his head, large and healthy and getting more handsome over the years. It is Grandpa Charlie's pate, I realise, that is gleaming in the candlelight, and Grandpa Charlie's two big hands that grab one of mine, and I don't know, as I stand and Ernest clasps me to him, whether this is a priestly or grandfatherly hug — no breasts anyway: my small breasts are not, with this hug, in the way.

How does he do it?

It is his job. My brother has a trained heart; compassion is a muscle for him; he inclines his head when you speak. He barely looks at the coffin, but apprises, instead, the look in my eyes. Then he turns slightly towards the body.

'Don't tell the rest of them I'm here, will you?' he says. 'Not yet,' and sends me, with a nod, out the door. And of course, this is why I hate him too, in all his priestly *can-dour* — this fakery. Still, Ernest was always nice to me, growing up. We were just the right distance apart.

Out in the hall, I give an ear to the voices in the kitchen — a sharpened American note, that must be Ita's. And Mossie's wife shushing her perfect kids.

I turn and go upstairs to find my own.

'Rebecca! Emily!'

The stairs are narrow, and steeper than I remember. I can hear the sound of their laughter, above me, like children hiding in the branches of a tree, but when I reach the landing they are gone.

It is a long time since I have been up here. This was the girls' floor: Midge, Bea and Ita at the back; me, Kitty and Alice at the front, with a view of cherry blossom, and slanting black wires, and a white street light. It did not seem small, at the time. Kitty's overnight bag is on her bed, the other two beds are bare. Framing the window is the maze of shelves and little cupboard doors my father built for us out of white MFI. A few schoolbooks are left on one shelf; none of them in English — perhaps this is why they were not thrown away. *Das Wrack* by Siegfried Lenz, and stories by Guy de Maupassant, one called 'La Mer' in which, as I recall from school, a sailor stores his severed arm in a barrel of salt in order to bring it home. The books look soiled as opposed to read, but we did read them too:

Tá Tír na nÓg ar chúl an tí
Tír álainn trína chéile

I turn and find the girls at the door.

'Come on, down you go.' And these children, who never do a single thing I say, turn and walk ahead of me down the stairs. At the bottom, Rebecca takes my hand in hers and walks me to the kitchen, like a mislaid giant she has found in the hall.

There was a thing Mossie would do with our hands. He would squeeze the small bones until you screamed, running the knuckles across each other, over and back. He is there in the kitchen, standing with Tom at the table: the two professionals in the room, talking man to man. *Why do men never sit down,* I think, then realise that all the chairs are in with the corpse. I look around. Ita is leaning back against the sink. She looks smaller. Even her face looks smaller — perhaps it is the light of the window behind that has her so reduced. But she is too well-preserved and I have, as I kiss her, a retching sense of the waxed flesh

280

next door.

Then the twins are hugging me from either side — as they do, being always delightful, and hard to see. I look around for Kitty and see her outside in the garden, smoking. The mysterious Alice is not here. Probably mad, I think suddenly. The mysterious Alice was probably always mad.

Midge's children stand in a gang and I turn gratefully towards them, but Bea throws a look at me, swinging her hair back over one shoulder.

All right. All right.

I go over to where my mother is sitting and stand by the wing of her chair while a neighbour finishes saying the ritual words.

'Yes. Thank you. Yes.'

The neighbour, Mrs Burke, is bent low, telling some great and particular secret into Mammy's ear; stroking her hand, over and over.

'Yes,' says Mammy, again. 'Thank you. Yes.'

When Mrs Burke moves on, I step forward to kiss my mother.

It has happened. She sat watching television for the past ten days, waiting for something which has now well and truly arrived. It has, as they say, 'hit her'. Like a truck. There isn't much of her left.

Always vague, Mammy is now completely faded. I look her in the eye and try to find her, but she guards whatever she has left of herself deep inside. She looks at the world from this far place, and allows it all to happen, without knowing quite what it is. It is hard to tell how much she takes in, but there is a peacefulness to her too.

'Oh. Hello,' she says to me, and there is a hazy kind of love in her voice — for me, for the table set with food, for everyone here.

'Mammy,' I say, and bend down to kiss her cheek, and although she was never good at kissing or being kissed she does not flinch from me now, but angles her face like a debutante to receive the childish pucker of my lips. I suspect she has forgotten me entirely, but then she takes my hand, and sets it flat between her two light hands, and she looks up at me.

'You were always great pals,' she says.

'Yes, Mammy.'

'You were always great with each other, weren't you? You were always great pals.'

'Thanks, Mammy. Thanks.'

Tom's hand is warm on the base of my spine. At least I think it is him, but when I crook my head around, he is not there. Who has touched me? I straighten up and look at them all. Who has touched me? I want to say it out loud, but the Hegartys and the Hegartys' wives and the Hegartys' children are some distance away from me: they shift, and talk, and eat on, unawares.

'Are you all right there, Mammy?' I say, by way of taking my leave.

'I need to see the children,' she says.

'What?' I say. 'What?'

'The children,' she says again. 'I need to see the children.'

'They're upstairs, Mammy,' I say. 'No. They're here. I'll go look for them, Mammy. I'll find them for you.'

Then Tom is finally, actually, at my side. He dips to take my mother's hand in wordless sympathy, then straightens up to take my elbow again and wheel me around to the rest of the room.

'Have you been in?' I say.

'He looks,' says Tom. Then he stops. 'It's not him.'

'I wouldn't really know,' I say.

Tom's fingers grip my arm. They are very full of themselves, these fingers of his. They do not leave me in any doubt. This is the man who will fuck me soon, to remind me that I am still alive. In the meantime he says, 'He looks like an estate agent.'

'It's the shirt,' I say.

'Ah. It comes to us all.'

Then the children come up: Rebecca, Emily, and Róisín, who is Mossie's youngest — so often seen, so seldom heard. Such a cutie. She stands before me and swings her tummy from side to side.

'Will you say hello to your Auntie?' I say. 'Will you say it, or will you squeak it, like a little mouse? Squeak. Squeak.'

I tweak her tummy with my witchy old hands. Then I straighten up and mutter at Tom, 'Mammy says she needs to see the children.'

'Right so.'

'Would you ever fuck off,' I say.

'What?'

'Why does she *need* to see the children?'

'Well,' says Tom.

'It's not what children are for,' I say, quite fiercely. And he gives me a look of sudden interest, before twisting the girls by the shoulders, to push them across to their Gran.

'Give your Granny a kiss, there, go on.'

The girls stand in front of my mother. There is a chance that Emily will actually wipe her mouth in front of her — she does not like wet kisses, she says, only dry ones 'like her Daddy's'. In the event, there are no fluids involved. My mother lifts her hand and places it on Rebecca's head, then she turns, quite formally, and does the same to Emily, who receives the gesture with large eyes.

I watch this configuration as from a great distance. It is as though I am not related to any of them. But there is a roaring in my blood, too.

'So what are they for?' says Tom.

'They're not *for* anything,' I say. 'They just are.'

And I mean it too.

Rebecca comes back to me. Her face is full of unshed tears and I take her outside for a minute. The other room is occupied by the coffin so we have nowhere to go except the stairs, where we sit while my gentle, drifting daughter weeps in my lap for something she does not understand. Then she sharpens up a little.

'I want to go home,' she says, still face down.

'In a little bit.'

'It's not fair. I want to go home.'

'Why is it not fair?' I say. 'What's not fair about it?'

She is insulted, in her youth, by the proximity of death. It is spoiling her ideas about being in a girl band, maybe — or so I think, with a sudden impulse to bring her in to the coffin and push her on to her knees and oblige her to consider the Four Last Things.

Jesus. Where did that come from? I have to calm down.

'This is not about you, all right? People die, Rebecca.'

'I want to go home!'

'And I want you to be a little bit grown up here. All right?'

And so it goes.

'I didn't even like him,' she says, in a final, terrible whimper, and this makes me laugh so much she stops crying to look up at me.

'Neither did I, sweetheart. Neither did I.'

Emily has come out to look for me, followed by Tom. So we stand up and dust ourselves down and turn around, one more time. I have my children about me and my husband at my side, and I walk back into yet another family gathering; every single one of them involving ham sandwiches with the crusts cut off, and butter, and supermarket coleslaw, and cheese-and-onion crisps for the side of your plate. There are cocktail sausages and squares of quiche, and fruit salad for Mossie, who complains about trans-fats. There are Ritz crackers with salmon pâté and a single prawn on top, others with a sprig of parsley over a smear of cream cheese. There is houmous for Kitty or Jem, whichever one of them is vegetarian this week, in a trio of dips with guacamole and taramasalata. There is my smoked salmon, and Bea's lasagne, and fantastic packet jelly wobbling in little glass bowls, made by my mother with quiet deliberation and left to set the night before.

There is no wine.

No, I tell a lie. This time, for the first time — perhaps in honour of Liam's prodigious drinking — there are two bottles on the table; one red, one white. Everyone knows they are there, and no one, but no one, is going to drink them. Mossie tries to pour a glass for Mrs Cluny, who nearly beats him away with her handbag. 'No no, I couldn't,' she says. 'No, absolutely not.'

It is great to be nearly forty, I think, and lashing into the fizzy orange.

Jem goes in to rescue some chairs from the room next door, and Bea passes around the plates, and we get the show on the road. For a while I try to keep the kids in check, and then I don't bother. I lean against the wall and watch my family eat.

When we were young, Mossie used to insist on silent chewing. He didn't mind sitting with us, he said, and we could talk as much as we liked, but he would not abide the noise of the food being mashed up in our mouths, and any slurps, even the slightest squelch, would get you a thump across the side of the head. He kept his eyes on the table for the duration, but he moved fast and blind. I don't know why we put up with it — it must have been fun, too — but, watching my family scoffing the funeral meats, I do sort of see where he was coming from.

Ernest, the celibate, is particularly terrible to watch. Even my mother eats with a sudden greed, as though remembering how to do it. Some surge of recognition sends her scampering from one Ritz cracker to the next, she gets in people's way, and they are, for a tiny moment, aggrieved. The neighbours take a little on their plates and set them down, and then, after a while, they forget themselves so much as to scoff the lot. A man I slowly recognise as my father's brother is helping himself with thick fingers. He works pragmatically fast, amused by the array of little treats, concerned to get a decent amount of food into himself before night.

Daddy came from County Mayo — which is to say he left County Mayo when he was seventeen years old. Liam was sentimental about the West of Ireland, but I don't think Daddy was, and I am not. But I am sentimental about my Uncle Val — or so I find. I watch him, thinking that, if I stare hard enough, my childhood will rise to meet him. Also, I want to see what kind of a man he is, now that I have met many other men, out in the big world.

Val is a bachelor farmer in his seventies, so he should, by rights, be half-mad. But he looks chipper enough. Also clever. He does one thing at a time, that is the notable thing about him. He wipes his fingers on a paper napkin and looks for a place to set it down, and when he finds none, he scrunches the tissue up and tucks it firmly under the rim of his empty plate. Then he looks at one or other of us as if guessing at our lives: the way they have gone and the way they will end up. Uncle Val loved endings. He was especially fond of suicides. He used to talk us through the neighbours' houses, and tell us who shot himself and who used the rope. He told Liam a story about a local man who, when his wife refused to have sex with him, upped and got the kitchen knife and castrated himself in front of her.

'The whole shooting gallery,' he said. 'The whole shooting works.'

'Uncle Val,' I say, shaking his hand, thinking I could have a panic attack, just by catching the smell of his suit.

'Veronica, is it? I'm very sorry. He was a great lad. I think he was my favourite.'

'Yes,' I say.

'He was very good company, always.'

'Yes.'

I have loved my Uncle Val, I realise, since I was six years old.

'He always enjoyed his visits to you,' I say. 'He relished them.'

'Ah well,' says Val. 'We did our best.'

And it occurs to me that I wasn't the only one who tried to save Liam — this man tried too, and this man, stuck out on his farm in Maherbeg, will always feel guilty that he did not succeed. The word 'suicide' is in the air for the first time — the way we all failed. So, thanks Liam. Thanks a bunch.

Ita reaches behind her and takes a glass of water which she has set in the sink. It has been teasing me all evening — why is she keeping it there? Then I realise it is not water, but gin. Amazing. She looks the same as she did when I arrived, though her face is a little more swollen and set. There is also the fact of her nose, which is without doubt a different, and more American, shape. Ita is looking at us all with undisguised rage. Maybe it is because we are so ugly. Though I can hardly complain — the way I react to the sight of the Hegarty mouths moving around food.

Meanwhile, Tom is back talking to Mossie again. 'The only sane one, actually, in the whole family,' as he says to me, annually, sometime around Christmas. And it is true, as I look at him, my brother does seem very normal, he has a nice job and a nice wife and he sends around a nice newsletter telling us how his little family is doing. 'A big welcome for baby Darragh!!' Truth be told Mossie has done nothing psychotic for twenty years. But still *ha ha* says Liam next door, as Tom my professional husband engages Mossie my professional brother in some political talk about the way the country is on the up and up. *Ha bloody ha,* says the corpse next door.

I want to get drunk. Suddenly. This is a calamitous thing to want, but it can not be denied. I want rid of my children and my husband so I can get properly rat-arsed for once, because God knows I have never been properly rat-arsed before. And there is Kitty rolling her eyes at me, from the other side of the room. Ita! I drift by the sink (because alcoholics are always useful when you want a good time).

'We need a bottle of something. Is there a bottle, for after?'

And, through gritted teeth, Ita says, 'I'll

have a look.'

There is a shift in the room. It is time to move, or go. I must talk to Midge's girls, quickly, before they leave with children and babies and toddlers in tow. My niece Ciara is five months' pregnant, and her face is violently mottled in the heat.

I dab at her forearm and she grazes my wrist, because pregnant women must touch and be touched, and my look, I know, is quite ardent as I say, 'Are you sleeping? Did you get the new bed?' Ciara strokes her stomach, then reaches towards me in another flutter of hands.

'Jesus, life on a futon,' she says.

'That man of yours,' I say. 'He should be shot.'

'It's his back.'

'Yeah, yeah,' and we both laugh — dirtily, like we have been talking about sex.

Tom is beside me, liking all this. I turn to salute Uncle Val who is being led off, rather spookily, by Mrs Cluny, to stay next door. When Ciara goes to leave, Tom organises her nappy bag and rounds up Brandon, her toddler. Then he drifts back to me.

He says, 'Do you remember when you were pregnant with Rebecca and you wouldn't go to the graveyard — whose funeral was it? You wouldn't go anyway, because the child would be bandy, you said.'

'*Cam reilige.*'

'What?'

'That's what it's called. In Irish.'

'You're a funny thing,' he says.

'Yes,' I say. 'I'm a hoot.'

Cam reilige, which is Irish for *the twist of the grave.*

I walk away from him then, feeling, once more, the shadow of a child in me, the swoop of the future in my belly, black and open.

I put my hand to my stomach. It is like a pain, almost.

'Well it worked, anyway,' says Tom, still at my shoulder. 'She has a lovely pair of pins.'

I don't need you to tell me that. I turn around to say it to him, *I don't need you to tell me that,* but instead of seeing my husband, I only see the opening circle of his eye. If we wanted another child, it is waiting for us now. I can almost see it. So it is not all his fault, the sex that happens later. It is not entirely his fault, that I do not enjoy it *as sex goes.*

Meanwhile he gives me a nod. 'I'll take the kids. Any time. Come home any time.'

'Don't stay up,' I say.

And he says, 'I might.'

It was my sister Midge's funeral, actually,

and I was big as a house. My niece Karen had given birth a month before me, at the age of twenty-one. I remember sitting in the church and looking at the tiny, moist baby, churring on her mother's shoulder, a white hairband across her little, new head. Anuna — all Midge's grandchildren have silly names — is dressed now in an expensive red, puff coat, a knockout of a girl, with the dreaded Hegarty eye; cold and wild and blue.

'Goodnight, Karen. Watch out for that one.'

They are flickering at each other across the room now, blue to blue, as strangers and extras take their leave. Bea prises Mammy out of her chair.

'You're very tired, Mammy.'

'Yes.'

'Come here and I'll bring you upstairs.'

'Yes.'

'I'll bring up your cup of tea.'

But there is something she wants to do before she goes. Mammy escapes Bea's grasp and comes over to the table. She puts her two hands down on the wood, so everyone knows to stop talking. In her gentle, sweet voice, she says, 'He would have been so proud of you all.'

We know she means, not Liam, but our

father. She has got her funerals mixed up. Either that or all funerals are the same funeral, now.

'He *is*,' she says with horrible conviction. 'Your Daddy is so very proud of you all.'

Bea turns her around, to leave the room. 'That's it, Mammy.'

'Goodnight,' she says.

'Goodnight Mammy,' we say, in a little family patter.

'Goodnight now.'

'Sleep well, Mammy.'

'Get some rest.'

'Night night,' all out of rhythm, like the first drops of rain.

'*Coladh sámh,*' says Ernest, by the door, and she turns to him for a blessing, which my brother — the lying hypocrite bastard of lapsed-priest atheist — does not hesitate to give (in Irish no less) and she leaves happy. At least 'happy' is the look on her face. Happy. She is pleased with the people she has made. She is happy.

We are silent a moment after she is gone. Mossie sits. Ita takes a slug of her water, then her mouth twitches deeply down, in some riposte from the silent conversation she is having in her head. Kitty lights up a fag, which annoys everyone a little. And I think, *I never told Mammy the truth. I never told any of them the truth.*

But what was I supposed to say? A dead man put his hand in a deader man's flies thirty years ago. There are other things, surely, to talk about. There are other things to be revealed.

Like what, though? Like what?

I start to help Bea with the dishes, while Kitty brings a pile of plates over to the sink.

'What are you doing?' says Bea to her.

'Clearing up,' says Kitty.

'Oh.'

'What?'

'Oh. No, please do. Please do clear up.'

'Fuck off.'

'No, there's always a first time.'

'Oh, *fuck off.*'

'Well, scrape them first, would you? Scrape it, would you? *Scrape* it, and stack it over there.'

Kitty lifts the plate over her head like she is going to bring it smashing down on the floor. No one looks. She holds it there for a long moment — then, with a toss of the head, she carries the thing, ceremoniously high, to the bin. She goes to scrape it, and then she just can't help herself and stuffs the lot into the rubbish, plate, food and all.

'Jesus!' she screams, looking at the knife

that is left in her hand, like it is dripping with blood. I glance at the ceiling — Mammy is still moving around upstairs.

'Oh JesusJesusJesus!' says Kitty, throwing the murder weapon into the bin, and she flees out into the garden to finish her fag.

'Bea,' I say.

'What,' says Bea, very fiercely, as she picks the crockery out of the bin. *'What?'*

And I know what she means. She means, *What use is the truth to us now?*

Ita comes in from the corpse room and plonks a bottle of peculiar whiskey in the middle of the yellow pine table.

'It's all I could find,' she says. The bottle has a funny Irish name. It looks a bit decorative.

'I could go to the off-licence,' says Jem in a small voice.

'No, no. Not to worry.'

We uncork it anyway, and put it into glasses where it sits, thick and sweet. This ritual is strange for us because, although the Hegartys all drink, we never drink together.

'Look at the legs on that,' says Ivor, swilling it round and holding it to the light. We sip, and consider a moment, and suddenly Jem picks up his car keys, and leaves in a shower of large notes and instructions about red wine or white. The Hegartys have had a long day.

Bea, still on her high horse, takes the first shift in the front room while the rest of us stay in the kitchen and mooch and talk. Ernest checks the cupboards — a little intensely, indeed; dipping his finger into ancient mango chutney and sniffing at the mustard. Mossie has the occasional large opinion at the pine table while Ita keeps him company, leaning back against the central counter, too immobilised by drink to wash a plate.

It is like Christmas in Hades. It is like we are all dead, and that's just fine.

One by one we finish and sit, ready to uncork the wine when it arrives. And when it does arrive, we do not toast the dead but merely drink and chat, as ordinary people might do.

There is some talk of the mysterious Alice, also the surprise appearance of Uncle Val, who is looking so spruce.

Then Ivor says that he is thinking of buying up in Mayo.

'What?' says Kitty, who is turning stage Irish with the drink. 'A bit of the old place?'

'Well, maybe not exactly there.'

'Jesus.' Kitty stares ahead as if looking at

it. She needs an angle of attack. We all do. We talk for a while about interest rates and flights to Knock airport.

Then Ernest says, quite mildly, 'Not a lot of money up there.'

'Well, I think that's the point,' says Ivor. And realises he is already on his back foot.

'I don't know,' I say. 'I could never do that isn't-it-all-lovely and aren't-we-all-lovely touristy shite.'

Kitty explodes. 'Uncle Val could live for a month on the price of your jacket. How much was that fucking jacket?'

'Also you're gay, you eejit,' says Jem. 'Maherbeg is where gay men go to shoot themselves in the barn.'

'Oh, so that's where it is,' says Liam. I start to laugh and turn to catch him, but he is not there. He is dead. He is laid out in the next room.

A silence happens, as quick as a door clicking shut.

'It's a nice jacket,' I say.

'Thanks,' says Ivor, trying to figure it all out. He has never been called 'gay' by a member of his family before. Never, not once. Like the bottle in the middle of the table, it only happens elsewhere.

Mossie lifts his eyebrows, and dips his face into his glass. Still down there, he says,

'What is it — Paul Smith?'

'Em . . .' says Ivor, checking the inside pocket. As if he did not know.

Nor do we talk about money — the idea that one of us, even an uncle, might be poor or rich, or that it might matter. Something has happened to this family. The knot has come loose. Then Ita gets up on her hind legs and gives it a yank.

'Yes,' she says. 'What a nice jacket.'

Here it comes. Ita has been drinking so long she has been made sober by it, and slow, and violent. She has some terrible revelation to make and I wonder what it will be. *You never told me I was beautiful.* Or something worse: *You stole my best hairband in 1973* (I did actually). Family sins and family wounds, the endless pricking of something that we find hard to name. None of it important, just the usual, *You ruined my life,* or *What about me?* because with the Hegartys a declaration of unhappiness is always a declaration of blame.

'What?' I say. 'What?'

By which I mean, *What use is the truth to us now?*

'I'm going to sit with Liam,' says Ita, finally, because the Hegartys also love a bit of moral high ground. She pushes herself away from the table at a good angle to hit the door. It's the gin she wants, I realise. The grand exit was just an excuse so she can go and raid her stash.

I reach for the bottle, in a panic, and pour myself another glass. Liam taps his nose at me. But because Liam is dead I have to do it for him. So I tap my nose, three times.

'What?' says Kitty.

'The nose,' I say.

'The what?'

'Ita. The nose job.'

'Oh come on,' she says.

'The tilt,' I say. 'The tilt.'

'I'm with you,' says Ivor, feeling grumpy now that he has lost his country house.

'What do you call that?' I say. 'Retroussé?'

Mossie says, 'What. Are. You. Talking about?'

'The Hegarty nose,' says Kitty. 'Ita's had a job done on our nose.'

'I really think,' says Mossie.

'What?'

'I really think. It's her nose. At this stage.'

And we roar laughing, for some reason.

After the laughter is finished, Kitty and Mossie are left staring at each other across the table. Enough is enough, I think. I can't do the Mossie thing as well as everything else. Yes, he hit us, Kitty. He was fifteen. He hit us all.

I get up to go to the toilet, and meet Bea at the door.

Ita has taken her turn with the corpse. She is leaning against the door jamb of the front room when I pass; a glass of thick water in her hand. She is crying. Or just leaking, perhaps. She does not turn as I climb the stairs. From the back, she looks beautiful. From the back she looks like Lauren Bacall.

I go to the bathroom and pee and wash my hands and look at the same cabinet mirror that has reflected my face for thirty years or so. The silver backing is peeling at the edges. *Who could blame it?* I think. And turn away to go and face them all again downstairs.

When I get out of the bathroom, my mother's door is open, just a crack.

'Bea?' says her voice into the gap. 'Bea?'

'No, Mammy, it's me.'

I go to her. When I open the door fully, I find that she is already back sitting on her bed, weirdly, like a video that has been put on fast forward and then paused.

'What do you want, Mammy, are you all right?'

'I thought you were Bea,' she says.

'No, it's me, Mammy. Do you want me to get her? Is that what you want?'

But she can not quite remember.

'Come on. Into bed, Mammy. Into bed,' and she complies like the sweet child she has always been. She sleeps on her own side, I notice. She still leaves plenty of room.

'They're all gone now,' she says, after she has settled into the pillow.

'No they're not, Mammy.'

'All gone.'

'I'm here, Mammy. Will I sit with you? Will I sit awhile?'

There is no chair in the room. I perch on the end of the bed a moment, and I rub my mother's ankle and foot through the counterpane.

Heh heh, she breathes in like a woman crying. *Haw,* she exhales.

Heh heh. Haw.

Hch heh heh. Haw.

And so, fitfully, she falls asleep, while I sit in the tang of her life: Nivea cream and Je Reviens and old age; the smell of my father, too, still minutely there, in the scorched wool of the electric blanket, maybe, and the slightly rancid paste that holds the paper to the walls.

I am crying, I find. My mother is not asleep but looking at me. Her eyes, as they stare out over the top of the blankets are wide and young.

'Sorry, Mammy.' I stand to go.

'What is it?'

'Nothing,' I say, under this keenly intelligent gaze of hers, that still doesn't quite know who I am.

At the door, I do not look at her as I say, 'Do you remember a man in Granny's?'

'What man?' She was expecting a question. And she doesn't like this one.

'No man in particular. Just a man in Granny's, used to give us sweets on a Friday. What was he called?'

'The landlord?'

'Was he?'

'We always called him the landlord,' she says. And she gives me a most direct look.

'Why?'

'Because he was.'

And, fussed of a sudden, she lifts the covers and swings her legs out over the side of the bed, the unreadable body under her nightie sliding this way and that as she pushes herself off the edge of the mattress and starts to wander about. She goes to the door of the wardrobe and opens it, and shuts it again. She doubles back to the bed, then squints at the top of the wardrobe, in case there might be something up there.

'I don't know,' she says. 'What are you saying to me?'

'Nothing, Mammy.'

'What are you saying to me?'

I look at her.

I am saying that, the year you sent us away, your dead son was interfered with, when you were not there to comfort or protect him, and that interference was enough to send him on a path that ends in the box downstairs. That is what I am saying, if you want to know.

'I just liked the sweets, Mammy. Get back into bed, now. I just remembered the sweets is all.'

Because a mother's love is God's greatest joke. And besides — who is to say what is the first and what is the final cause?

The murmur of voices strengthens in the kitchen below, and there is laughter, followed by the slam of the back door. Kitty again, storming off.

'I don't know.'

Mammy sits back on the bed. She is tired now. She doesn't like anybody now.

'I don't know where it is,' she says. 'The house stuff: it's somewhere up high. It's up on a shelf. I don't know.'

But I have her by the shoulders, and am easing her around, to lie in the bed.

'I'll get Bea for you.'

'Yes,' she says.

'I'll get her for you now.'

But I don't.

I close the door and look around the landing. I go over to the older girls' bedroom, and I look on top of the wardrobes and open the cupboards, then I come out again and do the same in my own old room. I stand on Alice's bed in the dingy yellow light and pull down a biscuit box marked 'Papers' in my mother's weak and flowery hand. I am looking for what she failed to find, but the only things in the box are documents of the most arbitrary kind, certificates of confirmation, Kitty's Irish Dancing; Ernest's Public Speaking at the Feis Maithiu; my degree, strangely enough — my nice fat 2:1 from the NUI; Liam's Leaving Cert., much good to him it is now. It seems that Mammy put away any bit of paper that was thick and rolled and useless. I cast my mind about the house wondering where the important stuff is, birth certificates and death certificates, photographs and contracts and deeds. I know where she keeps them, I think, suddenly, and put the box down on the bed.

But I have disturbed the ghosts. They are outside the door of the room, now, as the ghosts of my childhood once were; they are behind the same door. Their story is there, out on the landing of Griffith Way, waiting for me one more time.

Who are they?

Ada first, pragmatically dead. A thin old thing, she is the kind of ghost who is always turning away. Ada just gets on with being dead. The past is a puddle around her feet.

Charlie is there too, shambling and brown. Charlie, who had no badness in him and yet did everything bad — bad debts, and broken promises, and bad sex with shop girls and housewives and the occasional actress. Wanting his luck to turn, though his luck was always turning, and his luck was always the same. Charlie can not settle in to being dead until he can get it all back for Ada, his one true love.

These are my nightmares. This is what I have to walk through to get downstairs.

I turn the handle of the door and Nugent is a slick of horror on the landing. He moves like smell through the house. Nugent plays with his sister Lizzie, now they are both dead. They kiss each other and are consoled. They do not breathe; the tangle and slither of their tongues is endless and airless and cold.

I get across the two feet of carpet that brings me to the lip of the stairs. I fall down them, one step at a time. I am nine years old, I am six years old, I am four again. I can not put my hand on the banister, in case I touch something I don't understand. The light switch at the bottom seems to recede, the quicker I go. Who turned it off? Why is the light in the hall turned off, when there is a corpse in the house?

The last is always the worst. My Uncle Brendan, in knee socks and short pants. He stands in the hall outside the twins' room, the room where baby Stevie died, and his middle-aged head is full to bursting with all the things he has to tell Ada, that she will not hear him say. Brendan's bones are mixed with other people's bones; so there is a turmoil of souls muttering and whining under his clothes, they would come out in a roar, were he to unbutton his fly; if he opened his mouth they would slop out over his teeth. Brendan has no rest from them, the souls of the forgotten who must always be crawling and bulging and whining in there; he reaches to scratch under his collar and handfuls come loose. The only places clear of them are his unlikeable blue eyes, so Brendan just stares as I reach for the light switch, and his shirt heaves, and his ears leak the mad and the inconvenient dead.

The light comes on. Just as it always used to. And my body, in the light, is a merciful thirty-nine years old. And when I walk into the front room all is silent. There are no ghosts in with Liam's body, not even his own.

The candles have burned low.

In the far alcove, near the window, is a piece of furniture — I think we used to call it 'the dresser' — a thing of heavy oak, with shelves for glasses and vases, and presses down below. I check these presses and find nothing. Which is to say I find everything: an old liquidiser in a clear plastic bag made grey by age; my mother's few 78s from the unlikely time before she was wed, 'Jussi Björling', and 'Furtwängler conducts'; Scrabble; a game called Camel Run; a net bag with four, chipped pieces of artificial fruit; a support bandage for someone's knee that stopped hurting long ago. Then I think to look up. There, behind the ornamental fretwork that crests this thing, are some boxes. I push the doily aside and climb up, and reach for a green shoebox. I poke it down, and catch it, and fumble around the lid, on which my father once wrote the word, 'Broadstone'. Then I climb down and stand on the ground, and open the thing.

Inside, there is a brown paper bag containing a few photographs, all in sepia brown. Some receipts — the kind you would get in an old-fashioned butcher's shop. A thick little fold of letters written on watermarked blue notepaper such as a woman might use, and held with a rubber band. A series of blue hardbacked notebooks, each circled on the vertical by a round of what Ada used to call 'knicker elastic', no matter what she was using it for.

They are rent books; starting in 1937, when my mother was eight years old. The first covers fifteen years, at twelve weeks to a page. The same handwriting, the same fountain pen, on line after line of Fridays, a small increase every year. The fountain pen continues through the second volume and only changes to biro in the third — when the rent is paid monthly, and the handwriting begins to shift to pencil or red biro or whatever came to hand.

What are these doing in our house in Griffith Way, sixteen or more years after the woman died? Why should anyone keep these things, except out of fear — of the long arm of the law, or of the Revenue Commissioners; investigating the tax situation on a house you never owned, and that your mother did not own before you? I have, as I put it back in the box, a sickening sense of what these books meant to the possessor, the rights they might afford.

After 1975 there is nothing. Pages of nothing. I wonder was this the year that Nugent died? I lift the book and turn to show it to Liam, and I see Ada watching us from the doorway. There she is. I see her not as I 'saw' the ghosts on the stairs. I see her as I might see an actual woman standing in the light of the hall.

31

I don't know how the rest of the night went, or who sat up with Liam's body after I left; I suspect Bea and Ernest did the bulk of it, though at one stage, Kitty tells me, they all moved in there and played cards. Apparently, I made a bit of a fuss in the front room. Mossie pushed a sour little pill in my mouth, and Ernest tried to pray with me, but I refused point blank to rest in my old, childhood bed, so they put me in a cab and sent me home.

The empty house, when I got there, was such a blessed relief — I think that is one of the reasons I walk around at night now, to get that feeling again; of sanity and emptiness, of one room giving way so easily to the next. So I stayed up for a while, and then I went upstairs and had sex with my husband for the last time.

That was not my intention, of course. After the night I'd just had it wasn't my intention to have sex of any sort, never mind terminal sex. But I slipped into bed and Tom was awake. And he was in love with me. There is really no point in going over his reasons: he loved me; he wanted to drag me back to the land of the living. And maybe, now that my soul was so soft, he wanted to leave his mark there too. My body was not soft, however. I wondered why he did not notice this. But I did all the moves, and I made way for him, and I did not tell him to stop. So I must have wanted it too, or something like it.

He was not to know what had happened in Griffith Way after he left. Or that I had taken a pill (maybe it was the pill?) or that I felt like meat that had been recently butchered, even as he felt terribly moved. If that is what he felt. He was very gasping and juddery, at any rate, like his nerves were all alight.

Afterwards, we lay face to face, buried up to the neck in the duvet. We have said too much to each other, over the years. We are judiciously silent.

But he needs to say one more thing.

'I'm sorry,' he says.

I think for a moment that he is apologising for the horrible sex, then I think he is sorry about the death of my brother, but in fact he is sorry for some infidelity he has committed in the past — he will tell me in a moment how little she meant — and this will be so silly and unbearable under the circumstances (I have just, I realise, slept with my husband for the last time), that I forestall him by saying, 'It's all right. It's all right.'

He takes this as a sign. Everything is going to get better. He says I should do something. Work part-time, or take a daily walk at least — what about a house, what about getting a house and doing it up, now that the market's on the move? Money. I could earn money. He says he has been too busy, he's had a bit of a dip, but that we are out of the woods, he is over it now. And I say, 'A *dip*?'

He says, 'Please, not that again.'

I say, 'Your daughters will sleep with men like you. Men who will hate them, just because they want them.'

And he says, 'What?' He says, 'Jesus, you know. It's just . . .'

'Just what?'

I think he means that there is a limit to these things, to the way men think. That it isn't real. That no one gets killed, for example. I think he means that this side-by-

314

side business is all we've got.

He is probably right. So I lie there, side by side with him, and I contemplate the spreading bruise of my private parts.

'Funny thing about men's bodies,' I say. 'They never lie. That must be handy. I mean you're built to tell the truth. On / off. Like / don't like. Want / don't want.'

And Tom says, 'Not really.' There is no reliable connection, he says, between what you want and what your mickey wants; sometimes it's hard to tell.

'Oh,' I say, and roll over, and go to sleep.

32

It was Ita at the door, of course, I should have known. It was not Ada, it was my addled older sister; psychotic with drink, and with a stupid new nose.

This is what I remembered, when I saw her.

I remembered a picture. I don't know what else to call it. It is a picture in my head of Ada standing at the door of the good room in Broadstone.

I am eight.

Ada's eyes are crawling down my shoulder and my back. Her gaze is livid down one side of me; it is like a light: my skin hardens under it and crinkles like a burn. And on the other side of me is the welcoming darkness of Lambert Nugent. I am facing into that darkness and falling. I am holding his old penis in my hand.

But it is a very strange picture. It is made up of the words that say it. I think of the 'eye' of his penis, and it is pressing against my own eye. I 'pull' him and he keels towards me. I 'suck' him and from his mouth there protrudes a narrow, lemon sweet.

This comes from a place in my head where words and actions are mangled. It comes from the very beginning of things, and I can not tell if it is true. Or I can not tell if it is real. But I am sickened by the evil of him all the same, I am sweltering in it; the triangles of blackness under his sharp cheek-bones, the way his head turns slowly and his eyes spin, slower still, in their sockets, towards the light of the opening door where my grandmother stands.

I do not believe in evil — I believe that we are human and fallible, that we make things and spoil them in an ordinary way — and yet I experience the slow turn of his face towards the door as evil. There is a bubble rising in his old chest: a swelling of something that might, at any moment, shoot out of his opening mouth and stain the entire world.

What is it?

I can not move. In this memory or dream, I can neither stop it, nor make it continue. Whatever comes out of his mouth will horrify me, though I know it can not harm me.

It will fill the world but not mark it. It is there already in the damp of the carpet and the smell of Germolene: the feeling that Lamb Nugent is mocking us all; that even the walls are oozing his sly intent. The pattern on the wallpaper repeats to nausea, while hot in my grasp, and straight and, even at this remove of years, lovely, Nugent's wordless thing bucks, proud and weeping in my hand.

And the word that he says, when the door is fully open and his mouth is fully open, the bubble that bursts in the O of his mouth is the single word:

'Ada.'

Of course.

Is she pleased with what she sees? Does this please her?

When I try to remember, or imagine that I remember, looking into Ada's face with Lamb Nugent's come spreading over my hand, I can only conjure a blank, or her face as a blank. At most, there is a word written on Ada's face, and that word is, 'Nothing'.

This is the moment for blame. The soiled air of Ada's good room will rush out past her, as she stands in the yellow light of the hall. This is the moment when we realise that it was Ada's fault all along.

The mad son and the vague daughter. The

vague daughter's endlessly vague pregnancies, the way each and every one of her grandchildren went vaguely wrong. This is the moment when we ask what Ada did — for it must, surely, have been something — to bring so much death into the world.

But I do not blame her. And I don't know why that is.

I owe it to Liam to make things clear — what happened and what did not happen in Broadstone. Because there are effects. We know that. We know that real events have real effects. In a way that unreal events do not. Or nearly real. Or whatever you call the events that play themselves out in my head. We know there is a difference between the brute body and the imagined body, that when you really touch someone, something really happens (but not, somehow, what you had expected).

Whatever happened to Liam did not take place in Ada's good room — no matter what picture I have in my head. Nugent would not have been so stupid. The abuse happened in the garage, among the cars and bits of engine that Liam loved. And Nugent was horrible to my brother in ordinary ways, too, out there. He had his sadisms, I am sure, and his methods. I have to make this clear because, somewhere in my head, in some obstinate and God-forsaken part of me, I think that desire and love are the same thing. They are not the same thing, they are not even connected. When Nugent desired my brother, he did not love him in the slightest.

That's as much as I know.

I could also say that Liam must have wanted him too. Or wanted *something.*

'Now look at what you've got,' says Nugent, as I cry and drive my car around the night-lit streets of Dublin town. 'Now look at what you've got.'

As for myself — I don't think I liked the garage and I never went in there much. Though when I drive these nights, and when I stop the car, I wonder, among other things, did it happen to me too.

What can I say? I don't think so.

I add it in to my life, as an event, and I think, well yes, that might explain some things. I add it into my brother's life and it is crucial; it is the place where all cause meets all effect, the crux of the X. In a way, it explains too much.

These are the things I do, actually know.

I know that my brother Liam was sexually abused by Lambert Nugent. Or was probably sexually abused by Lambert Nugent.

These are the things I don't know: that I was touched by Lambert Nugent, that my Uncle Brendan was driven mad by him, that my mother was rendered stupid by him, that my Aunt Rose and my sister Kitty got away. In short, I know nothing else about Lambert Nugent; who he was and how Ada met him; what he did, or did not do.

I know he could be the explanation for all of our lives, and I know something more frightening still — that we did not have to be damaged by him in order to be damaged. It was the air he breathed that did for us. It was the way we were obliged to breathe his second-hand air.

Here I am back in St Dympna's, with ink on my tongue. Liam does not sleep with me any more. I wear my knickers to bed. Then I get up and put on my tights. Then I get up and put on my school blouse; it is important to be ready, when the time comes. I get up again and put my gymslip over the back of a chair. I put my shoes under the chair, and turn the lot to face the door, so that when I dress I will not have to turn around to leave the room. Then I get up and fold my sash and put it in the right shoe, with the end trailing out along the floor. Then I get up and put the gymslip on, after which I fall asleep.

In school, I smell tired. The box pleats of my gymslip are all shattered. I can not leave the feel of the sheets behind — ghost sheets rubbing and slipping against my gymslip, as my body turns in the bed, this way and that. Liam sleeps on the far side of the room, Kitty sleeps beside me. In front of me Sister Benedict teaches us how to pray:

As I lay me down to sleep
I pray the Lord my soul to keep
And if I die before I wake
I pray the Lord my soul to take.

33

'If the Virgin Mary was assumed bodily into heaven, then where does She go to the toilet?'

'What did you say?' Daddy is looking at me.

'If the Virgin Mary was assumed bodily into heaven, then where does She go to the toilet?' and my father has hit me before I see his hand move.

This was shortly after we came back from Ada's, when I was in the height of my religious phase.

I remember it because, although my father used to hit his children all the time, more or less, it was never personal. He might slap three at a time and let the fourth go or he might stomp among us with his hand raised as we ran, shrieking, around him. The boys were different, of course, but in the main my father hit us, not because he was in charge, but because we were in charge. That is why, when Kitty starts throwing accusations around about hitting, I can not quite sympathise.

But, BOK! the sound of all sound being sucked away from the side of your head, a numb silence that is cut through, after a while, by an expanding ring of pain.

The question was almost worth it, though — because it is the only evidence I possess that our father was a Catholic. Of course Mammy is a Catholic, in the way that Mammys are, but for fourteen years or so I sat by or behind my father, on a wooden church bench, every Sunday morning and in all that time I never saw his lips move. I never heard him pray aloud, or saw him bend his head, or do anything that might be considered remarkable were he sitting on the top deck of a bus. When it was time for Communion he stood at the end of the bench as we trooped by, like letting sheep out at a gate, but I don't know if he ever followed us up to the Communion rail. My father attended church in his official capacity. If I went looking for his personal belief I would not know where to begin, or in what part of his body it might inhere.

I think about him at Liam's removal. Ernest is on the altar in his priestly robes. The embroidery down his front has a Mayan theme, and he looks very fine.

The diminishing Hegartys are sitting in the front row in order of age. Ernest enjoins us all to pray and I place my father's stubby hands together, I fumble them a little around his lips, 'Oh Lord,' I say in his voice: but it all lacks conviction — which is to say, his conviction. My father was never pious and I do not think he was afraid of hellfire — so when he had the sex that produced the twelve children and seven miscarriages that happened inside my mother's body (which is kneeling now at the end of the line), then that was all he was doing — he was having sex. It was nothing to do with what the priests told him or didn't tell him, it was just something he needed to do, or wanted to do; it was just something he felt he deserved.

He did love my mother. There is always that unpalatable fact — the fact that my father loved my mother, and she loved him right back. But he did not love her enough to leave her alone. No. My father, I suspect, had sex the way his children get drunk — which is to say, against his better judgement; not for the pleasure of it, so much as to make it all *stop.*

This is the nearest I can get to the impulse that made the child who now lies in the coffin in the centre of the aisle. Because Liam, in his box, is a boy again. He does not fill it more than three-quarters of the way down. The years are drifting away from him. The years are being metabolised, until he pees the last of them out, standing by the railings of the Basin in Broadstone, at nine years old.

Wheee!

All the Hegarty children have a hangover, including the one in the box. It is a very peaceful, precious kind of feeling; a swelling of the senses, between pain and warmth. Liam has the biggest one, of all, of course, because Liam finally got really wasted. He got a skinful. Liam finally got out of his head. He will be sleeping his one off, for a while.

At the end of the line, Mammy has been rendered transparent by sweetness and suffering. Bea stands beside her, attending church in an official capacity, just like Daddy used to do. Next is Mossie who says the responses out clear. The rest of us mumble and are silent. On one side of me, Kitty is hunched and fervent (but fervently *what* — that is the question), while on the other, Ita sits, her a mind like a stone.

I try to believe in something, just for the heck of it. I pluck some absolute out of the air, some expanding thought that will open in my head like ether — God, or the future, or the greater good. I bow my head and try to believe that love will make it better, or if love won't then children will. I turn from the high to the humble and believe, for many seconds at a time, in the smallness and the necessity of being a mother.

But it's all a bit *nice,* for a Hegarty. Belief needs something terrible to make it work, I find — blood, nails, a bit of anguish.

So I catch my anguish. I look at Liam's coffin and try to believe in love.

Not easy.

I do remember God's love, that year in Ada's when I was eight, and Liam was nine. I remember it very clearly. Sister Benedict told us to take Jesus 'into our hearts' and I did, no problem. I check my heart now, and I find that there is still a feeling there, of something hot and struggling. I roll my eyes back under my closed lids, and there is the sense of opening in the middle of my forehead. The chest thing is like fighting for words and the forehead thing is pure and empty, like after all the words have been said.

There now.

Belief. I have the biology of it. All I need is the stuff to put in there. All I need are the words.

After Daddy hit me across the side of the head, he turned and walked away, in utter silence. He may have shocked himself. He certainly shocked me. But the truth was that I did not believe in heaven then, and never would. And when I thought about hell, it was just very quiet.

34

Here is Ada, sitting on the sofa in the good room in Broadstone. She has a piece of work in her hands, simple work, it must have been some hemming or darning. There is an eight-year-old girl in the room, who is me.

I remember the curve of her back; her hands, dropped in her lap; the pick and lift of her fingers as she teases the thread through. The sofa behind her is a dark red, overlaid with a tangle of cushions, though Ada does not lean back into them. The two Turkish rolls with tassels at the end, from the set of some seraglio at the Gate Theatre; a red velvet round cushion with loose smocking around the rim, like the tread on a fabulous, fabric car; a series of little logs, their covers made out of metallic thread in purple and brown striations, like bark in a theatrical wood.

She sits in front of them all, and bends a

little over her work, her head occasionally pulling back the extra distance required of old age. But she does not look old to me. She looks content, of a piece; she looks completely like herself. I go to sit beside her and she nods slightly my way — and when she is finished that particular stitch or twist, she reaches without looking up, and rubs her knuckles against my cheek.

'Hello.'

That is what I remember.

Nobody left and nobody came. Charlie was elsewhere, Mr Nugent did not matter, Liam and Kitty were doing homework, perhaps, on the dining-room table, and I was with Ada in the shrine of her good room, the red velvet theatre curtains giving on to the street, and the signed photos on the wall, Jimmy O'Dee, the Adare sisters, a drawing marked 'Othello' of a man with a brown face and an elegant, pointed foot. They were all figures in a play that was happening elsewhere. And here, offstage, was the place to be, with Ada who could not be anyone else, even if she tried, who walked through her life with a perfect civility; quiet, a little harsh sometimes — though she never let on just how harsh she might be. Sitting there, entire in herself, Ada sews. Her past is behind her, her future is of little concern.

She moves towards the grave, at her own speed.

And I, caught for a moment by the sight of the cloth in her lap, watch one stitch more, maybe two, before standing up and running out of the room.

35

The rent books only start in 1939 — which makes me imagine, briefly, that Charlie owned the house once, but lost it to Nugent on a horse. I doubt this could be true, but the after-image still lingers: Charlie out at Leopardstown with Nugent like a crow over him at the rails, with his coat tail lifting in the breeze.

'There you go,' says Charlie, desperately insouciant, handing over a last slip of paper to the man who loves his wife better, or at least sharper, than he.

'On the nose.'

But Nugent did not look like a crow, he looked like an ordinary man, I do remember that, though all I can recall of him absolutely is the peculiar growth in his ear, a perfect little bulb of shiny pink, and the leaning-backness of him in the wing-chair, on a Friday in the good front room.

■ ■ ■ ■

I bring the girls over to my mother's one
Saturday, as I have taken to doing since
Liam died, and I ask her, in an ordinary
way, where she lived first, before Broadstone; what house they were in, before they
moved to the house I knew.

'What?' she says, looking at me like I
might be a stranger, after all.

'When you were little, Mammy. Where did
you live when you were little?'

'Around the corner,' she says, and is
distressed by the fact. 'I think we lived
around the corner.'

The past is not a happy place. And the
pain of it belongs to her more than it does
to me, I think. Who am I to claim it for my
own? My poor mother had twelve children.
She could not stop giving birth to the
future. Over and over. Twelve futures. More.
Maybe she liked having all those babies.
Maybe she had more past than most people,
to wipe clear.

The letters I found are on blue writing
paper, watermarked with the crest of Basil-
don Bond. There are maybe fifteen of them
in all, each signed L. Nugent, or Lambert

Nugent, and each more banal than the last. There are gaps and lapses, into which I read anger or desire. I would do that, that is what I do, but they are, at the very least, intriguingly mute.

Dear Mrs Spillane,
I am afraid I can not offer any rebate on the six shillings owing since Easter last. The work you have had done on the hall skirting board was undertaken without any prior, and can not be considered as 'in lieu'. I will be seeking the full amount when your rental next falls.
Yours sincerely
Lambert Nugent

Dear Mrs Spillane,
Believe me when I say that I have your best interests at heart in the matter of the back garage, which feeds anyway into the back laneway.
Yours sincerely
Lambert Nugent

Dear Mrs Spillane,
You know yourself what I mean. I mean that Christmas meant nothing in the scheme of things, which stand as

they have always stood in this matter.

The cistern man will be there on Tuesday and I will pay for him <u>myself.</u>

My best regards to your husband, Mr Spillane.

Yrs

Lambert Nugent

Dear Mrs Spillane,

In the question of seven shillings and sixpence, it may well be your husband will have it after the 5th. I will want it on the day, however.

Yrs

L. Nugent

Dear Mrs Spillane,

I can not afford you what you seek in the matter of the tenancy. By sub-letting to Mrs McEvoy, you are in contravention of all agreements in this matter and I am quite entitled, as you will find, to seek an increase or find another tenant, which I am, as you know, very slow to do. I am very much in my rights.

Hoping to continue an arrangement that is suitable to all concerned,

Yrs

Lambert Nugent

Dear Mrs Spillane,

Here is the receipt for the ceiling on the boxroom.

Yrs
LN

Dear Mrs Spillane,

My son tells me that you have had a bit of a scare and I wanted to send you my very best and good wishes for a speedy recovery. I will not send Nat down on Friday, but come myself, if I may.

Yrs sincerely
Lambert Nugent

Although it was Nugent who died first, in the end.

It seems to me that it was a relationship of sudden pique and petty cruelty. I may be wrong — this may just be the way that landlords speak to their tenants. But there is a sense of thrall to it, too; of Nugent working in the garage, that he owned, at the back of the house and then walking round to the door, that he owned, at the front, and knocking. It makes the ritual of the tea and biscuits a savage enough little one, on his part, and Ada at her most charming — her most, you might say, sexy — because that is what women on their back foot are like. Thirty-eight years of so many shillings per week; her whole life dribbled away into his hand. Thirty-eight years of *bamboozling* him with her female charms, while he sat there and took it, and liked it, because he thought it was his due.

And *he loved her!* I say, poor fool that I am. *He must have loved her!*

But when it came to love, Nugent was just a small-timer; he didn't have much of it to throw around. He had the house, and he had the woman, more or less, and he did what he liked with the children passing through. Even his gratifications were small. Because children in those days were of little account. We three Hegartys were manifestly *of little account.*

When Nugent saw a child he saw revenge — I have no doubt about that — and a way out of it all; the whole tedious business of human exchange that a man has to go through in order to get what he might want.

Think of it. The bitterness of the man and the beauty of the boy.

36

One night I give up steering the car one way or the other and let it go where it wants, which is north, as always, this time past the hump of Howth Head and on to the Swords road, all the way to Portrane.

I make my way past the asylum and turn down to the sea, then I stop at the gate of the small field, in the middle of whose rubbish is my uncle's mathematical head. More than five thousand people are buried here, according to Ernest, who knows the local priest. I am not surprised. A cube of panic rises out of these walls. The air at the gates has the same hum as you find under high-voltage wires.

I stand for a while, and feel my hair stand to.

The moon is up. In the distance a line of white wave unfurls itself along the strand, and makes no sound. The sea slaps at the rocks below me, upset by cross-currents and by some distant storm. There is no wind.

I stand there and think that there is no worse place for me to go. This is the worst place there is.

In which case, it is not too bad. If this is as mad as I get then it is not too mad. My children will not be harmed by it; though I may have to change my life a little; get out more, trade in the Saab.

This week's property supplement — Tom's little offering on the kitchen table — had a house for sale on Ada's street. It is not Ada's house, or not yet; but everyone is selling and moving, it might come up any time. I could stalk it, Ada's house. I could buy this house up the road, and make it over, and sell on, until the day comes — not too far away, I feel sure — when I am standing in Ada's front room, pulling up a corner of the wallpaper, talking to some nice architect about gutting the place. I will wear a sober trouser suit and incredibly silly heels and click-clack my way across the bare boards, while telling him to rip out the yellow ceiling and the clammy walls; to knock down the doorway to the front room, but save the Belfast sink in the little kitchen, over which, looking out the back window, I learned how to imagine things. We will exclaim together, my architect and I, over the little ceiling rose, and the pretty fireplace where things were burnt: letters, bookies' dockets, pork fat, the hair from Ada's hairbrush going in with a sizzle. I will ask him to get the place cleaned out with something really strong, I don't want a woman with a mop, I will say, I want a team of men in boiler suits with tanks on their backs and those high-pressure steel rods.

And the garage — we will turn the garage into a studio space, with skylights and white walls, and I will put wide plank flooring over the old cement. Oak.

'What do you think about oak?' I will say.

I will rent the house out for a while. And I will be nice to the tenants. And when I am finished. When I am good and finished. When I have beaten the shit out of the place and made it smell, in a wonderfully clean but old-fashioned way, of wood soap and peonies, I will sell it on for twice the price.

Is that all right, Liam?

There he is. Standing at the water's edge, looking out over the waves.

Is that all right?

He looks like an extra in a film. He is wearing a baggy brown suit, that he would never wear in real life, and a Paddy cap over his young curly black hair. His eyes of Irish blue crinkle at the corners as he looks out into the night. He is not alone. There is another man further up, there is a boy standing on a headland; at each peak and promontory these watchers stand, looking out to sea.

It is like a Guinness ad, but no one moves.

Overhead, a huge plane comes in to land. The first of the day, trailing Arctic frost. New York, Newfoundland, Greenland, Portrane. It is six a.m. Time for me to turn home.

I get in the car, and reach for the key, gone cold in the ignition. It is March. It is nearly five months since Liam died. Ciara's baby, who met him coming in the door, is now one month old. My own last child, the one I might have with Tom, is getting tired waiting. I turn the key and start the car.

Liam turns to watch me as I go. He does not know who I am, or what the sea is, or what sort of a place Broadstone might be. He is full of his own death. His death fills him as a plum fills its own skin. Even his eyes are full. It is a serious business, being dead. He would like to do it well. He turns from the confusing lights of the car, and sets his face towards the sea.

I drive back up to the main road, but the car does not turn for home. I go to the airport instead and, after a little while, I get on a plane.

37

Suicides always pull a good crowd. People push in: they clog the doors and sidle along the back benches, gathering on the rim of the church: they turn up on principle, because a suicide has left everyone behind.

I wish they had stayed at home.

I stand in the church porch waiting for the mourners' car to arrive from Griffith Way. Tom is chasing Emily along a bench. Rebecca stands beside me and will not let go of my hand. I am glad I have got the distraction of children among these people, strangers and friends, who check my face and will not say hello, or not yet. I fuss around the kids, and scold Emily and send them off with their father: he will need a head start to get them past the box at the top of the aisle.

A woman makes her way towards me through the crowd. I know her from somewhere — if I could just remember from where, then her name might come to me, and what she might want. She has been crying, that is the disconcerting thing. Anyone can slobber over you, I think, once you are dead.

She is tall and pale and black-haired and this should be enough, I should recognise her by this, and by the slightly harried look she has of a woman both wounded and mild. She looks around until she finds me — I knew it was me she was looking for — and she comes over, pushing her way through the other people with awkward grace. She is all hip and shoulder, in a mushroom-coloured trench coat and a beige jersey dress.

And then I remember her from that awful visit Liam made, the one when I had the builders in, and there was no floor in the girls' bedrooms, in the middle of which mayhem, Liam arrives with this woman who seems to have no opinions about anything at all. Not even about what she wants to eat.

I don't know how long Liam lived with her or slept in her single bed, or did whatever he did with these disastrous girls. And I can not, for the life of me, remember her name. But I do remember loving her a little, by the time they left for Mayo; with her long

344

nervous hands, and her blue-veined skin, and her hair in a drippy chignon. I do remember hoping that she would give him some rest.

She is older now, though the same sense of flickering hurt is there, as the stained-glass colours fly up her chest and pull at the corner of her eye. But this is gone by the time she reaches me. She levels her face at me, and is full of the story she has to tell. It is pushing its way out through her, this thing. It is not, in any way, her fault.

And I still can not remember her name.

'Did Kitty get you?' I say. 'It's a long way to come.'

And suddenly I feel very Irish as I reach out to take her hand in both my hands, to thank her for making the journey, to welcome her in and allow her to grieve.

'You'll come back to the hotel? Do you know where it is? Will you want a lift?'

'I just came,' she says. 'I just arrived.'

'You heard?' I say, meaning his suicide, and she nods, as if this was slightly beside the point.

'This is Rowan,' she says, reaching round to extract a child from behind her elegant legs, and I look down, for the first time, at my brother's son.

He has a curious large head and forward-

leaning little body and I realise, after a
second, that this is because he is only three
years old. Because he is only three — going
on four — years old, his head pivots beautifully on the stem of his neck as his face tilts
up to examine me, with my brother's blue
eyes, though when his mother tells him to,
'Say hello,' he squirms round the back of
her trench coat again. He peers out and
dives back, and I realise that I am supposed
to play hide-and-seek with this child. I am
supposed to duck and weave around either
side of his mother's narrow thighs. And I
do. I say, 'Hello Rowan,' and 'Were you on
an aeroplane?' Then I say, 'Hello Rowan,'
again, 'Hello sweetie-pie,' wondering how I
can trick or induce this child into my arms
and, after a while, kiss him, or inhale him.
How I will steal or filch permission to rub
my cheek along the skin of his back, and
play the bones of his spine, and blow thick
kisses into the softness of his arms? Perhaps
over time. Perhaps I will be able to do it
over time.

'Oh, he's terribly like,' I say to his mother,
whose name, I realise, is Sarah. I knew all
along that this is what she was called.

'Yes,' she says.

And the look that passes between us is
one of absolute regard.

'Will you come and sit with us?' I say, indicating the top of the church, though I know this might not be the best moment to break the news.

'No,' she says. 'Oh, no. I'm sorry, I just got in.'

'That's all right,' I say. 'You'll come back after?'

'Oh, I think so,' she says. 'I think I should.'

'Yes, you should. You should.'

The mourners' car has arrived outside, but I can not, I find, leave the boy. I get down on my hunkers and I smile. He hides again. I reach out my arms and he edges further back. He knows my need for him is too great. And then, evil person that I am, I say, 'Afterwards, you know, if you come back with all of us, there will be *buckets and buckets* of ice cream.'

He likes that one all right.

Here they come: my mother, tiny and round and bobbing on Bea's elegant arm. Mossie on the other side, also tall, and handsome in the way that professional men can be; his gentle wife; his three too-perfect children; Ita in a slow march; the twins, Ivor and Jem, who bump together and separate, all the way up the aisle. Kitty, my little sister, stops to take my hand, in a quietly theatrical way. As I turn to leave, Sarah nods to say that she will not disappear, that she knows who she is, and what she has come here for.

I make my way up to the top of the church and am drowned in the emotion, whether love or sadness, that floods my chest. My face sets into the mask of a woman weeping, one half pulled into a wail that the other half will not allow. There are no tears. My head twists away from whichever side of the church is more interested in my grief, only to show it to the other side. Here it is. The slow march of the remaining Hegartys. I don't know what wound we are showing to them all, apart from the wound of family. Because, just at this moment, I find that being part of a family is the most excruciating possible way to be alive.

Tom turns, and when he sees my face, he stops. He hands me in to the seat in front of him, and the girls follow me on the other side.

'All right?' he says, slipping his hand over mine, while Emily turns in to cling to me — or, if the truth be told, to stroke my breasts while pretending to admire (or console, perhaps) the covered buttons of my good, funeral coat.

'Leave your mother alone,' says Tom.

Indeed. I have been so much touched

these last few days. I cross my legs over the memory of the sex we had the night of the wake. Or he had. And wait for the Mass to begin. Everyone wants a bit of me. And it has nothing to do with what I might want, or what my body might want, whatever that might be — God knows it is a long time since I knew. There I am, sitting on a church bench in my own meat: pawed, used, loved, and very lonely.

Actually, I do know what I want. I want whoever touched the small of my back in Mammy's kitchen to declare himself. To say, again, that everything will be all right. Because I felt someone's loving touch, and I was — but completely — reassured by it, before I turned to see that there was no one there.

Also, I want Rowan. I yearn for him, not with lips or hands, but with my entire face. My skin wants him. I want to nuzzle him, and feel his light hair tickle my chin. I want to flutter my eyelashes against his cheek.

This spooling fantasy runs through my head through all that follows: the Mass and the stupid old priest and Ernest's few words from the altar.

Liam was never interested in material things, says Ernest. He had a great sense of humour.

'My brother had a rage for justice,' he says, not mentioning how this might turn to bus-kicking, in drink. But it is done well enough. The words are well enough spoken, while behind me, my great, and soon-to-be-broken, secret shouts, 'Hallo! Hallo!' in broad South London at the back of the church.

We do the whole thing. We follow the box out down the aisle again and as soon as we hit open air, I say it to Tom.

'Do you remember the girl? That girl who came with him the last time, or the second-last time.'

'What girl?'

'Remember the girl who wouldn't eat, with a face on her, when we had the builders in?'

'I don't know,' he says.

'He was horrible to her.'

'Oh, yeah. Her.'

'She was pregnant,' I say. 'She was pregnant at the time.'

'By him?'

'Oh, there's no doubting the child,' I said. 'It's Liam. To the life.'

The Hegartys are stuck in the porch, shaking five hundred people's hands. I don't know half of them, and I don't care. I am waiting for Sarah to come through so I can take her aside and figure how to do this thing.

'I'm very sorry for your trouble.'

'Thank you.'

'I'm very sorry.'

'It's a great loss.'

All of them apologising for the fact that someone you love is dead, when the world is full of people you don't.

'I knew him at school,' says one man to me, transforming, even as the words happen, from a middle-aged stranger to Willow of the vodka naggin and the beautiful older brother. He is absolutely himself, and this confuses me. I can't get the picture of a middle-aged man back, now that I know who he is.

'Oh, Willow,' I say, like a schoolgirl fool. Love is one thing, but there are so many people in the world to like, that we never see.

It's a heady business, burying the dead.

I wait until we are at the hotel, and even then I am reluctant to break the news. I can not hand it to Bea, the owner of all the Hegartys. I can't expose it to Ivor's irony, or Ita's intelligence, or Mossie's wonderful *management skills*. I need a child to do this, or a grown-up child.

'Come here, Jem,' I say to my little brother; the youngest and best loved. And I watch him go round the others; Mammy last. Bea tries to make her sit down, but she will not sit down. Mammy stands up and undoes the top button of her blouse, and, wild-eyed, pulls off her coat, casting around her as she does so, stuck in the second sleeve. She finds Sarah and the child, as Bea yanks the last of the coat off her arm, and she hurries over, runs even, to set her hands on the child's shoulders, then up on either side to graze his lovely face. She looks at Sarah, with a terrible contract in her eye, and Sarah steps forward, very politely, to shake her hand. After which, as though none of this had happened, Mammy turns away.

It is hard to describe the effect of the boy on the assembled Hegartys.

'Rowan?' they say. *'Rowan.'*

It is like we had never seen a child before. He has the Hegarty eyes, we say — delighted, like they weren't a curse — and we look to see what human being looks out through them, this time. It is too uncanny. Everyone wants to touch him. They just have to — they reach out and he shies away; flinches, even. The one he chooses for safe haven is, of all people, Mossie, who sits him on one long leg and jounces him, hard, *Ride a cock horse,* threatening to spill him on to the floor. Mossie, who was for Liam a dark mirror, loves the boy and the boy loves him. Mossie's own children gather round, and for the first time I see how happy they are — that is why they are so well-behaved, with their gentle mother and their father who is *firm but fair:* they are content.

This seems like an amazing thing to notice about your own brother, after so many years — it is almost more amazing than the fact of Liam's son. Maybe that is because the accident of Liam's son is too fantastic to contemplate, in the middle of a hotel reception room, in the suburbs of Dublin, where two hundred people I sort of know are sitting down to soup or melon, followed by salmon or beef.

We eat it all up. Down to the apple tart and ice cream. We do not stint. We put slabs of butter on bad white rolls, and we ask for second cups of tea. I am inordinately interested in the food. I look up from my plate to Rowan and then I look down again to stab a potato croquette.

There are other things to notice, whenever I have the strength to pull my eyes away from the boy. Ivor talking to Liam's friend Willow for several moments too long. A look that passes between them and the priest, no less, who gets his coat and looks again, before he goes out the door. Ernest sees this last glance too and takes note. And there is Ita sitting at a right angle to Ernest, holding on to his forearm with both hands and talking into the side of his face, which has that drawn, mortified look I remember from confession. Someone has given Kitty a microphone, and she stands there while Mossie taps a glass with his knife. Then she lays the microphone down on the table, and lifts her face to sing, with utter sweetness, Liam's favourite song:

> Let us pause in life's pleasures
> And count its many tears,
> While we all sup sorrow with the poor;
> There's a song that will linger
> For ever in our ears;
> Oh, hard times come again no more.

But of course. This stupid thing. I have to push hard against my eyelids, the tears are so sudden and sharp.

> 'Tis the song, the sigh of the weary,
> Hard times, hard times,
> Come again no more;
> Many days you have lingered
> Around my cabin door,

Oh, hard times come again no more.

A ragged consensus gathers under the chorus, but, by some miracle, they let her sing the verse alone: my annoying little sister, looking at the ceiling with innocent eyes, as she takes each note and tenderly lays it down.

> While we seek mirth and beauty
> And music light and gay,
> There are frail forms fainting at the door;
> Though their voices are silent,
> Their pleading looks will say
> Oh, hard times come again no more.

There isn't a dry eye in the house. On Mossie's knee Rowan grows indignant, as he watches his mother wipe away the tears.

'Shut up,' he says suddenly. Then louder, 'Shut uhhhhp!' in his sweet English accent, and everyone laughs. I have never been to a happier funeral.

I push back my chair and go out to find a cigarette.

It is many years since I smoked. We all gave up, one way or another, after Daddy died, so I have to accost one of the neighbours with this oddly intimate request.

'I couldn't take one of these off you?

Would you mind?'

'Work away. Work away.'

I go and sit in the foyer, and I smoke. The cigarette tastes like the first cigarette I ever had, sitting on Liam's mattress in the garden passage, in 1974.

38

The day she hears that Lambert Nugent has died, Ada orders a cup of coffee in Bewley's — nothing fancy, just a white coffee and a custard slice, waitress service, and when they arrive, she picks off her gloves, with the same twitching precision that caught Nugent's eye, many years before. So, he is dead. She sips the coffee and cuts the custard slice into small pieces, which she eats, one after the other, until she is done.

Ada is worried about the rent — even though she has no need to worry about the rent; she took advice about the rent, years ago. Some other man will come and take it — some man she does not care about, one way or the other, and it will be the same money and the same little house, and the same life she leads inside it. Even so she felt it had broken loose, that the bricks and the slates and the granite lintels had been set sailing on a calm, grey sea.

It was over. Whatever the story between them had been.

Old Nolly May.

Or even, as they sometimes said, Nolly May Tangerine — from the 'Do not touch me' of the Bible.

And why not? Why should he not be touched?

'Isn't he a card?' as she used to say of Lamb Nugent, after this or that comment, some implication: her profligacy at the butchers, or the necessity of Christmas. 'He's all heart,' she used to say, by which she meant that, on the day he died, she would order a quiet custard slice in Bewley's, and really quite enjoy it.

Ada is seventy years old, which for a certain kind of woman, is not really old at all. She is always on the go and she might have twenty years in front of her (although she does not have twenty years in front of her), Ada does not count. At seventy, she lies in bed, like the rest of us, thinking of the warmth and texture of the last doctor's hands. Her own hands, as she unsheathes them from her black leather gloves, are skinny and restless: a tangle of strings and knobs and bones, like ship's rigging. Who needs a doctor, when your body is busy coming out through you, to display its working parts? Ada is fond of her hands, even a little proud — they have been so clever, over the years. As for the rest of her body, she is not bothered to check, having long ago fallen out with the mirror, that seems to supply her with no useful information any more — none whatsoever.

But her hands, as they slowly dip the spoon, so the coffee chases itself up through the crust of sugar, her hands have done good service. They have stitched and un-picked. They have done their insect work, and changed, as an ant might change, the surface of the earth.

And as she sucks the sticky tip of the spoon Charlie is there in front of her, bow-ing over a paper bag and saying, 'Oh, comfort me with apples,' at the Fairyhouse Races, a lifetime ago.

A very Protestant thing to say, she thinks suddenly — quoting the Old Testament like that. And she wonders for the thousandth time, whether her husband was the man he said he was, at all.

If Ada had reached any sort of conclusion in this life, it was a little one. *People,* she used to think, *do not change, they are merely revealed.* This maxim she has applied, with the flattest satisfaction, to turncoat politi-cians, and unfaithful spouses, and wild boys who turned out right in the end. She applies it now to the memory of Charlie Spillane and to his true heart, that only became more intensely, and importantly true to her over the years. If people were only revealed by time, then the man who was revealed to her in Charlie Spillane was endlessly good — just that — with all his evasions and his regrets, his eye for a filly and for the main chance, the thing that her husband was had burned more clear for her, since he had died.

It was a great mystery: goodness.

Ada presses the pad of her finger into the last flakes of pastry, then fails to put it to her mouth. She rubs the stuff off, to fall on the floor, and she misses her husband, and all the men she once knew who are now dead. They each left a quality behind; something distinctive and hard to catch. If Ada believed in anything she believed in this persistence, that other people might call the soul.

In which case Lambert Nugent had none, or none that she could find. Nugent was the kind of man who flared up on you; the rest of the time he was hardly there at all. The ardent youth, the trembling man, the white flame of his old age; she had seen each of these in glimpses, the rest was a murk of small remarks and glances elsewhere, of things withdrawn before they were shown.

What did the silly man have to hide?

As Nugent aged, his mouth got more greedy around her biscuits, and his tongue and throat, his whole tasting apparatus was the most tender and vivid thing about him. Sometimes Ada felt he wanted the biscuits more than he wanted the rent, he had such a sweet tooth. He was such a child. Maybe that was the secret — the fact that he was only and ever five years old. Or two.

Oh, Nolly May.

Some mother had a lot to answer for there, she thinks. The Lord have mercy on his soul (if He could find it).

She takes a sip of coffee before her custard slice is chewed and gone, and this annoys her, suddenly. Ada hates mixing things up in her mouth. She hates mixing things up at home. More and more her life is like this, sniffing at the clothes in the old chest of drawers and washing them one more time, for the last time. More and more, she puts the tea towels in a different wash from the bath towels, or does not put them in a wash at all, but boils them on the stove.

She stands up and organises her stuff, thinking, as she does so, about the aneurysm that got Nugent in the end, wondering if it hurt — surely there were no nerves in there to feel the pain. Except of course your brain was where pain *was* in a way, so maybe it was the worst way of all to go.

And so she steps out into the roar and light of Grafton Street, with the buses rushing past, and is, as she does so, a child again.

Ada with her suitcase, the day her mother died.

How she turned and carried the suitcase out of the house. And everything that seemed impossible was possible after all. She had the gift of feet, that placed themselves one after the other so that she could walk out of there, and she had the gift of her hands, to make her way through life, and she did not look back.

39

There is a hotel in Gatwick airport where you could live for the rest of your life. You could stay there until they found you, and they would never find you — why should they? You could eat the stale croissants from trays set out in the hallways, wash out your smalls in the sink, nip from room to room when the cleaning trolley went round.

It has a spa. I saw this when I checked in. I went back to the shops in the South Terminal and bought myself some togs. And I bought socks and pants there, too, and a bag to put them all in — quite a nice bag, very unfussy, in that bumpy, hammered leather. And when I was coming back, walking past reception with the flat key in my wallet, I realised that I did not know how to leave.

There are three restaurants, or so the ad in the lift tells me, but I don't have to go to any one of them. I can order a Caesar salad upstairs — there is always a Caesar salad. I can walk the room — because you can always walk the room, if there is enough space. And in this room there is just enough space to go from the bed over to the window, to the television set on its corner bracket, then over to the desk, which is under a mirror that also reflects the bed. Here, you can pause to look at the information in the leatherette binder, after which, you might move to the trouser press and the box with runners on the top where you are supposed to leave your case, if you have a case — most of the guests in the Gatwick hotels do not; their luggage circulates without them, somewhere up there in the sky. Being in a Gatwick hotel does not mean that you have arrived. On the contrary, it means that you have plenty left to go.

The foyer contains the human contents of a 747 whose engine failed over Kazakhstan. This is their second night on the ground in the wrong country; their clothes are ripe — crying out for a heated trouser press — and their skin is grey. They will think about a bath and settle for a shower, but not yet, because they have nothing clean to wear. They will check the wardrobe and the bedside light, after which, they will sit on the bed, then lie on it, or tug out the tight quilt and climb under it: though after a while we will all roll or crawl or slump across to the forgotten mini-bar, and wonder is it worth the price. Any of it.

This is not England. This is the flying city. This is extra time.

San Miguel, Gordon's, Coca-Cola, Schweppes. I need something more precise — there is nothing *precise* enough for me to drink here. I take the overpriced water and swallow until the plastic bottle collapses with a crack. I should go out and get a litre of this stuff. I should go and get a half-wax in the spa. I have the rest of my life to organise. I can't organise the rest of my life with hairy legs. I wonder is there any way to get into the Clarins shop in the departure lounge where a woman in a white coat does a serious facial in a little back room, though facials always make me look plucked. Still, I have a terrible yearning for a woman in a rasping white coat whose pressing and patting fingers will stick my face back on, where it is in danger of falling away.

I felt very level when I drove to Dublin airport. I felt very sane and full of purpose. I had some idea of seeing Rowan, perhaps, or of walking along the Brighton front one last time. But the minute the plane's wheels touched down I knew what I had come here

to do. Sleep. I needed to sleep. So I just followed a sign that said 'Hotel' and it led, as
it often does, to a firm bed, a full mini-bar,
and a clapped-out television remote control.

And I sleep.

I wake fully dressed, take off my clothes
and get in between the cool, tight sheets.

'I tried to catch you,' says the man in my
dream. 'But you were in the wrong year.' It
is Michael Weiss. He has swum through
decades to get to me, he has fought his way
up through layers of time. And when we
stand face to face I say, 'How are you
Michael?' and he says, 'I'm fine. I'm just
fine.'

I wake again and can not tell if the light
outside is morning light or afternoon. I jab
my thumb into the spongy buttons of the
remote to find the time on the TV news. It
is half past six in the evening. I have slept
for eight hours. I turn to sleep again, then
reach in a panic to ring the girls.

Tom answers the phone.

'Darling. Hi. Where are you?' Very calm
and level.

'Will you put Rebecca on?' I say and realise, in the pause that follows, that it is quite
within his power to say no.

'Hello.' She sounds so much younger than
herself.

'Hello, sweetie.'

'Where are you?'

'Are you all right?' I say. 'I'll be home soon.'

'Oh. OK.' Quite cheerful. This is not her responsibility. Quite right too.

'Put your sister on.'

Emily breathes down the line.

'Hiya,' I say. 'Hiya.'

More breathing. It is a protracted business, for Emily, the phone. ('You're not here,' she said to me once. '*I* am here.') This time she has figured out what the damn thing is for. Just about.

'Mummy?'

'Yes, sweetie.'

'I give you a word,' she says. 'And that word is "love".'

'Yes,' I say finally. 'Yes. That's a good word to give.'

'Bye bye!' And to save me the bother, she slaps down the phone.

Emily. I do not know if the child is brilliant or odd — she can't make things connect up, somehow, but when they do it is always amazing. So I am not worried about her, I think, before realising that, actually, I am in Gatwick airport. I have run away from my daughter. I have left her behind.

But there is no leaving the girls, they are

always with me. I turn in to the covers and feel for the fine hair of Rebecca fanned out on the pillow, where she sometimes likes to curl up beside me; the cat's gaze of her sister watching from elsewhere in the room. They are so beautiful. Wherever I touch, I can conjure the silk of their hair, and think it a great and quiet victory to have them in the world.

Rebecca Mary and Emily Rose. They stay with me now in my sleep. They are quite patient. They turn away for a while, and let me be.

I wake again, and shower. I put on new pants and leave the old ones in the bin. I discard this other life, and leave the hotel behind.

Outside, I am surprised to find that I am still in an airport, that the dream goes on. I have travelled for so long and I am still here.

Palma
Barcelona
Mombasa
Split

From the departures board, all the places I have never been are beckoning to me like streetwalkers, blank to my desire.

Fuerteventura
Vilnius
Pula
Cork

Such strumpery. The people around me, quite rightly, ignore them and shop instead. I follow them in the glass lift to the next floor, and look in Accessorize for something small for each of the girls, something sparkling or floral. I look at the people queuing at the till, and I wonder are they going home, or are they going far away from the people they love. There are no other journeys. And I think we make for peculiar refugees, running from our own blood, or towards our own blood; pulsing back and forth along ghostly veins that wrap the world in a skein of blood. This is what I am thinking, as I stand in the queue in the Gatwick Village branch of Accessorize with my two pairs of flip-flops, that sport at the plastic cleft a silk orchid for Emily, and for Rebecca a peony rose. I am thinking about the world wrapped in blood, as a ball of string is wrapped in its own string. That if I just follow the line I will find out what it is that I want to know.

Towards or away.

The temptation to go back to the hotel is

very strong, but I force myself to sit awhile in the concourse on the departures floor, thinking I might choose a destination by check-in zone, knowing that I am going nowhere, but home.

Nice
Djerba
Edinburgh
Dublin

Where is Djerba, anyway?

And this time the plane will land properly. I just feel it didn't land *properly,* the last time I flew into Dublin. Kitty was weeping beside me, and Liam was sitting there accusing me, and the place we touched down in wasn't the place I used to know. Perhaps none of it was real. I feel like I have spent the last five months up in the air.

I ring Kitty, suddenly.

'Are you all right?' I say.

'Sorry?'

'Are you all right?' And for a second, I think she knows what I am talking about.

'Yes, I'm all right. Are you all right?'

'Yes, I am. Yes, me too.'

And we talk on about other things.

I know what I have to do — even though it is too late for the truth, I will tell the truth. I will get hold of Ernest and tell him what happened to Liam in Broadstone, and I will ask him to break this very old news to the rest of the family (but don't tell Mammy!) because I can not do it myself, I do not have the arguments for it. I just couldn't face Bea's disapproval, or Ita's dank sorrow, or Ivor, crisply saying, 'How come you guys had all the fun?' God, I hate my family, these people I never chose to love, but love all the same.

And what a pathetic attempt this is, at running away from them all. Gatwick bloody airport. I should be in Barcelona, looking for a sign. I should be walking the streets of Paris waiting to be found; some man who will walk up to me and say, 'I have been expecting you for so long,' and later, weeks later, I will watch some children playing in the Luxembourg Gardens and start up with the cry, 'No! No! This can not be.'

But I do not want a different destiny from the one that has brought me here. I do not want a different life. I just want to be able to live it, that's all. I want to wake up in the morning and fall asleep at night. I want to make love to my husband again. Because, for every time he wanted to undo me, there was love that put me back together again — put us both back together. If I could just remember them too. If I could remember each time, as you remember different places you have seen — some of them so amazing; exotic, or confusing, or still. If I could say this is what it was like the time Rebecca was started, or Emily made herself known. Or once, I remember, some afternoon, when he sat at the end of the bed in the white curtains' light, and he looked like someone I knew from the very beginning, whenever the beginning might have been.

I stand in the queue for tickets and I have to close my eyes suddenly. I stand there with my lids squeezed shut, my driver's licence tight in my hand, and my hand pressed against the lurching, empty feeling in my stomach — the future, come back to annoy me. Some new soul, with eyes like plums.

A boy.

Hey, Tom, let's have this next baby. Just this one. The one whose name I already know. Oh, go on. It'll cheer you up, no end.

Well, yes.

And though it would be amazing to have another child, this is not what I want most as I stand in the queue in Gatwick airport with my eyes closed: a woman with no luggage, no sharp objects, and nothing I haven't packed myself. I just want to be less afraid. That's all. Because it is fear that I feel as I wait to go up to the lip of the counter for a flight out today or, if the price is too extortionate, first thing tomorrow. I do not know if I can get up those tin steps and on to the plane.

Gatwick airport is not the best place to be gripped by a fear of flying. But it seems that this is what is happening to me now; because you are up so high, in those things, and there is such a long way to fall. Then again, I have been falling for months. I have been falling into my own life, for months. And I am about to hit it now.

Thanks to Sinéad for checking my Irish, and to Mary Chamberlain for checking everything else. Thanks, as ever, to Robin Robertson and Gill Coleridge.

Anne Enright
Bray, 2006

We hope you have enjoyed this Large Print book. Other Thorndike, Wheeler, and Chivers Press Large Print books are available at your library or directly from the publishers.

For information about current and upcoming titles, please call or write, without obligation, to:

Publisher
Thorndike Press
295 Kennedy Memorial Drive
Waterville, ME 04901
Tel. (800) 223-1244

or visit our Web site at:

www.gale.com/thorndike
www.gale.com/wheeler

OR

Chivers Large Print
published by BBC Audiobooks Ltd
St James House, The Square
Lower Bristol Road
Bath BA2 3SB
England
Tel. +44(0) 800 136919
email: bbcaudiobooks@bbc.co.uk
www.bbcaudiobooks.co.uk

All our Large Print titles are designed for easy reading, and all our books are made to last.